By the Same Author

True Enough

The Man of the House

The Easy Way Out

The Object of My Affection

Alternatives to Sex

Stephen McCauley

Granta Books

London

Granta Publications, 2/3 Hanover Yard, Noel Road, London N1 8BE

First published in Great Britain by Granta Books 2006
First published in the US by Simon & Schuster 2006

A CIP catalogue record for this book is available from the British Library

1 3 5 7 9 10 8 6 4 2

ISBN 13: 978-1-86207-859-8
ISBN 10: 1-86207-859-9

Printed and bound in Italy by Legoprint

To Anita Diamant and Amy Hoffman
with love and gratitude

Alternatives to Sex

a start

My decision to practice celibacy had nothing to do with prudery or penance, morality or manners, dysfunction, or fear of disease. It had very little to do with sex. It was all about real estate.

What had started out, one year earlier, as a bout of benign computer dating—a euphemism for online chatting followed by brief encounters, less impersonal than old-fashioned anonymous sex because you exchanged fake names with the person—had turned into an almost daily ritual that had replaced previous pastimes such as reading, going to the movies, working, exercising, and eating. I'm exaggerating, of course, but by how much, I'd rather not say. For months, I'd known that my habits were slipping out of control, but I figured that as long as I acknowledged my behavior was a problem, it wasn't one.

And then, one rainy September morning—coincidentally, the same morning Samuel Thompson and Charlotte O'Malley wandered into my life—I woke up and decided that too much really was enough. I could feel trouble pressing down on me like the low dark sky outside my bedroom window. I lived in a house near the top of a steep, San Francisco–like hill, but rather than a view of the Pacific, I saw from my windows the colorful sprawl of Somerville, Massachusetts—jagged rooftops and the tight grid of streets—and in the near distance, the cozy, unimpressive skyline of Boston, minimized this morning by the clouds. The previous owners of my house had installed a picture window in the master bedroom, an architectural feature I frequently deride but secretly love. As I stood looking out through the streaks of rain, a plane dropped from the clouds in its approach to Logan Airport. The sight of it, popping suddenly into view like that, jolted me. For the past year, the sight of airplanes heading toward the buildings of the city had been alarming.

Do something about your life, I told myself, a directive that's usually, in my case, translated as: *Stop* doing something.

For some reason, a disproportionate number of the men I met online turned out to live in dank basement apartments with minimal, makeshift furnishings that didn't acknowledge the existence of aesthetics—sofas made out of rolled-up futons, mattresses on the floor, television sets that took up half a room, collapsible bookshelves lined with DVD boxes. I hate DVDs. I'd switched from vinyl records to tapes, from tapes to CDs, from convection ovens to microwaves, from typewriters to computers, from landlines to cell phones, from revival movie houses to videocassette rentals, and as far as I was concerned, that was the end of it. I'd traveled as far along the technology highway as I could, and the sight of those skinny boxes gobbling up space in the video stores (and on collapsible bookcases) was enough to send me into a spiral of despair and dread.

It's always good to take a stand in life, even a completely meaningless one.

I don't mean to be a snob about anyone else's taste or to suggest that my own is worth bragging about. I don't really have taste; I have reactions to other people's. I have opinions. If I walked into my own apartment with anything resembling objectivity (fortunately, an impossibility) my reaction would undoubtedly be disapproval. Too beige. Too many midcentury lines and angles.

Too self-consciously symmetrical. Way too clean and tidy. Who lives here? I'd wonder. What's at the center of this guy's life, aside from dusting? But imperfect as my own place was, the fact that I so often connected with men who chose to live unfurnished, subterranean lives had started to worry me. Maybe, if I kept to current habits, my future lay in that direction. Downward.

The night before, I'd spent an impersonal, passionate forty minutes with someone who claimed to be called Carlo. Most of the men I met claimed to have names that were either Latin-lover mellifluous or vigorously American West: Carlo, Marco, Hank, Jake. I usually called myself Everett. My name is William Collins. I wasn't cheating on anyone, wasn't breaking a vow of fidelity, wasn't sneaking a wedding ring into my pocket as I knocked on someone's basement door. But taking on an assumed name seemed to be part of the game, even part of the pleasure, and Everett, being a name that was neither mellifluous nor particularly cowboyish, struck me as unlikely enough to sound real.

Carlo was not young, not old, not unattractive, not unintelligent, not unclean. Clearly not Latin, but never mind. For the forty-minute encounter, it's most important to figure out what a person *isn't* (not a mass murderer, whew); figuring out what he *is* requires more time, not to mention the belief that such information might be useful at a later date. Carlo and Everett barely had a present, never mind the pretense of a future.

It all went predictably enough. He pranced around in a jockstrap, got down on all fours, pleaded, moaned, and complimented my height. If you can't be classically handsome, you're no longer young, and your idea of exercise is making plans to go to the gym, it helps to be awkwardly tall. He said "nice" at the appropriate moments and did a little panting thing at the end that turned me on, even if it was clearly one of his rehearsed bits. Afterward, there was that unsettling postcoital silence in which I realized I was with a stranger, noticed the dirty laundry in the corner, and saw that the TV on the bureau was tuned to FOX News. A flushed, scowling commentator was talking ominously about Iraq. I propped myself up on an elbow, ran my finger along Carlo's tan line, and to fill the conversational void, asked him if he'd been on vacation.

He rolled over onto his back and gave me an indignant look. "I'm not interested in sharing a lot of personal information," he said.

"Of course not," I said. "I'm sorry for asking. If it's any consolation, I'm not interested in hearing any. I was trying to be polite."

He pulled on a T-shirt and, satisfied by my lack of interest, said, "I was in Maine for two weeks."

"Ah," I said, and realized that I truly wasn't interested and had no follow-up comment or question.

As I was leaving his apartment, I noticed that he had bath towels—light blue with appliqué peonies and bleach stains—tacked over the eye-level basement windows for privacy. At midnight, it had been a detail that had struck me as amusingly tawdry, but now, in the gray light of morning, as I stared out at the rain, it screamed final straw.

The descending airplane disappeared from view behind the skyline of the city; when there was no ensuing rumble or billow of smoke, I got dressed and set up the ironing board in my kitchen. I'd bought a $125 iron from a catalogue that specialized in expensive laundry-related products for obsessive-compulsives. It had arrived in the mail the day before, and I was excited about using it for the very first time. I was pouring verbena-scented water into the thing when it hit me that I should give my sex life a rest for a while. I couldn't take any more dank basements and grim window treatments. You can choose who you go to bed with, but you can't choose his decor.

Besides, I had a lot of *New Yorkers* to catch up on. My kitchen shelves needed to be rearranged. I had to start paying much closer attention to my job. I'd been meaning to sign up for a class in tap dancing. It was now or never on the question of spirituality and me. And so on, in that irrelevant vein.

Vanity compels me to say that I knew my resolution was about a lot more than the towels, but pinning it on those allowed me to try and change my behavior without diving into the mucky swamp of my psychology. Enough self-deception, in other words, to make it an unthreatening place to begin.

dinner plans

The iron surpassed my expectations. It glided over the shirt with a life of its own, and when I hit the appropriate button, steam came out with such power, it nearly levitated. I could go on about why I love to iron—a nice straight crease in the pants, wrinkles smoothed—but it's all pretty obvious stuff.

As I was going over my shirt for the second time, I figured it would be easier to stick to my sex resolution and break a bad habit if I kept myself busy. I'd recently turned forty—and more recently than that had turned forty-four. I'd noticed that for most of my peers, the first half of life is about acquiring bad habits and the second half is about replacing them with something else—usually, these days, some "healing" ritual that invariably turns out to be a variation on massage or a 12-step program.

The past year had been a posttraumatic time of uncertainty and anxiety for the whole country. Since the tragedy of the preceding September, everyone I knew was trying to choose between combating the collective evil of mankind by putting selfishness aside and doing good, and abandoning altruism altogether and doing whatever it took to feel good. *Right now.* The result seemed to be a lot of infidelity and binge eating, followed by resolutions to curtail same, followed by trips to overheated yoga studios where ninety minutes of narcissistic posing and fat-reducing exercises were said to contribute to global harmony because you collectively hummed "Om" at the end. Everyone I knew felt they had, for the first time in their pampered lives, a mission, but no one knew what it was. The pundits, the politicians, and Julia Roberts said that everything had changed, and on some level, it was true. And yet the only change everyone could name was that you were no longer supposed to pack toenail scissors in your carry-on luggage, and almost no one I knew owned a pair of those anyway.

Everyone I knew had felt a sudden need for reassuring moral absolutes, for patriotism, for righteousness. Everyone wanted to feel strong again. Then the hostile bumper stickers started appearing on the gas-guzzling cars with the flags sticking out of the windows, the political convictions grew blurry, and it was back to the massage table.

Given the timing, I had to conclude that my sexual habits of the past year were a combination of makeshift anxiety management and fatalism of the better-get-it-while-you-can variety. Or perhaps I was just trying to shift blame and ascribe global significance to my predictable midlife malaise.

I wasn't sure, but it was a little too early in the day to define my mission in life or suddenly come up with moral absolutes. It was easier to make distracting dinner plans. I dialed my friend Edward's cell phone to see if he was going to be in Boston that night.

"Dinner plans?" Edward said. "You haven't wanted to make plans with me for ages. You've been vague and elusive for months now. I can't pin you down on anything. You must be in despair. What is it?"

Edward and I had been friends for over three years, but because he was a flight attendant with an erratic schedule, it was hard to make dates with him. It was also true that since I'd started my sex bender, I'd avoided tying myself down with social engagements. By eight o'clock on most nights, I grew restless to get on the computer and line up the next disappointment.

I wouldn't have minded telling Edward I was giving up sex for a while, but telling him what I planned not to do would have meant revealing to him what I had been doing, and because I was a few years older than he and better educated (although unquestionably less intelligent), I always tried to give him the impression that I was above superficial concerns about age, weight, sex, laundry, and most of the other things I was obsessed with.

"You're being melodramatic," I said. "I haven't seen you in a while, and I miss you. I'm getting ready for work, and I thought of you, and here we are."

"For the record," he said, "I don't believe that. But we'll let it pass." Edward had a croaky voice, and especially on cell phones, he sounded like someone getting over a mild case of laryngitis. Maybe it was the dry, recycled air he breathed on planes day after day. Whatever the cause, it made him sound adolescent, as if he hadn't entirely settled into his voice. "Where would we have dinner?"

"Your choice."

As he thought this over, I heard a lot of commotion in the background, the low hum of voices and the squawk of PA announcements. On principle, I felt compelled to object to invasive, obnoxious cell phones, but really, I loved the way they gave a you-are-there documentary quality to even the most dull conversations. Even conversations with my elderly mother—usually so hypnotically mundane they passed into profundity—had taken on a degree of drama as she chatted with me on her mobile and simultaneously interacted with a large cast of characters she met as she strolled around the grounds of her assisted living facility in Arizona. ("Oh, Christ, here comes that old lush I was telling you about last time. Hi, Carrie. You're dressed for the heat all right!")

"That's a lot of noise for eight in the morning," I said. "Where are you?"

"I'm walking through O'Hare, and it's seven in the morning here. I've walked past three thousand people, and not one of them has cast even a casual glance in my direction. I went through the security gate, had my luggage searched, and officially entered the invisible stage of life."

the seven stages

Edward's version of the Seven Stages of Man was this: Jail Bait, Barely Legal, Fuckable, Barely Fuckable, Irrelevant, Invisible, and Dead. If I had to choose a category in which to put him, I'd say he was still very much Fuckable, but I would never have said this to his face because I didn't want to give him any wrong ideas.

His sex life consisted mainly of intense attractions to men with some tenuous claim to heterosexuality—a girlfriend who lived in another city, an ex-wife, a child or two they were helping to support. Straight men, Edward claimed, were just *different,* by which he meant, in a self-hating way, *better.* He met most of these better men while serving them drinks on airplanes. They'd show up at Edward's hotel room draped in their superior heterosexuality, drop to their knees, and beg to be controlled, feminized, and fucked, things Edward was definitely not interested in doing.

As for his claims that straight men are different from gay men, I suppose there's truth in it, although the only consistent difference I've noticed is that straight men rarely buy their own clothes.

I was touched by the thought of Edward, a short man with light hair and boyishly thin arms, alone, wheeling his little black suitcase through the bustling, nervous crowds of such a large and chaotic airport.

"If you turn around right now," I said, "you'll probably see that at least half a dozen people have stopped to give you a long, lascivious second glance."

"Oh, you think so? Let me check. Well, there's one. Five thousand years old and drooling, but never mind. I feel much better. Pathetic for being so shallow, but better. I hate to mess up your dinner plans, but I won't be back in town for a few more days."

"A few more days," I said. "Not till then?"

"Oh, William, you are in despair. Why? Tell me. No, don't tell me. I don't have time to listen. I hope it's interesting, that's all. Will you be treating me to dinner?"

"I'd love to. Then I'll feel more in control of the situation." I vacillate between pointless generosity (keeping a tenant in my first-floor apartment who rarely pays her rent, for example) and bouts of pennywise parsimoniousness that last a few hours at most. Maybe celibacy would lead to a spell of frugality and wise investment. My sales figures at the real estate office where I worked were not what they should have been.

I sprinkled more scented linen water on my shirt, hit the steam jet on the iron, and was engulfed in a fragrant fog.

"If you're paying, I accept the invitation. We'll go someplace that's overpriced and where no one's likely to be holding hands. You're not ironing, are you?"

Edward had an uncanny ability to read my mind and guess at my activities. (He'd probably guessed at my sex spree, for example.) He was unusually sensitive to the smallest gestures and shifts in vocal inflection, but this seemed unnervingly on-target, even for him. Not wanting to give him the satisfaction of being one hundred percent correct, I clicked off the iron and unplugged it. "I was," I said. "How did you know?"

"I could hear you banging it against the board. Plus there was that weird distracted tone you get when you're doing housework. Are you using that hundred-and-twenty-five-dollar thing you told me about? You could have given that money to a worthy, hopeless cause. Me, for example. You should be ashamed of yourself for buying a thing like that."

"I am ashamed," I said. "I'm deeply ashamed." I find even the most egregious self-indulgence forgivable if it's accompanied by massive helpings of shame, regret, or self-hatred. Even murderers are shown a degree of leniency if they can cough up a bit of remorse.

"I hope it's not a pillowcase or a dish towel you're ironing, something truly demented."

I assured him that it was a cotton shirt, one that was genuinely in need of ironing.

"And it's yours, isn't it? Not your wife's."

"It's mine," I told him. "And it's a very nice one. White with an invisible white pattern that only registers subliminally. A Dutch designer with an unpronounceable name. My wife prefers peasant costumes."

my wife

Edward called the tenant on the first floor of my house my "wife" because he was convinced that my relationship with her had taken on the most destructive qualities of a bad marriage. He wasn't entirely wrong in this, but I resented the term even so. She—a painter called Kumiko Rothberg, speaking of fake names—was perpetually several months behind on the rent. As of that morning, she owed me $3,000, plus the $500 I'd loaned her to pay off a debt she owed to a previous landlord. A month or so earlier, I'd made the mistake of telling Edward that I'd let her come upstairs to use my ironing board and had ended up doing the ironing myself. I'd resisted the temptation to confess that since then she sometimes left a few rumpled articles of clothing in the front hall with an attached note reading, "If you have time," and that somehow, I always found the time. I hoped it would encourage her to be more diligent about paying her rent. So far, this hadn't worked.

Edward claimed he never would have allowed the situation to get so out of control. This undoubtedly was true; like most people who are one hundred percent submissive in the bedroom, Edward was a tyrant everywhere else in his life.

Oh, really?

"I was going to call you anyway," Edward said. "There's something I've been meaning to discuss with you for a while. I'm about to make some big changes and I want to talk to you about them."

"Oh, really?"

"Yes, really. And don't take that condescending tone. I'm very serious about this."

"What are they?"

"I'm not going to tell you now. It'll give us something to discuss over dinner. You certainly don't tell me what's going on with you."

Edward was always contemplating making big changes in his life, but usually they turned out to be something like replacing the bathroom vanity with a pedestal sink or starting a new fitness regimen that required the hands-on assistance of a paid professional who happened to be devastatingly handsome and muscular. I was happy that the planned changes never went deeper than that, since, in my mind, Edward was nearly perfect exactly as he was—due mostly to his many imperfections.

"I'll come by your apartment at eight on Thursday," I told him. "Where are you off to?"

"Dallas and then some other hell spot, back to Chicago, and then LA, then home."

"Have a safe trip."

"That's my hope, but unfortunately, my fate is in the hands of arrogant pilots, hungover mechanics, lunatic baggage handlers, and the minimum-wage kids checking the carry-on luggage for guns. Here's my gate."

The phone went dead.

When commercial airliners had been used as weapons, Edward had started to talk openly about job-related safety concerns for the first time since I'd known him. He was worried about more terrorist attacks and, equally, about the dismal state of maintenance standards in the face of major financial losses by the airlines. His status in the world had changed radically since the events of the previous September; after years of condescension and derision, being thought of as an unwholesome cross between a cocktail waitress and an airborne geisha, Edward was now treated with the hushed reverence generally reserved for military personnel, Nobel Prize winners, and really good dermatologists.

I was happy that Edward finally was being given some of the respect he deserved, but all things considered, it seemed like small compensation.

previous addictions

As I was leaving the house for work, I thought that if I stuck to my celibacy resolution for a couple of months, I might be able to tell a few friends about my recent adventures. All of my previous addictive behavior had been of the most deeply shameful kind: an obsession with vacuum cleaning; a tendency to furtively clean a sink or bathtub when I went to someone's house for dinner; maintaining a small file of index cards with tips for using hair spray, nail polish remover, lemonade mix, and other household standards as cleaning agents; the ironing thing. During the scattered periods of my life when I'd been in long-term relationships, I'd been ashamed by my adeptness at fidelity, which had made me feel unmanly. I'd used evasive language and innuendo to convey the impression that I was leading a wildly promiscuous life. But once I'd added promiscuity to my repertoire of diversions, I'd done my best to imply that I spent most of my evenings alone at home reading the complete works of Simone de Beauvoir, an intellectual with top-shelf name recognition whose work no one is eager to discuss with anything resembling specificity. If I ever did reorganize my life and take on one of those someday-before-I-die literary projects, I'd feel a lot more comfortable once again assuming the identity of a sexual libertine, using the details I'd accumulated in the past year. Before locking the door of my house behind me, I rushed back upstairs to my bedroom and put a copy of *The Mandarins* on my bedside table. You never know.

This morning, there was no basket of laundry from Kumiko waiting for me in the entryway, a huge relief for about one second, before I began to worry that she hadn't liked the way I'd done her ironing last week. I was tempted to knock on her door and assure her that with my new iron, I'd do a better job next time, but that was a bit much, even for me.

I opened up my umbrella and made a dash for my car, glistening with rain in the driveway. My house had a garage, a small bunker of concrete blocks with two windows, covered in vines, but I'd never used it once since purchasing the place. About six months earlier, I'd let Kumiko move her painting supplies into the building and set up a studio. Maybe, I'd reasoned, if she felt she was getting more for her low rent she'd be more likely to pay it. So far, I'd seen no signs that she'd used it for anything but storage.

. The car windows fogged up as soon as I closed the door behind me. On the passenger seat, there was a paper with my handwritten directions to Carlo's apartment. A reminder of past mistakes. I ripped it in half and put it in the trash container I had Velcroed to the dashboard. I felt lighter and calmer already. Breathe in, breathe out. I couldn't imagine why I hadn't thought of abstinence sooner. I sat for a moment folded up in the driver's seat with the engine idling and my eyes closed. I pictured returning to the driveway after work, walking into the house, and picking the book off my night table. *The Mandarins*. Excellent title. I had a clear image of it in my mind. I felt relaxed and in control of my life as I walked to the chaise longue in the corner of my bedroom, turned on the light, and began to read. These were pleasures I'd enjoyed in the recent past, and with a little discipline, they would be mine again. I'd had a year of posttraumatic self-indulgence, and now it was time to move on. I opened the glove compartment, stuffed my mobile supply of condoms into the trash container, and backed out of the driveway. It was going to be a very good day.

too damned happy

It had been a dry summer, and that morning's rain, far from being an annoyance, was a welcome novelty, a suggestion that nature was, perhaps, getting back on a path of normalcy. And maybe, therefore, life in general would resume a normal rhythm at some point.

I'd been at my desk for about an hour when I looked up to enjoy the sight of Massachusetts Avenue being washed by a suddenly fierce downpour and saw two people huddled under a large black umbrella gazing at the real estate listings posted in the window of the office. Given the position of the umbrella, I couldn't see their faces, but there was something about the way they were leaning in toward each other and wearing twin raincoats that made me think they were either headed for or had just come from next door, a brick building affectionately referred to as the Nut House because so many shrinks had offices there. I was familiar with the place, having spent a few afternoons in it myself a number of years ago. Fortunately, I was declared cured after a mere eight sessions, on the very day that my insurance coverage ran out.

The Nut House was a boost to businesses in the neighborhood. People were always rushing from their shrink appointments and heading to a bakery around the corner or the restaurant across the street to binge on instant gratification. Or coming into Cambridge Properties to signal a change in their lives by buying a new place to install their familiar miseries.

"What do you think?" I said aloud. "Headed to see their couples counselor, or just on their way out?"

Deirdre Fisk, occupant of the desk next to mine, leaned away from her computer and peered out the window. I glanced at her screen and saw that she was shopping online for ceiling fans.

Deirdre, an extremely successful saleswoman, spent a lot of her time in the office shopping for overpriced appliances, face creams made by eastern European countesses, handcrafted furniture, and antique wallpaper. She was disappointed in nearly every item she bought via the computer (I could relate to this) and always ended up sending it back.

"I couldn't tell you," Deirdre said. "I can't get past the outfits. I hate couples who dress alike. And raincoats with belts? Hor-ri-ble. They're probably one of those smug, self-satisfied couples who go around advertising how unhappy and discontented they are to any sap who'll listen. 'We're about to get a divorce.' 'He's an abusive drunk.' They're always so proud of themselves. You have no idea how hurtful it is."

I confessed that I hadn't noticed the belts, but otherwise found the raincoats dashing. It was a mistake to venture into the subject of clothes with Deirdre. She loved talking about clothing and generally had scathing views that she delivered with intimidating authority. Shortly after she came to the office two years earlier, I started paying a lot more attention to my own wardrobe, hoping to avoid her scorn. I'd developed a friendly relationship with the owner of a consignment shop in Boston who called me up whenever he got in anything that might fit my tall, skinny body.

It was also a mistake to bring up the subject of couples around Deirdre. In terms of age, she lived in my untrendy, forty-something neighborhood and had been married to a homely, arrogant lawyer named Raymond for nearly twenty years. The central problem in her life (her version) was that she and Raymond were, and always had been, too compatible, too much in love, *too damned happy*. According to Deirdre, people snubbed you socially, condescended to you intellectually, and questioned the depth of your emotions if you were happily married. It didn't help that she generally worked with divorcing couples funneled to her by Raymond.

The man shook the rain out of his big black umbrella, held the door open for the woman in a courtly way, and the two entered. It was close to lunchtime and Deirdre and I were the only ones in our small office, one of the few independent real estate offices in town that hadn't been gobbled up by a conglomerate.

"Do you want to help them, or should I?" I asked Deirdre.

"I was just about to go out and buy a soda," she said, code for huddling in the alley behind the building and smoking. She pushed herself back from her desk. "You take them. I'm not in the mood to listen to them bragging about how close they are to divorce. You can deal with it better than I can, being single and all."

When it comes to dealing with gay colleagues, most people follow a Don't Ask policy, as if posing a question about dating or romantic interests would be unacceptably invasive. In all the years I'd been working at Cambridge Properties, no one had ever questioned me about my social life, and although I was open with everyone in a general way, I'd never shared a detail of same, aside from occasionally dropping the name of a man I might be dating into a conversation, something that had never produced a single follow-up question. This situation made me feel inferior to my coworkers—a bit like a maiden aunt with no prospects—and oddly enough, simultaneously superior, as if I had a wildly sophisticated private life that was above the tedium of marital squabbles and framed photographs of smiling spouses.

Being single and all, I took on the couple, and Deirdre went out for her Marlboro Ultra Light.

rocks and pills

"We're not looking aggressively," the man said. "I should tell you that right off, just so you'll know. I don't want you to end up feeling you wasted your time with us."

We were standing in front of the empty reception desk near the door, and the man was having a tough time figuring out what to do with his dripping umbrella. Polite to a fault. An attractive fault. I like people who make an effort with the small details of everyday manners, holding open doors, not dripping all over your carpets, saying thank you for insignificant favors.

I was convinced that manners were a dying, possibly dead art, the victim of talk radio and a growing suspicion that anything less than all-out bullying was an admission of weakness, an open invitation to telemarketers and suicide bombers.

"Don't worry about my time," I said. "In the end, it's a lot less work for me if you don't buy anything. You'll be doing me a favor."

He grinned at me. "I feel better already."

He was a good-looking man with the sculpted face of an aging runner. His graying hair was brushed straight back off his forehead and slicked down close to his scalp, the lines of the comb clearly delineated. He was dressed and groomed—a dark suit under the now-open raincoat and that arranged hair—as if he was about to appear in court or make an important presentation, and so I wasn't surprised later when I learned that he was that profitable, nebulous thing, a business consultant. There was something in his manner—confidence mixed with empathic generosity—that made me certain he'd grown up with advantages he wasn't afraid of having taken away from him.

"He's not looking aggressively," the woman put in. "He's looking passive-aggressively." She pursed her lips, and then smiled, erasing the hostility of the comment.

"Anyplace in particular that caught your eye out there?" I asked.

"The three-bedroom on Avon Hill. The 'Manhattan-style' layout?"

She put an ironic spin on this last part, a jab at the silly description of the apartment that, it so happens, I had written.

About ten years earlier, I'd been hired by the owner of Cambridge Properties to write the copy they use in their listings. It was a part-time project I took on to fill a few hours per week after leaving (on the advice of my eight-session therapist) a lucrative but debilitating position at a Boston advertising firm. One thing had led to another, and within a short while, I'd earned my license and was selling. Real estate was, in my case, less lucrative than advertising, but it was also less soul-numbing because you're at least selling people something they need—shelter—even if at vastly inflated prices.

It didn't take me long to realize that the key to writing successful listings is to describe everything in relation to something it isn't: a Manhattan-style layout in a Cambridge apartment; a country kitchen in a downtown condominium; in-town convenience for a suburban ranch. It appeals to the basic human desire to have everything at once and nothing for too long. ("Great resale potential!") And also, it tricks people into believing that their lives are a little better or more exciting or glamorous than they really are.

As I led them back to my desk, we made our introductions: William Collins, Sam Thompson, Charlotte O'Malley. They told me they had a house in Nahant, a rocky peninsula that sticks out into the ocean north of Boston. It was one of those anomalous scraps of Northeast coastline, a fragment of Maine dragged down on a glacier a few million years ago. Far enough away from urban noise and congestion to be desirable as a summer retreat, but close enough to downtown to be within easy year-round commuting distance and to have views of the city skyline.

Oddly enough, the best way to convince someone to move to a new locale is to praise the place they're trying to leave. "I've heard it's beautiful out there," I said.

Samuel lit up at this. "It's spectacular," he said. "Views, ocean breezes, incredible sunsets. Really *fabulous*." He swept a graceful hand—long fingers with a wedding ring floating loosely on one—through the air, setting the scene for me. It was an unnecessarily theatrical gesture that, along with use of the word "fabulous," made me suspect he knew I was gay. I have a theory that heterosexuals use the word "fabulous" more frequently when in the company of gay men but I had no way of testing out the theory. "It's another world," he added.

I nodded enthusiastically, even though "another world" usually turns out to be a euphemism for racially segregated.

"One of the reasons we're thinking about leaving," Charlotte said, studying the listing sheet for the Manhattan-style apartment, "is that it's just too spectacular. Too fabulous. It's *so* incredible, you feel like leaping from the rocks." She made another little pout and went back to the sheet.

"Some of us," Samuel said. "Not all of us." He spoke in a cheerful, reassuring way, issuing his words through a big smile and showing off a set of teeth that had been whitened to the color of fresh snow.

"True. Some of us are happy all the time. Others of us not. Others of us sometimes forget to take our antidepressants and start to think about leaping from the rocks." She looked at me and gave me an ironic smile that made me feel we were accomplices.

meaningful relationships

I was tempted to ask her what antidepressants she was taking. I was embarrassed by the fact that I wasn't taking any mood-altering drugs myself—it seemed so arrogant not to be these days, and obviously I would have benefited—but it made me feel like part of the mainstream to discuss them. Nothing got people into a more open, animated mood than discussing their medication. For many of my friends, their relationship with their antidepressants was the central relationship in their lives. Healthier, probably, than a relationship with your iron, but more expensive. They reveled in describing the distinctive way this or that pill interacted with their unique chemistry, as if they were describing a virtue or a personal accomplishment. *"She* didn't like Wellbutrin, but *I've* never had any problems with it. It's not for everyone, but for *me,* it's been wonderful."

should we? shouldn't we?

"I hear there are a lot of those in Nahant," I said. "Rocks."

"Millions." Charlotte was scanning the listing sheet with the middle finger of an unmanicured hand. "Only one bathroom?"

"I'm afraid so. The building's from the 1920s, when people apparently cared less about having lots of bathrooms."

"We don't care much, do we, Charlotte?" He put his hand on his wife's thigh, a gesture so spontaneous and tender, I felt intrusive simply for having noticed it. He looked at me. "Our son started college this month, so it's just the two of us."

"We'll care as soon as we have a guest. Especially if it's Daniel.

Last year at this time, I was convinced I'd risen above caring about two bathrooms. Now, to be honest, I'd love three."

She had large dark eyes that had about them a look of exhaustion not uncommon among intelligent people who know themselves too well and are worn down by the acquaintance. Looking at the two of them together, you had to conclude that she was the brighter of the pair—more imaginative, even if less successful. Her light brown hair was gathered into a loose, droopy chignon with a few damp tendrils undone and stuck to her neck. She wasn't thin—a nice contrast to her husband's impeccable angularity—and there was something about the easy, sloppy way she was sitting that made me think she didn't care all that much one way or the other. I guessed her to be at least a few years younger than her husband—mid-forties?—but I was getting increasingly bad at guessing anyone's age, collateral damage from having lied so often about my own on the computer dating circuit. She appeared to be more tossed together than Samuel, as if she was too busy worrying and fretting to comb her hair in perfect rows.

They began debating the virtues of having several bathrooms versus having just one in a way that made me think neither really cared about this issue; each just wanted to have the final word.

Deirdre came back from the alley, trailing in with her a faint smell of cigarette smoke, just in time to hear Charlotte say to her husband, "You make a relevant but facile point." She sat down at her desk and began banging at her keyboard a little too loudly.

Deirdre glanced over and rolled her eyes at me, scoffing at the unfairness of being subjected to yet another public display of domestic discord. There was something in the tone of their conversation that suggested they enjoyed having an audience. I didn't mind. I had been part of a couple and knew how weirdly lonely it can get, and how, from time to time, you need someone to hear the trees falling in the forest.

"Why don't we go look at the apartment?" I said. "Just to give you an idea of what's out there. You have to start the search somewhere."

They gazed at each other, silently conversing: Should we? Shouldn't we?

"It's right around the corner," I said. "We can walk."

passing the nut house

It was still pouring when we stepped outside. My umbrella was one of those unreliable folding kind, and I couldn't get it to open. Within a few seconds, the shoulders of my suit jacket—Prada, inappropriately dressy for that hour of the day, but since it had cost only $90 at the consignment shop, I considered it casual wear—were wet.

"There's room for one more," Samuel said, lifting up his huge umbrella a little higher.

I'm usually too proud to accept generosity from men, especially if they're handsome, but in this case, doing battle with a cheap accouterment seemed the more emasculating position, so I tossed my umbrella into a trash barrel, mumbling something about it being a useless piece of garbage, and stepped under theirs.

It was awkward, walking up the street like that, bumping against one another, each of us getting wet in a different place, but I liked the feeling of being between them, hovering slightly above both, protected by their umbrella and, for the length of time it took to walk four blocks, a part of their lives, even if an insignificant part.

As we were passing the Nut House, Samuel smiled at Charlotte, more confirmation, I thought, that they'd just spent fifty minutes there. Because Charlotte had already brought up drugs, depression, and suicidal longings, it didn't seem wildly inappropriate to ask if they had a counselor there, but remembering how offended "Carlo" had been by my vacation question the night before, I attempted a bit of discretion.

"Nice building, isn't it?" I said. "I used to go there to see a shrink, not that I needed one."

"We went there for the same reason," Charlotte said. "We fired our counselor this morning. She kept trying to make us change the things that aren't working in our marriage. I mean, if it was that easy, why would we have been there in the first place?"

"They always want you to change," I said. "It's depressing."

Almost everyone I knew, with the exception of Edward, was in or had been in therapy at some point in his life, ostensibly to solve his problems. But for some, going into therapy was a costly but effective way to settle into a holding pattern until they'd figured out an airtight rationalization for clinging to their neuroses and counterproductive habits. After all, there's room for only so many geniuses and prodigies in the world. For the rest of us, our best shot at individuality comes in the form of unique character flaws and neurotic patterns.

"What really happened," Samuel said, "was that she, the counselor, finally got me, the husband, to see that Charlotte, the wife, had a point about getting an apartment in town. As soon as we settled that, Charlotte decided we didn't need her anymore."

"It was generous of you to go along with the idea," I said.

He shrugged. "I was outnumbered. I had no choice."

Like most men, it seemed, he took a completely passive attitude toward his marriage and let his wife figure out what was required to keep it together.

dishwasher people

I knew the apartment was wrong for them as soon as we walked in. I'd written the description based on information the owner of Cambridge Properties had given me without ever having visited it, but I saw now that despite its attractive layout, much of the character and style had been sanded, painted, and Home Depot'd into bland facelessness. Everything in the place was depressingly new and functional. It was perfect for the customers I thought of as Dishwasher People.

There are customers who want a living space that fits in with their lives, their taste, and their aesthetic sense of balance and proportion, and then there are the people who want a dishwasher. In the former category, there are people who walk into an apartment or a house and pay attention to the height of the ceilings, the exposure of the windows, the way the rooms flow one into the other, the width of the floorboards. In the latter category are the people who ask: "Is there a dishwasher?" and then, if the answer is yes, plop down a deposit. The former group looks for a place that will be a good staging ground for the drama of their lives, the latter looks for the location of the cable hookup. Oddly enough, I had the impression that most Dishwasher People didn't really care all that much about a dishwasher. They just felt obliged to show interest in some concrete detail, so they wouldn't appear to be an easy target for avaricious sellers or landlords. I doubt many Dishwasher People ever use dishwashers since they tend to be the workaholic sort who rarely spend more than two waking hours at home and subsist on frozen dinners you can eat out of the packaging.

Technically, I'm a Dishwasher Person manqué. That is, I

checked first to see if my house had a dishwasher and cable hookup, and when I saw it didn't, I bought it anyway.

Charlotte and Samuel entered the apartment with the tentative silence that often overcomes people when they first start looking at real estate. The couple that owned the apartment had equipped it with the kind of nondescript, supposedly tasteful furniture and art-work (some of which could be found at my house) that constitutes an erasure of all taste. They'd outfitted the living room with a sleek rowing machine and exercise bike, conveniently facing the very big television set.

"The furniture is all going," I said, watching Charlotte sink into an immense slipcovered chair that bore no relation to any of the other furniture in the room.

"I suppose the walls and ceilings and floors stay," she said.

Sam had his hands in the pockets of his raincoat. "Recently painted. And very clean."

"He's the glass-half-full part of the pair," Charlotte told me. "Also the cook," she explained as he went looking for the kitchen. She picked up a big, brightly painted balsa wood sculpture of a bird, one of those individual works of art that are imported from Mexico in the tens of thousands. "I hadn't thought about it before, but in your job, you get to peek into people's lives directly, more so than a shrink even. They have to wade through annotations and outright lies, while you see the inside of the medicine cabinets."

"I never pry," I said. "I'm scrupulously discreet."

"I don't believe you." And then, pouting, she said, "I'm dying to open this and see what's inside." She touched the handle on a small cabinet beside her chair. "You wouldn't mind, would you?"

"Go right ahead."

Charlotte was delighted with the contents: a stack of *TV Guides*, a large box of cheap, chocolate-covered almonds, and two cartons of cigarettes. "All the things about themselves they don't want us to know," she said. "Do you think there are pictures of them anywhere?"

"I'm sure there are. Everyone has pictures, even though it seems easier to me just to look in a mirror. Should we go explore?"

"If I can pry myself out of this chair."

In the course of our conversation, she'd arranged herself in the big chair in a provocative manner with her coat falling open and her legs crossed at the knee in a way that drew attention to their shapeliness. She was wearing a pair of dark shoes with thin heels that accentuated her calves. I wasn't at all conflicted about my (homo)sexuality, but I enjoyed looking at women's bodies, almost as much as I enjoyed looking at men's. Sometimes more, since there was no envy, angst, or lurid desire to possess or to be the other.

I was about to compliment her appearance in the fatuous, automatic way I sometimes have when Samuel's cell phone went off in the other room, and he began a quiet conversation. Charlotte cocked her head and played with the loose strands of her hair while trying to overhear what he was saying without being too obvious about it.

"A business call?" I asked.

"It could be. Or it could be his mistress." She turned to me and opened her dark, tired eyes wide, as if to say: What do you make of that? Am I shocking you?

"Oh? Does he have one?"

"You never know. I've been encouraging him to get one for some time now."

They're just playing around with me, I thought. Samuel was being honest when he said they'd never buy. They probably have no intention of buying. I knew the type well, the pseudoshoppers who figure it's cheaper and easier to look at real estate on a weekday morning or a Sunday afternoon than to head to the beach or feign interest in a symphony. I extended my hand and pulled her up out of the chair. "We'll poke our heads into the other rooms and see if we can find anything of interest."

The rest of the apartment was as wrong as the front rooms— dark, despite large windows, and poorly laid out. I made a point of showing her the cramped closets, using them as an excuse to brush up against her a little too closely a couple of times. I wanted her to like me, even though I wasn't sure how much I liked her.

"Scented candles," Charlotte said. "What do you think that's all about?"

The air in the master bedroom was heavy with the cloying smell of artificial vanilla.

"Undoubtedly what everything else is about—self-hatred and insecurity." That, in abridged form, was my version of the meaning of life.

The bureau was lined with small, framed photographs, a brief montage of the courtship and marriage of the owners, one of those young professional couples who look as if they spend all their free time alternating between healthy outdoor activities and massive drinking binges.

"Why are they selling?" Charlotte asked.

Office rumor had it that the wife was pregnant and that they were looking for a place in the suburbs. But it seemed too tidy a mirror image of Charlotte and Samuel's move, and I was a little worried that it might sound to her as if the young couple was starting the richest part of their lives while they were sliding into late middle age and empty-nest irrelevance.

"I have no idea," I said. "Some people just want to make a change."

touch

Charlotte and I were back in the living room when Samuel finished his phone call and emerged through the pantry door. He sat on the arm of the big, soft chair and leaned against his wife. It was unusual to see a long-married couple touch each other in public; most display a faint trace of revulsion at the idea. Samuel's face, I saw, had a shiny cleanliness that made me think he probably got facials. I'd heard that a lot of heterosexual men of a certain age got facials, reportedly for reasons of professional advancement, the only acceptable reason for men to engage in any activity that might be considered vain. The trend of shaving one's scrotum had also supposedly spread to heterosexual men. I'd been assured of this fact by a number of friends whose incontrovertible proof was always the same: "I've had sex with lots of straight guys who shave their balls." From this I inferred that the trend had spread primarily to the kind of straight men who routinely have gay sex. It crossed my mind to wonder about Samuel in this regard, too, but only briefly.

I was just about to suggest we all go out for lunch somewhere, so I could get a better chance to find out what they were looking for, when Samuel announced that he had to head back to his office.

"I don't think this is the place for us," Charlotte said.

"I don't think so either," I said. "But call me in a few days and I'll have lots of other places you can look at."

"Good man," Samuel said. He kissed the top of Charlotte's head. We buttoned up our coats and jackets and walked out together.

As I parted company with them in front of the office, rain

pouring off the rim of their umbrella, I began thinking about how soon I reasonably could get in touch with them with the excuse of new properties to show.

"style"

Jack Nelson, one of my officemates, was on the phone, berating a client. Jack had a loud, deep voice and a sales technique that revolved mostly around intimidation and veiled threats.

"Hey listen," he brayed, "if you don't want to buy it, that's your business. But I'll tell you one thing right now: you'd be a fool not to. Well, then don't. But don't complain to me when the place goes up forty percent in value by Christmas."

With that, he hung up the phone and began erasing names from his appointment book. "They'll buy it," he said to me. "They'll call back in half an hour and make an offer. If not, it's their loss."

I took off my sports jacket and shook it once. Instantly, it was as dry as it had been, hanging in my closet that morning. It was made out of an elaborate blend of synthetic materials that repelled water, stains, wrinkles, and all odors. Somehow or other, I'd missed the moment, like so many other moments, when expensive designers had started to use plastic and rubber to make their clothes. "Why are they hesitating?" I asked Jack.

"Some horseshit about it being the wrong layout and the wrong neighborhood and the wrong size." He crumpled up a piece of paper and tossed it into the trash. All of his gestures were like this—firm and decisive. "'We want an eat-in kitchen,'" he mocked.

"Maybe it's not right for them."

"Hey, it's in their price range, it's got a roof and a toilet. You can't have everything in life. Am I right?"

"Jack, you are so right." I fished through my pockets for the keys to the apartment I'd just shown Charlotte and Samuel.

Jack was in his late fifties, a retired gym teacher who'd entered real estate a decade or so earlier, after his wife had walked out on him. He was a stocky, gray-haired man, handsome in a pugnacious, barrel-chested sort of way, but with the dark, scowling demeanor of a man who was convinced life had dealt him an unfair hand. Maybe it had to do with his height.

He lived in a state of slowly simmering misery at the thought that anyone else in the world was earning more than he was or working less or getting even a fraction more pleasure out of life. My brother in California was another of this sort; he was always talking about the income and job promotions of relatives and childhood friends as if he were accusing them of criminal activity. Jack worked hard, put in long hours, and much to my astonishment, his bitter, aggressive style paid off. He wasn't afflicted, as I was, with the desire to make people's lives better through their real estate purchases; he just wanted to close the deal.

"What were you showing?" he asked me as I put the keys back in the cabinet. I sat at my desk and started a file on Samuel and Charlotte. I always write up a little psychiatric intake sheet on clients when I first meet them, even if I think it's unlikely I'll see them again. You never know which connections might come in handy. "I was showing them the Avon Hill Manhattan-style layout," I told Jack.

"Overpriced," he scowled. "Lousy management company, the maintenance fees are ridiculous, and the building's in horrible shape. They going to take it?"

"Not their style," I said.

He scoffed at this. "Whatever that means. Style. 'It's not my style.' Since when does a condo have to have a 'style'? It's got three bedrooms, doesn't it? They want 'style' on top of that?"

"You have a point, Jack. Have you shown the place to many people?"

"A few times. No takers. At the moment, I'm working with a bunch of whiners."

Jack had absolutely no interest in the aesthetics of a house or apartment and was genuinely baffled by objections to crude renovations, the destruction of architectural integrity, or other such considerations. He was all about practicality and function, the original Dishwasher Person. Jack considered me a fool for paying so much attention to the demands and requests of my clients, for trying to get to know them and find out about their tastes and their fantasies of an ideal life. But he suffered fools gladly because we made him feel better about himself, and so he and I got along well. Like most people who appear to be opposites, we were undoubtedly more similar than either of us realized.

Under Samuel and Charlotte's name, I wrote: *Attractive couple, handsome husband, drugged wife, empty nest, both have excellent teeth. Looking for a pied-à-terre with 2 bathrooms. Or nothing? He very touchy. Loves her?* I wrote down the address of the place I'd shown them, and then, as an afterthought: *Potential friends?*

When Jack's phone rang, a few minutes later, he pointed at it and nodded. "I'll bet you anything it's that couple I just hung up on, crawling back to me. Do me a favor and tell them I'm out showing a house on Walnut to a couple of doctors from Weston."

It was Maria, Jack's current girlfriend, calling from her cell phone while working out at the Harvard gym. Jack had amazing success with women, mostly younger and attractive women who were, I suspected, looking for an aggressive father figure. Aggressive father figures seemed to have a special appeal since the previous September. Most of the interactions I saw between the two involved Jack advising her on how to undercut some classmate or make trouble for a professor, advice she rejected out of hand but clearly loved hearing. The fact that she openly referred to him as "Daddy" answered any questions about what she saw in stocky, gray-haired Jack.

He used exhaustion and age as an excuse for bragging about his sex life—"At this age, it isn't easy keeping it up for three hours." The one time I'd hinted at having a libido, he became distracted, as if we were heading into an uncomfortably dark part of the human experience.

where am I?

As I was trying to figure out the gist of Jack's mumbled comments to "Baby," Gina Fulmetti emerged from the cubbyhole that was her private office, and motioned to me. "I need to talk to you, William," she said hoarsely.

I held up a finger, indicating that I was in the middle of something I just had to finish. All of the agents at Cambridge Properties worked on commission, and so, technically speaking, we were paying our own salaries. Although there was no real boss to answer to, Gina owned the business, kept an eye on sales figures, paid the overhead, and was the person we all turned to for assistance. It was she who'd hired me to write ad copy and then encouraged me to get into sales. She was fond of me, I knew, mostly because I wasn't aggressively ambitious and because I took time to get to know people. But the qualities of mine she liked also meant I wasn't bringing in as much business as she thought I should.

There were usually six full-time agents on staff, plus a few part-timers who appeared to be in it for the business cards and the insider information on sales, always good dinner-party conversation. Almost no one, except Jack, kept full-time hours, and it was rare that more than three people were at their desks at any given moment. And yet, given the prices around Boston and the frenzied atmosphere of buying, selling, and speculating, the overall sales figures for the office had been increasing every year I'd been there, and Gina was, according to Jack, "loaded."

Her private office was a small windowless box, cluttered with papers and magazines. I felt the usual clutch of claustrophobia as I stooped to enter and shut the door behind me. Gina pointed to a chair, folded her hands on her desk, and stared at me silently for what felt like five minutes. She was usually soft-spoken, but she had a way of looking through me that often made me feel I was melting under her gaze.

"William," she finally said.

"Yes."

More silent staring ensued.

"William."

"Yes."

"Where are you?"

She had dazzling eyes, huge for her face and a lurid shade of green that was probably from colored contact lenses, but gave her a hypnotic power and made it almost impossible to turn away from her.

"I'm sitting in front of your desk."

"That's not what I'm asking. I'm asking you where you are. Where *are* you?" She ignored her ringing phone and continued to stare at me, waiting for an answer. "I had such high hopes for you. You were doing so well."

"Well . . ."

"Now I can't even see you." She took a folder out of her desk drawer without breaking eye contact. "Your sales figures."

"Bad?"

"Disappointing."

"I agree."

"Participation at office meetings."

"Disappointing?"

"Erratic."

"I was having those problems with my contact lenses."

"I'm not scolding you, William."

"I know."

"I'm worried."

"Don't be."

"You've gone, William. You've disappeared. I can't find you."

I was used to disappointing myself, but I hated to disappoint Gina. She was an unwaveringly positive woman of about sixty-five who'd been through as much trauma and tragedy as anyone I knew. She'd lived through two bouts with cancer, a car accident in which her daughter had nearly died, an explosion of a propane tank that had destroyed two-thirds of her house. Somehow she managed to consider herself the luckiest person alive. The chemotherapy, she'd tell you, had caused her to go bald, but then given her the rich, curly mane she'd longed for her whole life. The car accident had almost killed her daughter, but it had gotten the wayward girl off alcohol and into a nursing career. The propane explosion? "I hated that end of the house, anyway." It horrified me to think I was disappointing someone who'd managed to find an upside to ovarian cancer.

"It's funny you should say that," I said.

"Funny. Why is it funny? What's funny about the disappearance of someone you care for?"

"I've let my attention drift," I told her. When in doubt, a confession, any confession, usually brings people over to your side. "I realized it this morning. The drifting."

"And?"

"And I'm making some changes, Gina. Good ones, I hope."

Her phone started ringing again, but she didn't avert her mesmerizing eyes for a second. "How?"

"How?"

"How are you changing? What are you doing?"

"I'm reading Simone de Beauvoir," I said.

"I had high hopes for you, William. You know what I'm talking about, don't you? I'm talking about my son. He's going to be fine, it'll straighten him out, and he'll be a better person, but he isn't ever going to be a person sitting here at this desk, at my desk. I had high hopes you might. Do you see what I'm saying?"

A couple of months earlier, her forty-year-old son had confessed to heroin addiction and had entered rehab. From what I could tell, she was saying that she had been thinking of selling me the business at some point. She'd implied as much before, but we'd never discussed it.

"I'm working on it," I said.

"It's not as if you have distractions, William. No marriage, family, health problems I know of. This should be your focus."

"I'm working on it," I said again.

"I want results. I need results from you. Come back to me, William, come back." She picked up the phone and put her hand over the mouthpiece. "Now go."

an alternative to sex

My ritual upon entering my apartment at the end of the day was to go from room to room making sure there was nothing out of order. Because I went through the same routine before leaving in the morning, I rarely found anything that needed immediate attention, although sometimes the towels demanded refolding or there were spots on the faucets in the bathroom or a few wrinkles on the pillow-cases.

My cleaning compulsion was the source of endless no-win situations. I hated finding anything disorganized or dirty, but I got so much pleasure out of setting things right, I felt cheated out of a major source of satisfaction when I didn't. And so, when I walked into the kitchen and saw that I'd left the ironing board in the middle of the floor that morning, I didn't know whether to be happy to put it away or alarmed at the glaring oversight that was completely out of character. Where *was* I, indeed, that I hadn't noticed? Obviously, I was changing my sexual behavior at the right moment.

Once I'd stowed the ironing board, I heard the computer calling me from the room on the top floor of the house I used as a study. I felt an actual physical craving to sit down at the thing and start typing, similar to the physical craving I felt for coffee the instant I opened my eyes in the morning. At this very moment, upstairs in that study, on that very computer for which I'd paid good money and which therefore was completely within my rights to use, there was a huge party going on, a sweaty orgy of anticipation and flirtation. Within a three-mile radius of my house, thousands of men were logged on to their computers, making connections and offering unlimited opportunities for excitement, distraction, and, yes, disappointment, but even that had its appeal. And I was missing out on all of it.

I decided to vacuum, always a reliable alternative to sex. I'd bought my vacuum cleaner for $500 several years earlier, and it had quickly become my most cherished possession. I suppose there's a lot to take issue with in the German character, but one thing you absolutely cannot take away from Germans is their skill at making appliances. Vacuum cleaners are like bread: the less gimmickry, the better the product. This model was a sleek silver canister that was a shining example of simplicity and efficiency, the vacuum equivalent of a simple, crusty baguette. The two floors of my apartment comprise 1,875 square feet, and I went over every bit of it (minus the study, which I didn't dare enter) in a little under an hour.

I tried to make dinner, but couldn't muster up enough enthusiasm for cooking to bother putting together my usual scrambled-eggs-and-potato specialty. Like a lot of lonely people, I tended to eat breakfast food at all meals. I tossed a tray of frozen something into the microwave (no dishes or pans to wash) and brought it into the living room and turned on the TV. I'd stopped watching television with any regularity when I started my sex binge, and judging from what I now saw as I spun through the channels, in the intervening months, the usual programming on every channel had been replaced by shows on which people in bikinis sat around eating insects.

I checked my watch and saw that I'd been home for a total of two hours. It wasn't a promising start to the evening. I could feel my frustrated desire to log on morphing into anger and decided to focus some of my rage on the president and his wacko right-wing buddies and their apparent plan to start a preemptive war. But that led to more depression, which led to an intensified desire for carnal distraction.

Reading, that had been my plan. I went to my bedroom and picked up *The Mandarins* (wonderful title) and sat down on the chaise longue, exactly as I had pictured myself doing at various points throughout the day. This particular chaise was not quite longue enough for my ridiculous legs, a detail I'd forgotten in my meditative fantasies, and my feet hung off the edge at an uncomfortable angle. I resettled and opened the book. The recent paperback edition I owned had a fifty-two-page introduction by Rosemary Boyle, a contemporary poet and part-time academic who'd become famous for writing a memoir about being a widow.

The biographical note on her was twice the length of the one on Beauvoir. She started out praising the novel and quickly lapsed into an explanation of why the intelligent reader should attempt to suffer through its many long, boring sections. "The exasperating tedium of these chapters, the difficulty of forcing oneself to read page after page after page of unnecessary dialogue and descriptive passages will be handsomely rewarded by the satisfaction one feels upon reaching the end."

These discouraging words had not been part of my fantasies either. Part II of the introduction opened with Boyle's description of the ways in which Madame de Beauvoir had inspired her to write her own most recent best seller, an "infinitely more succinct" novel that had won "several major literary prizes."

The third section of the introduction began with a beguiling question: "Why dust off this unwieldy antique now, especially in this flawed, barely coherent translation?"

My back was aching from the way I'd had to contort my body and I could hear the whirr of the computer from my study. As an indication of the dangerous water I was headed toward, I began to think about Didier, a scrawny troublemaker who'd been dropping in and out of my life in assorted unwholesome ways for a couple of years. Don't, don't, don't, I reminded myself and then, in a moment of inspiration, picked up the phone and dialed my tenant, Kumiko.

an alternative to vacuuming

After my usual cheerful inquiries about the apartment, the hot water, and her artwork, I said, "I think we need to have a conversation soon—"

"About money," she said, cutting me off. "Am I right?"

"Yes, you are."

"You see, I know you well. I've been told I have psychic powers."

She was leading me down the path of irrelevance, a tactic she often used to derail conversations about the rent. Figuring out that the landlord to whom you owe more than $3,000 is calling about money doesn't exactly qualify you for the Uri Geller Hall of Fame.

"We need to talk about the rent."

"You're angry at me, William. It would probably be best for both of us if you'd just admit that you're angry."

"I don't see how it matters whether I'm angry or not."

"It matters to *me*. It matters a great deal. You think I'm not trying."

"Of course I think you're trying, Kumiko." I cursed myself for saying her name. Every time I uttered it, I felt I'd handed her a small victory. "I'm not accusing you of not trying."

"Well then, what *are* you accusing me of? Please. Tell me. Do you think it's easy selling art since September eleventh?"

It sounded to me as if she was about to get tearful, something I couldn't abide. I decided, for her sake, to let the attempt at exploiting the terrorist attacks pass. "I'm accusing you . . . I'm *not* accusing you . . . Listen, Kumiko"—that name again—"let's just take a deep breath and calm down, all right?"

"It's not easy to calm down when you're about to be evicted and your landlord won't even tell you why."

landlord 101

When I'd bought the house three years earlier, the first-floor apartment was inhabited by an elderly couple who'd been living there for twenty years. I was happy to have them in residence, despite a blaring television twenty-four hours a day. They paid the minimal rent exactly on time, and more important, I didn't have to go through the process of interviewing tenants and making a selection, something I dreaded because I'd been a renter for so long and was infinitely more comfortable in that role.

A year after I bought, the couple announced that they were relocating to a retirement village in Texas. "We hear it's hot, hot, hot three hundred and sixty-five days a year," the husband told me. "That's what we want. Hot, hot, hot." My widowed mother had moved to an assisted living facility in Arizona a few years earlier, also giving intolerably high temperatures as the central attraction. "Doesn't the heat bother you?" I'd asked her after listening to her brag about having had a week of 120-degree days. Her indignant answer: "I've got the air-conditioning set at sixty-five, twenty-four/seven. I live in sweaters and long pants and sleep under an electric blanket. Why would the heat bother me? I'm freezing."

Before moving to hell, the elderly couple had told me there was a woman in the neighborhood they'd met a few times who was looking for a place to live; her current landlords, they explained, had raised her rent two hundred percent.

"People have no morals," I said. "Greed. What does she do?"

"She's an artist," they said.

I interpreted this to mean what it usually means: she was living off a trust fund. When I met Kumiko for the first time, everything about her confirmed my suspicion. She was wearing Southwestern turquoise jewelry, was elusive on the subject of income, and had about her an air of education and long-standing unemployability. She had on one of those cheap muslin smocks only a rich person could afford to wear, and she had her long gray hair in braids. An ex-husband was mentioned in passing. Having spent years at the office helping landlords rent out their apartments, I knew that I ought to ask her for references, a security deposit, a month's rent in advance, and so on, but this all seemed invasive and impolite. I feared doing so would start this promising, amicable relationship off on a sour note. After a fifteen-minute conversation, I invited her to move in.

She had been living in the apartment for eighteen months and thus far had paid the rent on time twice. Most often, it dribbled in unpredictably in cash payments made in small bills that she counted out in front of me, making me feel guilty and avaricious for each and every dollar I was collecting. Half the time, I was so racked with anxiety watching her dole it out that by the time she finished, I had no idea what portion of the rent she was paying or had paid or still owed or if she was paying me this month's rent or last month's. I wasn't entirely sure about the exact figure she owed me, which was probably just as well, as it would only have made the situation seem more hopeless. Thinking it might elicit a little sympathy from her, I had once explained the economics of the arrangement, and had ended up revealing to her the kinds of financial details I'd been embarrassed to ask of her and never discussed with anyone, including my tax accountant.

She had an uncanny ability to head off my attempts at pressuring her to pay up. Twice when I'd been on the verge of asking her to leave, she'd asked me for a loan. There was something so bold and outrageous about this, I took it as proof of my initial supposition about her being an eccentric heiress. Vague statements such as "until my check comes in" fed my trust-fund assumptions.

As for her name, this was part of her painterly persona, not something that had been given to her by her parents. She claimed that "Kumiko" is Japanese for "girl with braids," and she always included "braided imagery" somewhere in each of her paintings. Or so she said; thus far, I'd never seen her work.

"Past the age of twelve," Edward had proclaimed, "you can get away with braids only if you're Willie Nelson or insane. I think we know which category she falls into."

an alternative to kumiko

After taking a few deep breaths to calm myself down and hopefully give Kumiko time to get past the threatened tears, I said, "If you were making even partial payments, I would feel better about the situation. I'd feel marginally more hopeful. But even those have dried up."

"You told me you found the partial payments too confusing, that's why I stopped. I thought that was what you wanted. I was trying to be a good tenant. You have to be more clear, William."

"I didn't know that Plan B was no payments at all."

I wandered downstairs to the living room, carrying the phone, sprawled in a chair, took off my shoes, and stared at my feet. A week earlier, I'd connected with a handsome young man whose sexual turn-on was bathing and massaging my feet and then trimming and filing my toenails. After getting past the initial ticklishness I'd found it relaxing and, despite a lack of genital contact, incredibly titillating. On top of that, he—apparently a grad student in economics with a fellowship—lived in a suite of Moorish rooms in a Harvard residence, and the architectural splendor alone was worth the trip. He'd done a fantastic job, and my feet still looked clean and well tended. Somewhere on my computer upstairs, I had his number. Surely it wouldn't count as sex if I got together with him again. It was basically a free pedicure with a little toe sucking tossed in, a happy experience for both of us. On the whole, I'm much less judgmental about a person's sexual interests than I am about his window treatments.

As I was mulling over the possibility of calling "Tad" and listening to Kumiko discuss problems she was having with air circulation in the garage studio, I heard a horn blaring on the street below. I went to the window and saw a taxi in front of the house.

"Could we wrap this up, William?" she asked. "My cab is here. I'm late for a yoga class. Why don't we try to work on being more clear with each other?"

"How long have you been taking yoga classes?" I asked.

"Years. It forms the core of my spiritual life."

"Spiritual life," I said. "I've been thinking about getting one of those."

After we'd hung up, I watched her load a string bag filled with water and towels and then herself into the back of the taxi. My relationship with her was deeply humiliating, there was no question of that. Worse still was the fact that allowing myself to be exploited by her made me feel morally righteous.

In fact, the whole absurd conversation made me feel so simultaneously abused and morally superior, I decided to sign on to the Internet and drop my membership for the "dating" site that had been my home away from home for so many months. That would settle it once and for all and make sure that there were no further temptations to resist.

As soon as the familiar graphics popped up on-screen, loud and lurid, I felt a surge of contentment and the evaporation of the anxieties of my day—my job performance, the Kumiko debacle, curiosity about Edward's plans for big changes. Oddly enough, I even felt a lessening in my worries about the amount of time I'd been wasting in this very pursuit and the gnawing concern that I wasn't going to stick to my resolve. Home again, home again.

But I'd entered so I could leave, and I started that process. Whoever had designed the site had made buying a membership easier than waking up, and closing it out the logistic equivalent of filing taxes. Retraction requests had to be made to several billing services; my "stats"—a compilation of elaborately exaggerated numbers—had to be wiped off the screen; and my pictures had to be deleted. I had posted two pictures, neither one of my face, since that craggy monument to lost youth wasn't my main selling point.

By the time I'd dragged my good intentions through half the process, my mailbox was blinking. I can't stand when people address themselves using their name, but a fake name seemed less cloying. "Everett," I said aloud, "don't open that mailbox."

When I clicked on it, I saw that six people had written to me. Two were men I'd already met at some point in the last few months, although judging from what they'd written, neither remembered the meetings. Two more qualified as the lunatic fringe ("Im tied up, blindfolded, naked, partying—complete PIG—do it all—no condoms—TOTALLY disease free—") with proctology-exam photos attached. All displayed the usual contempt for grammar: "Thats nice!!!!" and "Your hot!!!!!" (If you're going to use an apostrophe in this corner of the virtual world, you'd better use it incorrectly lest someone assume you care about such things or are, God forbid, a homosexual.)

I was always flattered by the attention ("Thank's!!!!!!!"), even when it came from people I wasn't interested in. I reserved special contempt and derision for anyone who was tacky and desperate enough to spend as much time combing through this flesh pile as I did. ("Hmm. Him again. Obviously has no life whatsoever.")

By the time I'd deleted those messages, several more had arrived in my mailbox. I could feel myself being sucked into a familiar cycle and could tell already that I was going to have trouble pulling out. What if one of these messages was from someone who might be the person who . . . But I couldn't finish the thought because I didn't know what the best-case scenario was in this case. What was I looking for?

Read them, I told myself, but don't respond to them. And then I qualified the rules so that I could respond only if the messages contained full sentences. Or if not full sentences, at least no spelling errors. Oh, all right, not *too many* spelling errors. And if the person clearly wasn't a native English speaker—Carlo, Marco, Sergio, David—the rule about spelling errors didn't apply.

I gave myself ten minutes to finish up; then I'd start making business calls. An hour and a half later, I got a message from someone who made the requisite anatomical compliments and wrote in complete sentences that he'd just moved into a new apartment and was looking for someone to come over and help him christen it. Real estate. Practically business-related. I could ask a few questions about his broker. Even my boss, Gina, would approve of that. I practically owed it to her to see him. Maybe he hadn't sold his old place yet and was looking for someone to put it on the market.

Half an hour later, as I was driving into Boston in the rain, I reasoned that I wasn't really breaking my celibacy resolution, I was simply delaying it. One day was as good as the next to make a start.

Besides, I had the option of turning around at any moment and heading back home. At nearly every intersection, I assured myself that if I turned around now, I wouldn't even have delayed my vow.

As I was parking the car, I told myself that I could just go for a walk and didn't have to bother ringing "Buck's" bell, and as I was ringing the bell to what turned out to be a third-floor apartment, I assured myself I didn't have to wait around to go in.

When "Buck" turned out to look absolutely nothing like the pictures he'd sent, I told myself I wasn't obliged to go inside, and when I entered, I told myself I didn't have to have sex with him just because it was a beautiful apartment.

"You're tall," he said, a statement of fact I chose to interpret as a compliment.

As we were fucking, I told myself it was for the best that I was getting the whole thing out of the way here and now and could start fresh in the morning.

There was a window beside the bed, and through it I could see the lights of cars speeding along Memorial Drive, on the opposite side of the river. There were still a lot of unpacked boxes from the recent move, but they were stacked in neat piles.

"Who's your real estate broker?" I asked as I was getting dressed.

"That's kind of a personal question," Buck said.

As I was driving home, I told myself I now had new confirmation that the celibacy resolution was a good idea. And since I was starting that tomorrow, and tomorrow was another day, I might as well make use of the remaining hour of this last day of my sexual profligacy. I thought about Didier again, as I often did at the tail end of these disappointments, but of course I was much too sensible to venture there.

I decided instead to call Christopher, a right-wing nut whose politics were in such conflict with his erotic appetites, it felt almost like my moral duty to have sex with him from time to time to point out to him what a hypocrite he was.

a fresh start

As I drove to the office the next morning, I decided my tactic of delaying the start of my resolve by twenty-four hours had been brilliant. Now I was truly ready to begin—enthusiastic about the world of real estate, determined to get back in Gina Fulmetti's good graces, and sexually exhausted.

The office was wedged between a pet-grooming salon and a

Mexican takeout joint along a busy and fashionable stretch of Mass Ave in Cambridge. It was walking distance to Harvard Square, but far enough from that circus of chain stores and students to be largely unaffected by it. I'd become friendly with Veronica, the woman who ran the grooming shop. She was an immense, gray-haired woman who tended to have a host of troubled teenagers doing volunteer work for her as they picked up a trade. When she was short on volunteers, she sometimes let me help bathe the dogs. That morning, she was propped up on a chair, drinking soda out of a cup the size of a small wastebasket and overseeing a couple of emaciated girls with pale faces as they hosed down a soapy Irish setter. Just as well I wasn't needed. I was ready to start my day.

The only person in the office that morning was Mildred Robinson. Mildred was an intensely focused psychologist who worked at the office part-time. She was transitioning—to use her verb—from psychology to real estate because it was more (another quote) fun. Everyone resented her impressive sales figures because we felt she ought to stick to a career she'd trained for for almost a decade. No one begins his adult life as a real estate broker, and certainly no one at Cambridge Properties had started out in this field; but most of us had ended up there as the result of financial or emotional collapse, not because we were seeking something as friable as "fun."

I sat at my desk and took out a legal pad. I listed the closings I had pending (only two, including one with a compulsive apartment shopper that probably wouldn't go through) and the follow-up calls I needed to make, putting Samuel and Charlotte at the top of that list. Then I wrote down the names of six people I could contact to remind them that we were in the middle of a real estate boom, and that if they were thinking about taking advantage of it by selling their property, they couldn't do better than listing it with me. This last chore ranked high on the dreaded death-of-a-salesman scale of business matters. It always made me feel as if I were panhandling or trying to talk someone into a morally questionable act of exploitation. "Sell your house while prices are still unconscionably inflated. Don't wait for the market to adjust."

I shouldn't have dreaded making cold calls as much as I did; I'd learned over the years that most people are flattered by the attention, like talking about their property—especially if they have no interest in selling it—and are always delighted to engage in discussions of the pornographic sum we'd put down as an asking price. Obscene phone calls everyone was happy to receive.

Since the previous September, people were willing to give serious consideration to taking what they could get while they could get it, even if they had no idea what they planned to do with it. Thanks to the wacky color-coded terror alerts, the news reports about anthrax attacks, and the gathering war clouds, the whole country was poised on the brink of smoldering panic. There was an underlying feeling that everyone wanted *out,* although, really, there was nowhere to go. Canada had begun to look like an appealing place to live to a lot of people who previously wouldn't have considered spending a brief vacation there. Even Edward, who had as much reason as anyone to worry about the future, had made noises about moving to Montreal, a city he'd once derided as being "a strip club with a good subway system."

The most promising names on my death-of-a-salesman list were those of a young cousin and his wife who'd made a small fortune in the computer field in the mid-nineties, had cashed out, and now spent their time taking trips to coral reefs, rain forests, and other rapidly disappearing natural wonders. They reportedly owned several condominiums in and around Boston. I'd avoided bothering them for years, but now they looked to me like prime targets. They were connected to the maternal side of my family, and the easiest way to get their number was to call my mother. It was barely dawn in Arizona, but since Margaret claimed not to have slept for at least ten years, I dialed.

Sleep deprivation

I started the conversation with my usual greeting: "I didn't wake you up, did I?"

"Who is this?" she asked.

"Your firstborn."

"William?" Perhaps there was another I didn't know about. "Did they blow up something else?"

"Not that I've heard."

"Ah. Why do you sound so peculiar? Did you just get up?" This was retaliation for my opening question and the ultimate insult. Normal sleep patterns were indicators of luck and a lack of character.

"Hardly," I said. "I've been up for hours, I cleaned my apartment twice, and I'm at my office."

"At least you went to bed. If I don't get some sleep soon, I don't know what I'm going to do."

"What's it been, five, six years now?"

"Twenty, but who's counting? I see you've been getting some rain the past couple of days. It's going to be lovely today and warm for the rest of the week. In case you haven't heard."

She always kept up with the weather in Boston, something I found touching since it meant she was thinking about me. Several years earlier, she'd relocated from Connecticut, where I'd grown up, to stifling Arizona. She'd moved partly for the insufferable heat, partly to be closer to a sister she never spoke to, and partly because my brother and his family lived in California. I'd been relieved that she'd moved out of my sphere of responsibility, but I still hadn't gotten over feeling abandoned on the East Coast by my family.

"What about the weekend?" I asked. "Any word on that?"

"Not that I've heard. I only watch the three-day forecasts. At my age, there's no point in listening to the long-range projections."

She was close to eighty and fiercely healthy. Arizona had cured any minor breathing ailments she'd had, and the activity in the retirement village kept her mind engaged in local gossip and dramas. Still, she'd picked up the sarcastic pessimism that seemed to be the dominant personality trait in widows of her age. Almost every comment or suggestion I made, whether it was about her own life or related to some broader political issue, was greeted with the same dismissive vote of no confidence. Education cuts? "What do I care? I'm on the way out, anyway." Television? "I've got ten minutes to live and I'm going to waste it watching TV?" Go out to dinner? "I'm sick of food." Call up her widowed sister, who lived a few doors away, and arrange an outing? "I've got better things to do than listen to her. She's so negative."

It was all a defense against the dying off of dear friends and the awful toll age was taking on the survivors. She spent a lot of time on the phone, talking to friends back east who were in various stages of mental deterioration, something she referred to often but I was banned from mentioning. I was not allowed to utter the words "senility" or "Alzheimer's." "Next thing you know," she'd say, "you'll have me in a home." There was no point in reminding her that she was, essentially, in a home, one she'd put herself into.

Despite our consistently combative tone, I enjoyed talking with her and was proud of her. She didn't drink much, ate sensibly, rarely expected me to visit, and as far as I could tell, never gave money to the Catholic Church. She and my father had been staunch Democrats when I was growing up, but in the past twenty years, her politics had turned vague. If I mentioned a politician, any politician, she'd say, "Ah, they're all crooks." I took this to mean she voted Republican but had the decency to be ashamed of the fact.

Once we'd wandered around our usual conversational land mines, I said, "I'm calling about the rich cousins. I need their phone number."

"Melinda and Rob? People with that kind of money don't just give out their phone number. It's unlisted."

"That's why I'm calling you. I thought you could give it to me. I wanted to ask them if they were looking for a real estate agent."

"Oh God, William, that's so humiliating. It's panhandling."

"It certainly is not. Where do you come up with these ideas? It's business." I could hear water running and the sounds of scratching or scrubbing. My brother kept her in cell phones with unlimited calling plans, and she spent most of the day wired to a headset with the phone hooked to a belt loop. "Are you scouring the bathtub? What are you using?"

"Some powder that was on sale last month."

"I told you to use orange Tang for the bathtub and the sink, didn't I? You dump it in and sprinkle on some Pepsi. It's much more effective than scouring powder."

A loud rush of water was followed by gurgling. "I can't be bothered shopping for all that. It's not in the store here. And don't tell me you'll send it to me. The whole idea of washing the house with food disgusts me. It worries me. Throwing food around the house and vacuuming six times a day. It isn't normal. You're almost fifty."

I bristled at the accusation. "I most certainly am not almost fifty. If you think about it, I'm closer to being almost forty."

"A big tall man like you dusting all day. What kind of a hobby is that?"

"Let's talk about Kevin. How's he doing?" I often used my brother as a conversational diversion when I was talking with my mother. He was the most normal person I knew, which is to say: overworked, stressed out, financially strapped, and emotionally confused. Today, Margaret wasn't having any of it.

"You should be dating," she said.

I took this advice to mean that she thought I lived an empty and perhaps tragic life. "I'm getting a little long in the tooth for maternal advice," I said. "I've hit a small bump at work, but that's temporary. I have a lot of close friends, many people who are important to me. For all you know, I could be dating compulsively. And while we're on the subject, *you* should be dating."

There was a long pause in the conversation, during which the door to the street opened and Charlotte O'Malley came into the office. I stood and motioned for her to take a seat in the reception area out front. She had on the same outfit she'd worn the day before, including the raincoat, even though the sun was out. She sat and began a futile attempt at gathering all the loose strands of her hair into an elastic band. "I should get going," I told my mother. "A customer just walked in."

"What kind of customer?"

"Half of a nice happily married couple looking to relocate."

"Maybe you can learn something from them. Maybe you should try. I don't see you surrounded by many nice, happy couples of any sort. And for your information, I *am* dating."

"Oh?"

"I suppose you could call it that."

"Well. Good for you."

The news came as a pleasant shock. My father had died a decade earlier and in the time after his death, Margaret had flatly refused any suggestions that she might, at some point, long for male companionship. The retirement village was mostly widows, all of whom, according to my mother, had been looking forward to this solo period of their lives since the day they were married, give or take a few hours. Widowhood, she explained, was generally considered the reward for a lifetime of living in the shadow of an overbearing husband and playing the role of dutiful wife. Desert Springs was full of sturdy women in T-shirts and sun visors who, despite their sarcasm and who-gives-a-fuck attitude, seemed fundamentally happy with their lives. They occasionally talked about some man or other who'd outlived his wife, usually in a disparaging tone, as if he'd broken the terms of a contract.

I'd had a cordial, distant relationship with my father, a dentist, and at his funeral had been stunned to learn that his receptionist had been his mistress for years. Rose herself had told me this. I suppose she thought I would be more understanding and less judgmental than my brother, and this was undoubtedly true. Like most men who adore their wives, worship their children, and are one hundred percent satisfied with their lives, Kevin couldn't stand to think that anyone was getting away with marital infidelity.

I'd always found my father a distressingly flat character with no discernible inner life. The mistress news at least provided evidence of outside interests and emotional complexity; it made me happy for him, even if it made me all the more certain that the entire marriage had been a raw deal for my mother.

"Does this guy live in Desert Springs?" I asked my mother. "Your boyfriend, or whatever he's called."

"He lives in Oregon. We met on the Internet."

"How contemporary."

"Everyone's doing it these days."

"I've heard. I just hadn't figured you for the type."

"I didn't either. But that computer has been sitting in my

kitchen since Kevin gave it to me, and between old age and dirty bombs, I figured I didn't have all that much to lose. You should try it, William. You can't believe how easy it is to meet people. Nice people."

It was alarming to receive this advice from my mother. I managed to wrangle the phone numbers of my rich cousins out of her, and promised that I'd make my shameful call only once, would leave only one message if they didn't pick up the phone, and would not mention her name or my brother's once I'd started my sales pitch. We said our farewells, and as I was about to hang up, she promised she'd send me a photo of Jerry, her romantic interest. "Don't worry," she added, "I'll send one of the G-rated ones."

advice

"We spent the night at a hotel in Cambridge," Charlotte O'Malley told me, "in case you were wondering why I'm wearing the same clothes I had on yesterday."

To be polite, I said, "I hadn't noticed."

"I'm sorry to hear that. I figured you for the observant type."

"In general, or particularly regarding women's clothes?"

"In general. Then again, you're wearing the same jacket you were wearing yesterday."

I checked. One of the drawbacks of neatly putting away all of your clothes at the end of the day, instead of heaping them on the floor, is that it's hard to keep track of what you've worn and when. "So you spent the night here in town," I said. "It sounds as if you can't wait to move. We're going to have to work on that."

"Sam had an early meeting and we thought it might be a good idea. To signal the start of this new venture. After all these years, it's odd to not have to get back home for Daniel's sake." She slipped off her raincoat and draped it over the back of her chair. She sighed as she turned around, as if she had a kink in her back. "I've struggled with feeling irrelevant since he turned twelve. Now I suppose I really am."

"It must be a relief."

"I'm trying to decide whether it is or not. I'm guessing you don't have children."

"That's true."

She smiled with a hint of sadness in her eye, and I could sense she was writing me off, as people with children often did, as having an impairment that I had to live with, a handicap, something like a missing limb. I never minded the pitying looks parents give the childless, largely because I pity people who were saddled with the grueling task of child rearing. The whole expensive, messy world of parenthood was lost to me, a mysterious and unappealing universe that I felt lucky to have avoided. I don't mind children, and I've met a few I even liked. But the plastic toys and the juice in boxes were another story. Probably I wouldn't be so dismissive at age eighty, assuming I made it that far.

She named the hotel they'd stayed at. "It's expensive, but it's lovely. Very romantic."

I nodded at this and looked away. By romantic, I assumed she meant that they'd had sex. I'll listen to the most graphic details of someone's anonymous sex encounter, but any reference, no matter how oblique, to the intimate life of a long-term couple is deeply embarrassing to me. Especially when the word "romantic," which I associate with toss pillows and floral bedspreads, finds its unwelcome way into the conversation. "That's . . . nice," I said.

She frowned, disappointed at my reaction, I suppose, and said: "I wanted to point something out about yesterday."

"Please."

"You didn't ask me what I do for work."

"I didn't, that's true."

"I think you were afraid I don't do anything and you didn't want to be rude by asking. You figured you'd just leave the ball in my court."

I started to protest, reassuring her that it had been a mere oversight.

"You asked Samuel," she said.

"And he answered, but I'm not sure I truly understand what it is he does. On a day-to-day basis."

"He consults. If you ask for more details, he'll happily provide them, but between you and me, I don't think you'd find them all that interesting. I know I don't." She shrugged and looked around the office. By now, Jack had come in and was turned away from us, muttering advice to his girlfriend into the phone. Mildred, the in-transition psychologist, was eating a candy bar and gazing into space. Aside from the three of us, the office was empty. "Is it always so uncrowded in here?" she asked.

"A lot of the job involves driving around town and checking out property. If you spend too much time at your desk, it doesn't look good."

"I don't spend enough time at my desk and it still doesn't look good. Fortunately, I work at home, so only I notice."

"That's my cue to finally ask you what you do."

"Nothing. Well, nothing I'm especially proud of. I'm a ghost-writer for a company that packages business books. Big, dreary tomes about management style and corporate culture. The books come to me late in the process, after the putative authors have finished, and I make them marginally more readable. The secret is knowing and caring nothing about the business world. Obviously, I got into it through Samuel's connections. Believe it or not, I was a nurse a million years ago."

"Pre-Daniel?"

"Yes, exactly. At one point, I thought I'd go back to it, but I'm not very good at sympathy."

I opened my filing cabinet and took out the folder I'd started on them. "You work at home?" I asked. "In that case, we should look at places with at least one study."

"Is that about us?" she said. She leaned toward me, trying to see what I'd written down.

"It's just the basic boring facts," I said.

She probly working-class Irish. Catholic, I wrote. *Former nurse who married well. Nice couple? I can learn something frm them?? She needs study. I shld close mine off. Always leads to trble.*

"Here's another boring fact for you," she said. "I'm hoping to rent a small office when we move to town. Working at home has been part of the problem." She looked down at herself and then back at me with a frown. "The kitchen, the pantry. The cocktail hour."

Jack had finished talking with his girlfriend and was going through the real estate listings that had come in that morning. He gazed over at Charlotte a few times, checking out her legs and listening in on our conversation. I had the feeling he didn't care much for women in a general sense, especially if they took the upper hand in real estate transactions.

"Were you interested in looking at more properties today?" I asked. "I haven't set up anything, but I could easily make some calls."

"No, I have to get home so I can procrastinate in a controlled environment. I was driving by on my way out of town, and there was a parking space, and I couldn't resist. I thought it might help if I gave you some advice about the best way to deal with my husband."

"To be honest," I said, "I didn't think you were that serious about buying."

"I'm completely serious. He's ambivalent. We have to work around his ambivalence."

"We're ganging up on him, in other words."

"Oh, absolutely. It's the only way to get anything done. I hope you weren't planning on being impartial. Even the counselor gave up on that charade."

Charades, I wrote on their sheet. *Drinker?*

"Let's face it," I said. "I'm a salesman. My main objective is to make a sale."

"Good. I wanted to get to you before Sam did. The key is this: he responds well to a hard sales pitch. Be aggressive with him. If he thinks you've put a lot of work into finding us a place, he'll be more likely to buy."

I nodded, as if this were the kind of information one spouse usually revealed about the other.

"Don't hesitate to try guilt. Mention the hours you've put in, the weekends you've spent sorting through listings for us. If you want to leave a message for him right now, call his cell phone. I'm sure he has it off while he's at his meeting."

"I might feel a little self-conscious with you listening in, knowing it was a charade, of sorts."

"But I could coach you."

"I'll call him," I said, "but not right now." It seemed important to stand up for myself, even if we both knew she was in control of the situation.

She thrust out her chest as she slipped on her raincoat, whether for my benefit or Jack's, I couldn't tell. "I think this is going to work out well for all of us. Call him soon so we can build up some momentum."

I saw her to the door and watched as she walked up the sidewalk to her car, a silver Volvo that appeared relatively new but had a significant dent in the trunk. When I got back to my desk, Jack moved to the chair Charlotte had been in, shook his head with disgust, and scowled. "That's why I'll never marry again, William. Manipulative bitch. Stabbing her husband in the back, no loyalty, no shame."

"Funny," I said. "I thought from the way you were looking at her you liked her."

"I love her. She proves everything I've always thought about women of that generation. If I were you, I wouldn't get involved with them. You might make a decent sale, but you get too caught up in people's lives, and the lives of that pair are messy, I can promise you that. They're going to walk all over you."

I should have taken his advice to heart, but it was the most personal comment he'd ever made to me, one that showed he at least had thought about me, and I was genuinely touched. "If you see me going off the rails completely, let me know."

"You're off already," he said.

I closed my eyes for a minute, visualized the calm reading corner of my bedroom, the chaise longue, the light shining on the page of my book. It was going to be a very good day.

Itr

I thought about Charlotte and Sam much later that night, as I was riding the subway home from downtown Boston, where I'd taken a minor detour on the road to celibacy. It was a little after eleven, the hour when the theaters and concerts had just let out, and the subway car was crowded with well-dressed people clutching playbills and each other, scanning programs to review what they'd just seen. I stood holding on to a pole, feeling like the isolated odd man out. I'd taken the subway downtown instead of driving because I was tired of battling Boston's ridiculous traffic problems, and also because I'd had a loopy, half-baked idea that I might spend the night down there and didn't want to have to deal with parking. Of course it hadn't worked out as planned.

A woman in a bright red sweater with one arm around her boyfriend glanced up from her playbill, saw me staring, and gave me a cold glance. Chastened, I turned around.

Earlier in the evening, I'd been sitting in my apartment expending an enormous amount of energy trying to not have sex, which seemed more pointless than actually going out and getting it out of the way. To minimize the amount of time expended, and avoid the black hole of the computer, I called someone I'd known for a couple of years and saw from time to time, usually at his convenience, although a lot less frequently in the past year. His name was Ron. He'd been in Chicago the previous September 11 and got stranded while the planes were grounded. During that period of stunned confusion and vulnerability, he'd met a man in a coffee shop, gone to an art museum with him, and then stayed at his apartment for close to a week. The timing of their meeting gave the relationship an extra layer of significance in Ron's mind, as if it were compensation of some kind, generously arranged for him by fate.

Since the advent of Marshall, Ron had gotten in touch with me a handful of times, explaining that long-distance relationships were difficult, and that I was the only one of his "buddies" he was comfortable continuing to see, albeit on an infrequent basis. Not only had I chosen to believe this, I'd actually been flattered by it. I assumed he meant I was in some special category of irresistible. (Ron himself was spectacularly irresistible, combining the rugged looks of an Italian soccer player, the submissiveness of overcooked spaghetti, and the mesmerizing self-absorption so common among exceptionally handsome men.)

But that night, as he discussed, in a moment of postcoital expansiveness, the many virtues of beloved Marshall, I began to wonder.

"So, Ron, let me ask you something. You're in love with Marshall, you've just said you have a perfect relationship, there's nothing you'd change. Why do you call me from time to time? Why did you agree to seeing me tonight?"

He thought this over for a minute and then reached down and squeezed my penis. "This," he said.

"That, of course." Partly, it was what I wanted to hear, but having heard it, I was insulted. "Those aren't that hard to find, and I'm guessing Marshall has one, too."

"He does, but I especially like yours. And obviously, it isn't only that. Not by a lot. You're different from a lot of people I meet." I was touched by the comment and was about to thank him. Unfortunately, he had more to say. "I've told Marshall about you, and it's all right with him if I see you sometimes. He knows this isn't any threat to what he and I have. You're obviously not a relationship kind of person. You're not a boyfriend kind of guy." He said it in a cheerful, lascivious way, as if he was paying me a compliment, but I dressed quickly and let myself out.

As I watched the happy couples on the subway car, I mounted a defense of myself. I was not incapable of long-term relationships. Especially short ones. I had had a few. To define my terms, I consider anything that lasts more than a year a long-term relationship. Less than that I think of as dating, even if serious. When people have been together five years or more, I usually file them under "married," and when a couple has been together for longer than ten years, I assume they're roommates with occasional sexual benefits.

In my several decades of adulthood, I had had four long-term relationships. The last—a twenty-four-month event—had ended about four years earlier. I considered this a pretty good track record. It showed a certain level of emotional gravitas. A child-hood friend had had no LTR—an acronym that makes coupledom sound like an expensive sports car—and secretly, I considered my-self four times healthier in the interpersonal relationships depart-ment than he was. I had been shocked to learn that he felt that his capacity for long-term relations was enormous but unproven, while mine had four times been tested and four times failed. A friend from college—a liberal arts school of some renown on the outer fringes of New England—had been with the same lover for twenty years. By rights, I should have thought of him as four times healthier than I, but I just thought of him as four times more inert.

Numbers probably don't tell much, although as I got older, they seemed to play an increasingly important role in my life. There was age itself, and then weight and height. There were num-bers related to IRAs and CDs and mutual funds, things that had never interested me in the past. There were numbers I suddenly felt compelled to pay attention to: blood pressure, cholesterol, PSA scores, and levels of red and white blood cells. Then there was the roster of inches, pounds, and years that comprised the fantasy portrait of my online self. It would be a relief to forget those, once I finally started paying attention to my no-sex self.

An older couple gathered their belongings as the train ap-proached Harvard Square. Charlotte and Sam very likely imagined they'd spend their evenings doing this sort of thing once they moved to town, attending lectures and concerts. Probably they would, too.

I suddenly wished I were returning from a long concert or one of those intellectually challenging cultural events that are equivalent to reading Simone de Beauvoir. I indulged in a fantasy of going to Symphony Hall with Charlotte and Sam, all of us returning together on the subway, they making my evening a little less lonely, I making theirs more interesting, just because a third person (any third person) often does.

I liked being caught up in Charlotte's little plot against her husband. It showed how well she knew him, how much respect she had for him—no matter what Jack had said—and how much she trusted me. For a fleeting moment, thinking about the two of them, I felt myself flush with the warmth of infatuation I often experience for inappropriate people. The warmth made the world, even the subway car, brighter, more hopeful. No doubt Ron had felt this warmth last September when he met Marshall, and had thought it would last forever.

Edward undoubtedly would find something dismissive to say about Sam and Charlotte, but he would like them, and I had a strong suspicion they would both be charmed by him. Once they moved to town, we could go out as a foursome. Edward had, in the past, made a number of suggestions that he and I go on vacation together, but the idea struck me as dangerously intimate, the two of us wandering around a hotel room draped in towels. With another couple along, it would be a more jovial group. Unless, of course, it turned out that they were fundamentalist Christians, or Sam was a closet case, or, as is so often true, both things.

The fantasy dimmed when I got off at my stop, climbed the stairs to the balmy street, and started the long walk home through the crowded neighborhoods of Somerville. Halfway up the steep hill I live on, I saw the looming silhouette of my house. The lights were off on both floors, and if I hadn't known the house was there, it might have looked like one of the only empty lots on the street.

exactly on time

Edward lived in a bright studio apartment on the fringes of the South End of Boston. With characteristic prescience, he'd bought his place at the last moment that one could get the legendary good deal, and since he'd owned it, its value had quadrupled. I sometimes brought Edward listings of apartment sales in his neighborhood and watched with pleasure as he studied the numbers with the excitement of a recovered drunk mixing a cocktail for someone else.

I rang his buzzer, as arranged, at eight o'clock. He let me in with a look of irritation and immediately went into the bathroom and shut the door behind him. "You're early," he shouted.

I dropped onto his sofa and picked up a magazine. "I'm exactly on time, young man."

"Same thing."

Through the door, I could hear the usual cacophony of aerosol cans and rushing water. I'd never once visited Edward when I wasn't forced to wait while he went through an elaborate cleaning, shaving, and moisturizing ritual. In every other respect, Edward was compulsively prompt and precise about time, so I knew his behavior with regard to me was a deliberate ploy. It made me feel like a high school boy being forced to wait while his prom date put the final touches on her makeup. I liked complaining to Edward about this annoying ceremony, but I was flattered that he cared enough about what I thought of his appearance to bother.

Although small, Edward's apartment was furnished and outfitted in ingenious ways that gave the illusion of space. Edward had made all of the built-in shelves, bookcases, and cabinets himself, along with doing most of the electrical work and a good deal of the plumbing. His skill at complicated home repairs was only one of his surprising traits. He could also sew, play a tidy repertoire of sing-along standards on the piano, and—despite never having driven a car—accurately diagnose automotive problems and then go a long way toward fixing them. I'd always been amused and charmed by watching Edward, not the most stereotypically masculine man on the planet, installing dishwashers and confidently building closets. This tidal wave of eclectic abilities should have induced in me massive feelings of inadequacy, but it was impossible to begrudge him his accomplishments.

He was a self-made Renaissance man who spent a lot of his downtime on airplanes studying history books, manuals of do-it-yourself home repair, magazines analyzing the performance of assorted mutual funds, and reading a number of Great Books, invariably identifying heavily with the oppressed and self-destructive heroines.

Edward's Story

Edward had grown up in Cincinnati, the only child of a pair of religious fanatics (a phrase that was becoming, in the newly terrified and confused America, more and more of a redundancy) who belonged to a cult version of Christianity. If you could believe Edward—and most of the time, I did—his parents talked endlessly about their love of Jesus, as if they were close personal friends. ("As I was saying to Jesus this morning . . ." "Jesus has such a cute smile.") And yet, their Jesus was also a petty, vengeful snoop with the worst traits of a nosy neighbor and a grotesquely malevolent baby-sitter, constantly wagging a finger of reproach, and whispering suggestions in your ear that you blow up a Planned Parenthood office.

Listening to Edward talk about his upbringing made me feel lucky to have had parents who paid lip service to piety but drove my brother and me thirty miles each Sunday to a little Catholic chapel that specialized in fifteen-minute masses. I'm sure there's a place for religious conviction, but on the whole, freedom of religion pales in importance next to freedom from it.

Edward's parents claimed to have known that their only child was gay from the moment of his birth, but upon being presented with the evidence when Edward was sixteen—in the form of an incident involving a basement recreation room and a cousin in the National Guard—they acted as if Edward had chosen his sexual preference as a way of getting them in trouble with their unforgiving, heavenly best friend. ("Jesus is going to think it's our fault," they'd reportedly said. "It's not that we don't love you, Edward, but we have to show Jesus we don't approve.")

Becoming a flight attendant got him out of town and kept him on the move, the homosexual equivalent of joining the military. I couldn't decide whether Edward's choice of career was perfect or complete lunacy. He loved being at home, and was consumed by his many home improvement projects, and hated almost all forms of travel, from flying to taking the subway across town. But in other ways, it was a perfect job for him since it allowed him to indulge in his basic love of taking care of people without letting down the impervious stance that was the heart of his defense against the world.

contemptuous compassion

I checked my watch after a few more minutes of rushing water. "I hope you aren't drawing a bath in there," I said. "And what's the big news you have for me? What stunning changes are you about to make?"

"Relax. I'll tell you in the restaurant. You're not reading one of those shelter magazines, are you? There's no point in that, William, since you couldn't stand the dust involved in the home improvements you need."

Of course, he was right; I'd picked up a copy of *Metropolitan Home* and was deep into the story of the amazing things Harry and Charles, a jovial, meticulous pair, had done to their Detroit loft. I believed these shelter magazines with their blasé acceptance of the Harry-and-Charles partnership were among the most subversive publications in the country. Harry and Charles and countless others like them talked for pages about choosing wallpaper and fabrics and designing their bathroom, and then, in the most casual and unflustered way, the author would mention that "the couple likes to give impromptu dinners for their friends" or that "the pair shares their bedroom with their three-year-old golden retriever." I approved of the politics of these articles, although the focus on partnered domesticity sometimes made me feel like half a person. It might be nice to see a story in which one of my lonely, aesthetically challenged basement dwellers was profiled. Or maybe a story in which an obsessive-compulsive cleaner rambles on for pages about his new iron or his German vacuum cleaner. "What William Collins lacks in taste and anything resembling a domestic life," the article might read, "he makes up for in cleanliness."

I threw the magazine down so Edward wouldn't be so eerily right about what I was reading. "I'm not reading anything," I said. "And please hurry, I'm starving."

"I wish I'd known," he said. "I'd have made reservations at one of those big restaurants where they expect you to eat."

He emerged from the bathroom looking slightly damp and shiny. "What's wrong?" he asked.

"Nothing's wrong. Why do you ask?"

"You're making one of those faces. As if I look weird, but you're not going to tell me why or how."

"You're imagining things."

Edward almost always looked tidy and nicely arranged, even when he was in the middle of a messy plastering or painting job. He had a narrow, lean body that seemed to shrug off fat and all attempts to develop musculature. Despite the time he spent with his assorted personal trainers, his slight body remained stubbornly true to itself. On the whole, I'm a little troubled by bodies that clearly have been tortured into nonindigenous shapes, even beautiful ones. It's like looking at someone wearing clothes that don't fit or an expensive hairpiece improperly attached.

But maybe that's my rationalization for never using a rowing machine I'd bought ten years earlier.

Edward's minimal height, sandy hair, and large, puppy-dog forehead made him look deceptively boyish, as if he hadn't quite grown into his final form. Boyish looks are a great advantage when you're in your twenties, but as Edward edged past his middle thirties, they were becoming a little less marketable. "Like trying to sell a thirty-seven-year-old bottle of Beaujolais *nouveau*," he'd once told me.

The top of his blond head came up to my shoulder.

At work, Edward had developed an interpersonal style I thought of as contemptuous compassion. His facial expressions and body language always seemed to be saying, May I help you? and, Don't invade my space! at the same time. It served him well in the cramped aisles of a jetliner; in the real world, it made him seem aloof and unapproachable. Edward was chagrined and proud of the fact that he intimidated people, as if it were a curse he'd worked hard to acquire.

"You think this shirt is ridiculous," he croaked in his ruined voice. "You think it's out of season, and I'm too scrawny, and the color is all wrong for my pallor."

He was wearing a jersey, a red cotton thing with white stripes, a polo costume filtered through a designer he probably couldn't afford. Edward had pale blue eyes and uneven ears that were far too big for his head, and the shirt accentuated a slight Howdy Doody aspect of his I found completely lovable. "I didn't say anything," I reminded him.

"You didn't have to. It was all in your mute horror."

"You look adorable."

"Adorable? In other words, it's too young for me."

"You look perfect."

He shook his head in disgust. "I count on you to lie to me, but what's the point if you don't do it convincingly?"

"Well, what's the point at all if you know I'm lying?"

He slid open a drawer on one of his built-in cabinets and pulled on a dark, shapeless sweater that covered all of the jersey and half of his gray pants.

"What's the point in God or Mozart or a seat cushion that doubles as a flotation device?"

"I give up."

"They give you a little lift, the passing illusion the universe isn't completely chaotic and that you just might be able to swim to shore. That's all I'm asking from you, a little uplifting dishonesty."

The rant was so clearly motivated by circumstances beyond my control, I figured it was best to change the subject. "You've made some improvements since I was last here."

"When was that?"

"I'm not sure. A month ago, maybe?"

"You haven't been here since May. You insist we meet at movie theaters and restaurants, someplace you can escape from easily, to go do whatever you do."

"Parking is difficult," I said.

Edward straightened out my necktie and then, dissatisfied with the results, made a tighter knot. The products he'd been using in the bathroom gave off a woody scent, combined with the faint smell of the sweat he'd worked up applying all of them. I drank in his clean scent while he took care of my tie. "Parking," he scoffed. "I almost wish I had a license so I could haul out the parking problem every time I'm late."

"You're rarely late," I pointed out.

"Thank you for noticing."

I wasn't sure why Edward had never had a driver's license, but I assumed it must have had to do with an early childhood trauma involving his father, the all-purpose tyrant. He certainly had no fears of being driven around by other people, and I genuinely liked to drive him places, since it gave me immediate control over him.

He patted the tie back into place against my stomach. "You're too skinny," he said. "Twenty-year-olds interested in men your age expect beer bellies. It's part of the appeal."

"I'll keep that in mind."

"Well, now that you're in my apartment for the first time in months, let's leave."

dave?

Edward's street was a quiet refuge from the bustle of the city—dotted with low, meticulously renovated brownstones and recently planted trees that were still in full leaf that September night, with only the faint suggestion of autumn color. The rain of the preceding days had washed the streets and sidewalks, and the air smelled clean and sweet.

What I liked best about Edward's neighborhood was the way new forty-story hotels and commercial buildings had been built up to the edge of the brownstones. That wall of steel and glass should have dwarfed and overwhelmed the brick houses like Edward's, but instead, they created deep, cool shadows during the heat of the day and offered glittering light shows in the evening. Edward's little apartment, I liked to imagine, was protected by this fortress of new construction.

"I do buy some age-appropriate clothes," Edward said as we crossed through a garden with a sputtering fountain. His neighborhood was lousy with sputtering fountains. "I just haven't started wearing them yet."

"Take your time," I told him and put my arm around his shoulder. "Once you start wearing age-appropriate clothes, there's no turning back. Enjoy your folly while you can."

Since last September, every middle-aged person I knew had decided to work on aging with grace and dignity. In light of what had happened, who would be shallow enough to even consider facial surgery or cosmetic injections? But thus far, none of my friends had perfected the plans for dignity. Edward was buying but not wearing age-appropriate clothes. My friend Miranda had stopped going out to nightclubs and was, instead, drinking at home alone. Tom had sworn off trying to pick up men half his age and had started paying for them instead. Laura had given up blaming her mother for all her problems and had started blaming her children. And so on.

Prompted by the resolutions of my friends, I had decided that continuing to see Didier, my Belgian sexual obsession of two or more years, was unbecoming for a man of my age. Undignified. He was a compulsive liar, a scrawny weasel, had the worst smoker's cough I had ever heard, and for reasons that baffled me, I couldn't get enough of him. I literally couldn't get much of him since he was so spectacularly evasive, a key element of his appeal. In a fit of trumped up, posttraumatic, get-a-grip dignity, I told him I didn't want to see him anymore and forbade him to call me. "I'm ready for something a little more real," I'd told him. To distract myself, I'd lurched into the world of semianonymous computer hookups, behavior that hadn't proved any more age-appropriate, although considering what my online age was, it didn't, initially, look quite as bad.

I was finding my middle years tough. Optimistic youth is spent talking yourself into believing that at any moment you'll do something bold, brave, and significant, while the calm post-sixty years are spent talking yourself into believing that you might have done something bold, brave, and significant but for bold, brave, significant, and unspecified reasons, you chose not to. At my age, I was living in the cold waters of semireality, trying to swim from one set of delusions to the temporary safe harbor of the next.

What did I want? I wondered as we crossed Tremont Street, my arm still on Edward's shoulder. Edward was describing the antics of an obstreperous passenger on a flight from Dallas, a tale I was only half listening to. Why had I thought first of calling him when I decided to attempt making some changes in my own life?

A car ran a red light, and I grabbed Edward and reeled him in. He looked up at me, stopping his story midsentence, and I felt my cell phone vibrate in my pocket. "Go ahead and answer," he said.

"You couldn't have heard that," I said, taking out the phone.

"You don't think I felt it, do you?"

The number displayed on the screen was unknown to me, a warning sign I ignored. A muffled voice said, "Is this Everett?"

The most prudent thing to do would have been to hang up, but because I'm basically an honest person, I said, "Yes, it is."

"Hey, Everett, this is Dave."

Dave—who knows why?—is another wildly popular fake

name. This guy even pronounced it as if there were quote marks around it.

"Dave. Right."

"You're in luck, Everett—I'm in town on business again."

Apparently he remembered something I'd forgotten. "Okay."

He named a hotel, a garish faux castle off the highway about fifteen minutes from the city that was inexplicably popular with out-of-town businessmen despite the fact that they had to drive through rush hour traffic to get to their meetings. "I'm in room 473. Come on out. I'm getting a group together."

A few days ago, a call like this would have been a bonus—like having the waiter forget to charge you for the dessert. I would have figured out a way to finish dinner with Edward quickly and would have rushed to the hotel. But now it was just an unwelcome irritant. And fortunately, Edward was with me to keep me irritable. He was gazing straight ahead with a fixed, blank stare, indication that he probably was concentrating on how best to embellish the story about the passenger and finish it with a bang.

"I think you've got the wrong number," I said.

"I don't think I do. I recognize the voice. If you change your mind, you know where I am." And then, continuing the theme from my earlier discussion with Edward: "The hotel has tons of free parking."

"I don't know why I bother carrying this thing," I said to Edward, flipping it closed. "Almost all I get is wrong numbers and solicitations."

"I know which that was."

the beast

The restaurant Edward had selected was the kind of place I used to loathe as pretentious but now found soothing. Everything in it, walls and lamps and drapes and chairs, was the color of sand. It was so warmly monochromatic, all of the patrons seemed to glow with life—the point, undoubtedly—and the colorful food appeared to be leaping off the plates like Technicolor cartoon figures.

As soon as the waiter, a refreshingly homely man, had placed the salads in front of us and carefully adjusted the plates, I apologized to Edward for the invasive call.

"Why would it matter to me?" he asked.

"I don't know. But you seemed annoyed. So I'm just saying, sorry."

"Your sex life is your own business," he said.

"You're making assumptions."

"I notice you didn't say 'false assumptions.'"

"Don't be so critical. You're important to me," I said. I took a long sip of wine and felt it warm up little pockets of sentimentality all over my body. "You must know that."

"Let's not get maudlin," he said. "It's a little late in the friendship for that." He pushed around the pile of tomatoes, drizzled with something green. "Why does everything have to be stacked? What happened to food lying on a plate?"

"It looks too much like airline food," I told him.

"Shows what you know. There is no airline food anymore."

"So what's your big news, little man? What are these life-altering plans you wanted to discuss?"

He dispensed with a few slices of tomato and then said, without looking up from his cutlery, "Marty is moving out to San Diego in December and asked me to go along." He glared at me for a moment, as if he'd just accused me of something. When he was satisfied that I'd absorbed his bombshell, he added, "I applied to the airline for a transfer."

"Marty," I said, dismissively, and immediately started digging through my salad to find the sugarcoated pecans.

Marty was Edward's friend, someone I'd always disliked and felt in competition with. Marty exerted an unhealthy degree of influence over Edward. Edward was susceptible to the influence, not wholly benign, because Marty was his ideal of rugged, strutting masculinity: a retired marine who'd served in the first Iraq debacle in the early 1990s and then started a business that Marty (and Edward, Marty's mouthpiece) claimed was raking in several hundred grand a year. In terms of domineering personality, unapologetic machismo, and bulky muscularity, Marty would have been a perfect lover for Edward. Unfortunately, for the sake of Edward's romantic prospects, Marty was a woman. Martine, in fact. A stocky African-American woman from Arkansas with the captivating voice and precise articulation of a Shakespearean actress.

Marty had left the military about five years earlier and had started a self-help business that combined rigorous physical training and "empowerment and self-actualization" seminars. If you read between the lines of the promotional material on her Web site—the address was ReleaseTheBeast.com—the route to self-assertion was letting yourself be bullied into submission by Marty and doing exactly as she told you to do.

"She has a lot of contacts on the West Coast," Edward went on. "San Diego is crawling with military and ex-military, her natural constituency, and she figures she can double her business within the first year."

"I see. And where do you fit into the picture?"

"I need to make some changes, William. I need a new line of work. She's going to have to have a business partner in all of this, to set up a new office, handle promotion, that kind of thing. It's an opportunity for me, and it's not as if I'm drowning in opportunities these days."

"You don't own a computer," I reminded him.

"I've been taking classes. You'd be surprised at how adept I am. The whole thing makes a lot of sense."

I was so irritated by this news, I pushed my plate away from me and leaned in toward Edward across the table and poked my finger into his flat, narrow chest. "It makes no sense at all, my friend. Do you want me to tell you why?"

"Not really."

"In the first place, if Marty is doing so well with her business, as you've been claiming for years, why is she uprooting and moving three thousand miles? That's a red flag right there. I guess you're so dazzled by Marty's beastliness, you don't see it." I stuffed some lettuce into my mouth. "You've got to think these things through. And you're going to be flying *and* managing her business?"

"Only for a year. Then, if everything goes as planned, I'm quitting the airline. You're jealous of my friendship with Marty. You always have been."

"I've always been concerned about your friendship with Marty. She's a petty dictator who makes a living—supposedly, but I haven't seen her tax returns—by shouting at people eight hours a day."

"Forget Marty for the moment," he said. "The important thing is, it makes sense for me."

"San Diego? All that sun? All those glaring, cloudless days? You burn easily, Edward. Your lips crack when you get too much sun. You think I don't notice these things, but I do. You'll blister and burn and dry up in that climate."

Edward glared at me with a hard expression in his pale blue eyes. "Have a little sympathy for me," he said. "Be a little more sensitive."

"I am sympathetic, sweetheart. I know you want some changes, but you're nearing forty. Just ride it out and do what everyone else does: get your teeth whitened and go on Zoloft."

fasten your seat belts

Out of nowhere, Edward's small face collapsed into a look of crestfallen misery and his eyes clouded over. "You don't get it, William. You don't know me at all. I'm unhappy."

There was so much bald emotion in this statement, I was speechless and hesitantly went back to my salad.

"For starters, there's my job. Just when I got used to the idea of being in a low-prestige rut with benefits, the world turns upside down and I'm suddenly on the front lines of the 'war on terror,' whatever that's supposed to mean. You try it for a few months. Every time I get on a plane, I look around for a heavy object I can grab in case someone tries to slit my throat. It's not what I signed up for. I went into it so I could wear a uniform and get paid to stare at guys' crotches while I checked to see if their seat belts were fastened."

"Edward . . ."

"And then there's Boston. What am I doing here?" He looked around the restaurant with a smirk of dissatisfaction, already apart from the rest of the population. "I feel as if I'm hanging around waiting for something to happen, but what? What's here for me?"

I had no illusions about Boston being the world's most vibrant cosmopolitan center, but I took the comment personally. It's standard operating procedure to weep and rage against a lover or spouse's steps toward abandoning you, but for the most part, you're supposed to applaud friends for doing the same, and then help them pack.

I wanted to say, "*I'm* here for you," but instead of just blurting it out, I thought about whether or not I *was* there for Edward, and what the consequences of such a comment might be. Before I had time to say anything, the waiter strolled over to our table and asked for permission to take our salads. He had dark hair and a big, wide mouth, and his sand-colored T-shirt and stretchy pants could barely contain his compact body. I watched him as he walked off with the plates, trying to decide if the lack of an under-wear line across the seat of his tight pants meant he was wearing a thong.

"You should slip him your phone number," Edward said. "He's one of those insecure, overdeveloped bottoms who loves to be hu-miliated. Letting himself be used by an emaciated fifty-year-old who lives in the kind of neighborhood you live in would appeal to his masochism."

"I wish everyone would stop accusing me of being fifty," I said. "Besides, I wasn't thinking about him. I was thinking about your relocation plans."

"Oh," Edward scoffed, "you always claim you're above lust and longing and all those other untidy human emotions. You don't fool me for a minute. That pathetic phone call a few minutes ago. I'm broiling hot in this sweater, but without it, I'll look like a candy striper. Why didn't you insist I take off this ridiculous red-and-white jersey?"

"I don't suppose it will be easy to get a transfer from the air-line," I said, hopefully. "They must have more important things to worry about than relocating you."

He smiled at me in the cold way I imagine he smiled at pas-sengers he ordered to take their seats as instructed by the pilot. "I heard yesterday," he said. "It's been approved. You'll be happy to hear, I've decided to give you the listing on my apartment, but I know you'll forgo the commission."

room 473

I've always found my ability to detach from and deny some of my own feelings and fears a useful but creepy part of my personality. It raises the possibility that I might not be a truly good person. I like to think of myself as highly ethical, although what that boils down to isn't making careful ethical choices but acting on impulse and then advertising my guilt and regret about having done so.

I experienced a moment of intense sadness and even panic upon hearing how far Edward's plans had advanced, but then I found my attention shifting, as if it had a life of its own, to the "pathetic" phone call I'd received an hour earlier. It seems to me defense mechanisms shouldn't work if you're aware that they're defense mechanisms and you know at least some of what it is you're defending against, but this one worked perfectly. So well, in fact, that I managed to talk Edward out of dessert ("Someone I know got food poisoning from the mousse here last week") and, shortly thereafter, found myself on the highway, driving to a faux-castle hotel at seventy miles per hour, not thinking about Edward leaving town and what it would mean for me, not thinking about why I cared so much, not chiding myself for rushing headlong into the kind of behavior I'd sworn off, but running through a mental list of possible bodies and faces I could attach to the name "Dave." Disappointment in myself flickered across my consciousness a few times, but I blocked it effectively with the familiar rationalizations about time and tomorrow and tomorrow and tomorrow.

As soon as I pulled up to the hotel, I realized the appeal of the place was its immense, moatlike parking lot, a vast sprawl of macadam that could accommodate any number of cars. I admire the way Ian Schraeger revolutionized hotel decor, but given cable

TV and free parking, most people would be happy to pay for overnight accommodations in a storage container.

I shared the elevator with a young man and woman who were holding hands and staring straight ahead. "Nice night," I said, thinking, Ha ha, you have no idea what I'm about to do.

"I think it's going to be a beautiful fall," the woman said, no doubt thinking, Ha ha, you have no idea what we're about to do.

Looking at them, pressed against the wall opposite me, a happy unit of human intimacy, I thought about Charlotte and Samuel, headed to their romantic hotel room a couple of nights earlier. So much for my fantasies about forming a friendly foursome with them and Edward. Now I'd have to move full speed ahead in pursuing some other role. I took out my cell phone, an act that instantly made me feel important and less alone, and left a message on Samuel's work phone. "Good evening, Mr. Thompson," I said, all bluster and good cheer. "Give me a call on this phone or at the office. I've got some great properties for you and Charlotte to look at."

All garish pretense of castlelike decor was abandoned in the ornate lobby; the walls of the fourth-floor hallway were covered in a green material that had the slick feel of vinyl, and the carpeting made squeaking noises, like wet grass, as I walked on it.

I knocked at room 473 and the door opened a crack. A faint whiff of smoke and sweat emerged, but very little light. At least I knew I had the right place.

"Dave?" I said.

"Come in."

The door swung open and I slipped into the dark room. But not completely dark, for the television set was on, flashing colored lights across a tangle of mostly naked bodies on one of two big beds.

"Ah," I said, pointing with my chin. "Mosh pit."

"Make yourself at home," my host said.

He had the kind of plump, nondescript face, puffy with alcohol, common on sportscasters and former athletes past their brief prime. I had a vague memory of having met him, but beyond that, I was blank. His features registered no particular recognition of me. A married businessman from somewhere west of Pennsylvania, I guessed. He'd probably called everyone he'd ever talked to within the Boston area code and taken his chances; the tangle on the bed was the result.

He lumbered back into the bedroom, naked. Nudity comes in several varieties: the wholesome, the artistic, the erotic, and, case in point, the are-you-sure-you-wouldn't-like-a-towel? There was something stooped and exhausted about his posture and even the way the flesh hung off his body. He stopped in front of the TV—checking out the porn to fire up the furnace, I assumed. But when I moved into the room a few steps, I saw that the on-screen action was one of those pampered, bow-tied, right-wing broadcasters using anger instead of information to promote imminent invasion of Iraq. These red-faced entertainers had been boosting their ratings for months by delivering a blanket kill-everyone-now message. As for the on-bed action, it was a little hard to make out. The exact number of bodies was unclear. And irrelevant. Once you get to three, it doesn't make all that much difference. There were a few mandatory moans along the lines of "Oh, yeah," and then someone tried to crank up the excitement by shouting, *"Yeah!"*

Dave responded in an angry stage whisper: "I told you guys to keep it down. I don't feel like getting tossed out of here."

He picked up the remote control for the TV, switched the channel to an antacid commercial, and turned up the volume: ". . . that bloated, burning sensation in your stomach. Rumbling gas and . . ."

Leave now, I told myself. But thinking about the drive home

and my ultra-clean house, I stretched out on the empty bed with my hands behind my head. It couldn't hurt to watch.

please charlotte

Samuel Thompson worked for a company called Beacon Hill Solutions. I loved the open-ended mystery of the name. Solutions to what? I suppose the idea was to make you think that whatever problem you had, this group of consultants could help you solve it. Since the company was located on an upper floor of an office tower in the flat heart of the city's financial district, "Beacon Hill" seemed to have been slapped on to give an aura of Brahmin respectability. I went to the BHS Web site to try and find some information that might help me deal with Samuel, or at least give me something to talk about with him. There were ten consultants affiliated with the company, although what any of them actually did remained unclear. *"Your business is our business,"* I copied down onto my notes for Sam and Charlotte. *"Making it work for you is what makes it work for us." What's that mean? More charades.* A short biography of Samuel reassuringly mentioned that he had an MBA and previously had worked for Merrill Lynch for "more than a decade." *Mde a killing in mutual funds? Problm solver? Maybe he cn "make it work" for me? What's "it"?*

There was a standard studio photo of Beacon Hill Solutions' six senior partners: Samuel surrounded by three overfed men in dark suits, a plump, platinum blond woman, and a pale beauty with her hair pulled back so tightly, she appeared bald at first glance.

Salesman, I jotted down. *Partners resent his gd looks.*

When he finally returned my message a few days later, he

sounded genuinely sorry that it had taken him so long to get back to me. "It's been a little hellish here," he said. "Our busiest season. Everyone wants to end the year with his problems solved. Come to think of it, that's why Charlotte and I came to you—solve our real estate problems before Christmas. Along with everything else. You up for the job?"

"It sounds a little daunting, but I'm willing to take a stab at it."

"Good man. I'm sorry that place we looked at wasn't right for us."

"The first place is never right," I said. This wasn't true. The first place people look at is often perfect, but they almost never buy it for fear of finding something better as soon as they've put down the deposit. In most cases, closing the deal, like securing a marriage proposal, is a matter of chipping away at expectations. "Usually the first half dozen places aren't right. I suggest we get those out of the way, too, so we can move on to something probable."

"Absolutely," he said. He spoke with enthusiasm and vigor—absolutely—but there was an edge of distraction in his voice, and I could hear typing in the background, as if he were answering e-mails.

"I've done a lot of research and put together an assortment of possibilities in your price range," I said. "When I see how you respond to these, I'll have a better idea of what your taste is and exactly what you're looking for."

There was a long pause, and at first I thought he hadn't heard me. I was trying to follow the general outlines of Charlotte's advice on how best to manipulate him, without sounding as if I'd scripted the call. His typing stopped abruptly, and he said, "The main thing is, we have to please Charlotte."

WE please Charlotte, I wrote. *Sam and me.*

"The move is her idea, and she has stronger tastes than I do, so I'm willing to give her a lot of decision-making power. But between you and me, the final decision is mine. Her business instincts could be a lot better. She made a series of horrible investments over the last ten years. I'm not planning to bring that up to her, but just so you know."

"I'll keep it in mind."

"I need to be convinced it's a good investment. That's number one."

Money most important, I wrote.

"Charlotte's wanted to get a place in town for a long time now. And I've resisted, for selfish reasons. The cost, my attachment to Nahant. I'm very happy out there, William, away from everything related to work, the stress. I leave my whole in-town life behind me. I kayak, run on the beach, bicycle, swim."

Fitness freak, I jotted down. *Shld I be jogging?*

"But something like what happened last year makes you reevaluate your priorities, think about what truly matters in life. For me, it's my family. That should be obvious, but it's easy to lose sight of sometimes. Until you get one of those unwelcome reminders."

A year ago, everyone had been reminded of something important, but it was my impression that most of us had already forgotten what it was.

"Daniel's off at college now," he went on. "It's time for Charlotte and me to attend to each other. It's not as difficult as people think, making someone happy. So as I see, our whole job here, yours and mine, William, is just to make someone happy. Nice work if you can get it, don't you think?"

For the moment, I put aside the condescension in his voice—a consultant talking to a lowly real estate agent—and the irritating way he kept saying my name. I liked the plan. True, the speech sounded prepared, as if he'd run through it a few times in his mind, or had expressed the same rationalization while having dinner with a couple of drunken friends, but what was wrong with a little rehearsal? I tried to find an element of irony in his words, but

I couldn't detect any. He believed what he'd just said, and thinking back to the tender way he acted toward Charlotte when they came into the office, I believed him, too.

"Her liking a place is the starting point. My instincts are the end point."

I could tell already that at some point, probably in the not too distant future, I was going to weary of this man with his contradictions and his pride in his business savvy, but at that moment, I was still flushed with admiration and an unthreatening crush on the two of them. We made an appointment to meet again. *Wear green C. Lacroix tie,* I wrote next to the time.

come again?

The following week, I was sitting at my desk at Cambridge Properties, nodding at one of my customers, attempting to communicate empathy, while internally retracing the depressing and titillating mistakes I'd made throughout the preceding week, many of which I blamed on Edward and his silly, upsetting plans to relocate. San Diego. It was such an obvious choice—perfect weather and pretty views. Where was the challenge in that? Where was the character-building hardship?

The customer was Sylvia Blanchard, a woman I'd been working with for more than two years. The depressing and titillating mistakes were, primarily, three attempted phone calls to Didier, my Belgian obsession, and an encounter with a handsome masochist who claimed to be named Sandy and wanted to be treated "as if I were your dog." Considering the amount of money and affection lavished on domestic pets in this country, "Treat me like your dog" are words no self-respecting masochist should utter.

As for Sylvia, she had previously put down deposits on three apartments and one two-family house. At the very last minute, she'd backed out of every deal. Her total loss of deposits and fees was approaching $15,000, but it was money she was happy to lose as long as it freed her from making a purchase.

I'd known exactly what to expect when Sylvia walked into the office that Saturday morning. I'd been waiting for a phone call or a visit for days. Her current deposit was on a triple-decker house she'd fallen in love with in a working-class neighborhood close to the one where I lived, and the closing was two weeks away. Now was the time for her to back out of the deal. When she opened the proceedings that morning with, "You're going to kill me, William," I checked out of listening mode and escaped into my own thoughts.

"That makes sense," I said, every time her mouth stopped moving. "You're right."

Sylvia was an excessively thin woman whose mod wardrobe consisted mostly of bell-bottom slacks and fuzzy mohair jackets, as if her fashion influences began and ended with Twiggy, circa 1968. She wore thick-rimmed eyeglasses in a garish shade of turquoise, the kind of I'm-having-fun accessory a person wears when trying to make herself into a recognizable public personage. She had a charming habit of scattering her conversation with non sequiturs that bubbled up from her subconscious and let you know in which direction her thinking was drifting while her conversation was otherwise engaged. We were very close in height, a fact that probably accounted for a lot of our attraction to each other.

She was now in the Deep Regret stage of her monologue, pulling glasses off and on. Her thin and very red lips were moving quickly, spitting out apologies and self-recrimination.

"That makes sense," I said again. "You're right."

Sylvia was a professor in the Women's Studies Department at

Deerforth College, a school about fifteen miles into the suburbs of Boston. She was the author of three books, each more successful than the last. The first was a study of some justifiably obscure Australian poet, the second a meditation on American women and food—Sylvia herself was British and clearly had a complicated relationship to nourishment. The most recent was an analysis of female sexuality called *Come Again*. The title of the third, the subject matter, and probably the eyeglasses had given Sylvia entrée to some of the more intellectual cable talk shows and even a brief turn on a couple of the morning network news programs. She'd become a celebrity of sorts in academic circles, applauded and despised for her sudden visibility. She frequently went on long tirades against Camille Paglia, obviously her role model.

"Of course you're right," I said. "And I *do* understand. That makes sense."

Back when I was still reading books—not merely their scathing introductions—I had plowed through Sylvia's first two tomes, avoiding the extensive footnotes and vast appendices. I'd had a lot more luck with *Come Again*. True, it was written in that bizarrely dense academic prose that's the literary equivalent of mud, but with chapter titles such as "Cunt" and "Fucked," it made for provocative skimming. The book had a shrewdly calculated concept; a bunch of incomprehensible intellectual palaver on sexuality, gender, Foucault, and Georgia O'Keeffe wrapped around—in alternating chapters—a graphic memoir of Sylvia's own profligate sexual history, one that made my recent adventures look tame enough for an after-school television special.

I was convinced that Sylvia would never buy an apartment, never budge from the overstuffed rented studio where she'd been living for the past dozen years, but I was always pleased to have her visit me, tell me her woes, and write deposit checks.

She was an extreme version of a type familiar to real estate agents: a real estate junkie, drawn to almost every house or apartment she was shown, certain it would give her a new and improved life. Most of these people bought and sold properties the way the rest of the population buys groceries, but Sylvia would never sacrifice the hopefulness of the search for the harsh reality of a done deal. What if she found, purchased, and moved into the perfect place and then discovered that her life was still a bog of lonely disappointment?

Despite all the irritations of dealing with Sylvia, I found her manic, unrealistic brand of optimism inspiring. She was neurotic, restless, confused, and conflicted, but there was an aura of happiness that surrounded all of these emotions. She wasn't exactly happy, but she believed absolutely that one day she would be. It was a quality I lacked and was trying to nurture.

"You're right, Sylvia. Of course. I understand completely. That makes sense."

These real estate deals resembled love affairs. She adored everything about a place at the start, every flaw and eccentricity, every potential hazard and drawback, the sloping floors, the tiny closets, the badly renovated bathrooms. These were all charming and endearing. Once the candlelight and violins faded, they became the intolerable features that made it imperative she cancel her plans.

a bright idea

We'd progressed to the part of her monologue in which she ripped off her turquoise glasses and listed a variety of psychological and chemical problems that made the purchase of this particular house impossible. Hypoglycemia, hypocholesterolemia, posttraumatic something or other.

She halted her speech to look for a mint in one of the canvas tote bags she always carried with her. She was an ex-smoker who kept replacing that oral fixation with a variety of others: chewing gum, mints, breath sprays, lollipops, and so on. The occasional solid meal might have taken care of the entire problem, but there was about as much likelihood of that as the actual purchase of a piece of property.

"And why take on the burden of all those tenants?" I prompted. "They would just be more headaches you don't need."

"Exactly," she said. "Look at your nightmare in that regard."

"Exactly." During our long talks about her housing headaches, I'd revealed to her many of my own, including the Kumiko Rothberg situation.

"I'd be as inept at collecting rents as you are. I wonder if I should go to a movie tonight? And you know I consider that particular ineptitude a sign of strength of character, in your case."

"Yes, I know. I appreciate the vote of confidence."

"Thank you for taking it the right way. Not that there's a *single* movie I want to see right now. Oh well."

Despite having read lurid descriptions of Sylvia's multiple orgasms and sexual escapades in parks and department stores, I found it hard to imagine her touching another human being, let alone being driven to heights of wild passion in a fitting room at Harrods. She struck me as too anxious and distracted—not to mention absorbed in the minutiae of university politics—to care about such things. I didn't know her age, but reading between the lines of her book, I'd come to the conclusion that she'd reached a period of blissful sexual dormancy, give or take the occasional grad student.

"And I wasn't ever really sure that that neighborhood was right for you," I said. "It's fine for me, but it would add another twenty minutes to your Deerforth commute."

"I wasn't sure either. Although I was almost sure. It was that point-two percent uncertainty that unraveled me in the end." Unable to find what she was looking for in her bag, she gave it a little kick and sat up straight. "I can get more mints when I buy the soap. They're usually on sale there."

I always ignored these oddball interjections and was never entirely certain if she knew she'd said them aloud.

"You don't hate me, do you, William? This is the third time I've done this."

"Fifth. But I'm not counting. When the right thing comes along, we'll know it," I assured her. "That fireplace in the second-floor rental unit would have been a constant worry."

Reassured that I was going to forgive her and was still on her side, she relaxed back into her chair. "I've been thinking of going back to square one. Can you stand to think about square one again? A tidy studio apartment right in the middle of everything. I know that's what I've got now, but I want to own. Downtown Boston somewhere. I'm sick of landlords, no offense."

"We've discussed how much you're going to lose on this, haven't we?"

"Down to the penny. But it's worth it and it's only fair. Those poor people deserve something. You'll find a buyer for the place, won't you? It's not uninhabitable; someone could cope with it. On top of that, I'll get us tickets for an opera or some expensive 'event.' America's becoming a culture of 'events.' I'll have to make a note on that before I leave. Remind me, will you? No, never mind, it's an idiotic observation that's going to go nowhere. I'm desperate for a new topic. I've exploited food and fucking already. Unfortunately, I don't have drugs or murder in the family to yack about. I may have to resort to literature again. How's your sex life, *carino?*"

"Dreary," I said. "An orgy here, a foot fetishist there, a couple of outdoor encounters along the river, a guy on a leash." I shrugged.

"Sounds like my week." One of her bags had toppled over, and she bent down to gather up the stack of books that had fallen out. "One day, I'm sure you'll tell me the truth."

"I wouldn't count on it," I said.

With some people, the best place to hide the truth about your life is out in the open. Sylvia often asked me, casually, about my sex life, one of the privileges, I suppose, of a person who'd written graphically about her erotic experiences on a fishing trawler. It was only to her that I'd made a full confession of all my doings, and she, in a gratifying and disappointing way, had consistently acted as if I was serving up lies as homage to her book.

It was as I was watching her pack up her bags and pat down her short, artificially red hair that I was struck with what seemed like a brilliant idea. I'd solve a couple of problems at one time and make several people happy—boss Gina, Sylvia herself, Edward, even Edward's beastly friend Marty.

"You know, Sylvia," I said, "I'm not sure this is the right moment to bring this up . . ."

"In that case, you must."

"A friend of mine told me he might be selling his studio in the South End. It's modest, but tidy, nicely appointed."

Her canvas bags slid off her thin arm and dropped to the floor. She sat down again, wound her legs together, and leaned on my desk. "Tell," she said, her eyes bright behind her big eyeglasses.

"It's not officially on the market yet, but we could probably take a look at it. Built-in everything, very modern . . ."

"Perfect."

"Small."

"Perfect. Windows?"

"Well . . ."

"Unimportant. When?"

"When?"

". . . is he moving out?"

"Oh, probably before Christmas. There might be some negotiating room."

And so we were off on love affair number seven.

"She's your classic dead-end street," Jack said, once she'd left.
"Or cul-de-sac. That's French for sack of shit. I would have fired
her years ago."

Jack had read through some of the more graphic sections of
Come Again and was convinced Sylvia had made half of it up. I
suppose his unwillingness to believe the book was motivated by
jealousy, although some chapters did include practices that
sounded physically impossible.

"I think this time it's going to work out," I said. "I have a
completely different feeling about it."

"Feelings. There's a concept I just don't get. You threaten
them, William. You tell them you won't work with them anymore,
they'll go bankrupt. Give me one week with her and I'll have her
in a crap condo that'll shut her up once and for all."

"I'll think it over," I said.

"It's about real estate, not people. You forget that." He shuffled
around some papers in a completely unnecessary way, and then,
without looking up from his desk, he said, "What's this about a guy
on a leash?"

"Guy on a leash? I have no idea what you're talking about. You
must have misunderstood. Was I talking about a lease at one point?"

He scowled at me, and I was shocked to realize that it wasn't
with disapproval of what I'd told Sylvia, but disappointment that I
wasn't sharing the information with him.

confidence

The seller took the news about Sylvia badly. He had a life of his own. He was moving to New Mexico. This was going to complicate everything for him. He was a hefty man with such a thick and idiosyncratic Boston accent, it was impossible to imagine him living elsewhere. Last September, he'd decided to move away from the East Coast because he considered it too vulnerable to future attacks. Like many people who had made radical plans for similar reasons, his will seemed to be wavering after a year of quiet on the home front, and I wouldn't have been stunned to learn that he was secretly relieved the sale had been postponed. Even so, I assured him that I'd start showing the house again the next day, and that if my customers didn't bite, two other agents in the office were confident they could find a buyer within a week.

"I know it's bad for you," I said, "but don't forget, she's not getting off easy, either. She'll be losing a lot of money."

"Good. I hope she loses everything. She's not one of those nuts who does this six times a year, is she?"

Six times a year was overstating it, even for Sylvia, so I told him truthfully that she was not one of those nuts. After I'd hung up, I began pondering my motives for interesting Sylvia in Edward's condo. Inevitably, she would complicate Edward's relocation idea, just as she'd complicated this guy's. It would be a roadblock to Edward's plans, even if not an insurmountable one. Every time I thought about helping my friend pack his belongings into boxes and shipping them to San Diego, I felt queasy.

The place Sylvia had rejected was wrong for Samuel and Charlotte in all ways, but I decided to show it to them anyway. In most cases, finding the right place to live is like finding a romantic partner through a personal ad. People go in with a list of qualities and physical details they consider essential, but then some chemical attraction to the least likely candidate kicks in and the interest in classical music and fine dining or the must-have walk-in closet is rendered irrelevant.

Charlotte showed up at my office alone the next afternoon. "I didn't want to get Samuel involved and have to consider his schedule," she said. "Sometimes it's better to make your own plans. At some point, I'll let him know you put in the time showing me the place so he'll appreciate your diligence." She picked up a calendar I had on the corner of my desk, arched her eyebrows, and flipped the page to the current month. "Do you really think I'll like the house?"

"I'm not sure. But it's always useful to rule things out absolutely."

She waved off the particulars of this place, as if to say that she trusted me and the process. She'd had a manicure since the last time she'd been in, and her nails were smooth and shiny, orange near the tips that appeared to blend subtly into red toward the cuticle, something like autumn leaves. Elaborately painted nails were increasingly common, but I was disconcerted by the sight of them on smart, professional women of my age whom I assumed to be too busy for such glossy vanity. She caught me looking and curled her fingers in a bit. "I have to deliver a manuscript in Boston later this afternoon," she said. "I was happy to have an excuse to leave the house this much earlier."

"Interesting book?"

"No, of course not. Something called *The Confidence Game*. A good title for a film noir or a spy thriller, but in this case, it is exactly what it sounds like: instructions on how to be more confident in your business dealings. Ten easy ways to get what you want from the underlings, all infused with a troubling tone of self-righteous American arrogance. At one point, the author even refers to 'terrorists' in the employee lounge. I tried to add a note of humility, but I'm sure it won't be appreciated. Humility is completely out of favor these days."

She made her speech with conviction, but also with the inflections of a performance, as if she wasn't used to delivering this kind of lecture on her work. Maybe she wasn't used to talking about it at all.

"If you think of some confidence-building advice for me, let me know."

She glanced around the office. By most standards, it was a highly successful business, but Gina, with her devotion to practicality, made very little effort at dressing up the place. The walls were cold white and the furniture was functional pressed wood stuff that she'd leased from a supplier. It probably didn't look like the kind of office where a truly confident person would work. At first, Gina had hoped I'd spruce up the decor some, but then she'd visited the apartment I was renting at the time and never mentioned the plan again.

Charlotte fiddled with her unruly hair. "I used to think my greatest maternal accomplishment, maybe my only maternal accomplishment, was instilling confidence in Daniel," she said. "It was an obsession of mine, practically from the minute he was born, obviously an attempt to undo my own parents' mistakes, since they were of the break-their-spirits school of child rearing. But lately, I've been wondering if I shouldn't have encouraged specific talents or skills that would give rise to confidence, rather than the abstract thing itself. He's extremely confident, but has he earned it?"

"I have no idea."

"Rhetorical question. And please don't repeat my doubts, especially to Samuel. He and Daniel are basically twin brothers."

I was delighted by the double betrayal.

As I drove her to the house, she became silent, and I could tell she was disappointed in the neighborhood. Vinyl siding was hugely popular in Somerville, and there was something unsettling about the sight of row after row of multifamily houses encased in plastic, as if the whole area were an overgrown Monopoly game.

"I know it's not exactly what you were looking for, in terms of location, but there are a lot of advantages." I left it at that because at that moment I couldn't think of one. "I don't live far from here myself."

"Oh, it's fine," she said. "I was just a little amazed by your car. I don't think I've ever seen a car this clean. Is it brand new?"

"Nearly." My Toyota was eight years old, but with its creased upholstery, layers of carpeting, and tiny compartments, it was an endless source of cleaning opportunities. I told her that a friend had taken it to a car wash for me, as a present.

"Oh," she said, nodding with the noncommittal distraction that usually indicates disbelief.

Fortunately, the seller wasn't home. He'd already begun to pack away books and dishes and posters, and all of the house's flaws were on display, along with a shocking amount of dust and filth that had been uncovered when the furniture had been moved. Charlotte wandered around the owner's apartment as if she were in a secondhand shop, occasionally pointing out a bowl or a lamp that she admired, but saying nothing about the place itself. She walked hesitantly, as if she was afraid of stepping on broken glass.

"I don't suppose you want to see the other apartments in the house," I said.

"No, I don't think so. I mean, there's no point, is there?"

"Probably not."

"A more interesting idea would be to look at your house. To give me a different view of the neighborhood."

I sensed that this was a bad idea. I was letting her get the upper hand in the relationship, never sensible, professionally or personally.

"All right," I said. "It's only a couple of minutes from here."

just in time

It was a bright day, warm for fall and disorienting to me because of the way the temperature scrambled my expectations of the season. Both Charlotte and I were overdressed for the weather, and standing in the cramped entryway of my house, fumbling with the keys, I could smell perfume rising off her with the heat of her body. It smelled of cinnamon and patchouli, a distinctive and seductive scent that I hadn't noticed before, even as we were driving.

I was about to comment on it when the door to Kumiko's apartment swung open. She stood there clutching a wicker basket filled with laundry wearing a look of exaggerated concern, as if she'd caught me in the middle of criminal activity. I had a moment of uncertainty about how to introduce her; "friend" was completely inaccurate, and "my tenant" sounded insulting. I settled on "my neighbor," which was truthful but vague.

"Charlotte and her husband are clients of mine," I said. "They're apartment hunting."

"William is my landlord," she corrected in a soft tone, as if she were my indentured servant and the laundry in the basket was mine. "I'm afraid I've fallen a little behind on the rent. Is that why you're showing the apartment, William?"

"Let's not get into it right now," I said. There was no way this discussion would make me look anything but ridiculous. In addition to that, I was desperate to get Charlotte upstairs before Kumiko handed me her laundry with a request to go lightly on the starch.

I looked down at the wicker basket and then glared at Kumiko—significantly, I hoped. "Kumiko's a painter," I said. "She uses the garage as a studio."

"And I appreciate it, too. Despite the mildew situation. I hope I don't develop an allergy to mold." She hesitated for a moment, and then reading my look perfectly and confirming the close, unhealthy nature of our relationship, tossed aside the laundry and withdrew.

As soon as I opened the door upstairs, I was overwhelmed by the stench of bleach, floor wax, and vinegar from an early morning cleaning binge. Usually, these smells made me feel happily in control of my life, but standing there with Charlotte, I felt ashamed of myself. "The cleaners were here this morning," I said.

It was early afternoon, and the bright sunshine pouring in all the windows was bouncing off every polished floor and piece of furniture, creating an almost blinding dazzle of light. "I hope you pay them well," Charlotte said.

"Who's that?"

"The cleaners."

"Right."

"You must live alone. To keep everything so tidy. I told Samuel you had the look of a solitary man. There's a monklike air about you."

By this, I assumed she meant I appeared to have no social or sex life. Why was I giving this impression to so many people?

"I hope you realize," she went on, "that your tenant is clinically passive-aggressive. I worked on a book about passive aggression in the workplace. I know quite a bit about it." I took her into the kitchen and pointed out the view and the skyline of Boston, glinting in the haze of the afternoon light. She nodded at it and shrugged, eager to get back to the subject of Kumiko, mostly, I suspected, because it made her feel more insightful than me. "Someone that manipulative and sick can string you on for years."

"I prefer to think of her along the lines of eccentric."

"No, no. She crossed that line long ago." She took a seat at the kitchen table and I quickly removed a neat stack of papers on which I'd tried to make a record of exactly what Kumiko owed me. I was unnerved that Charlotte was settling in, but there was nothing I could do except offer her a drink.

"Soda water, please."

"I have something stronger, if you're in the mood. Wine?"

"Please, no. I've quit drinking. You know what the worst part of giving up alcohol is? People look at you as if you're a drunk. You can collapse at any number of dinner parties and no one says a word, but order ginger ale in a restaurant and everyone gives you a sympathetic look, to let you know they *understand*. I suppose I'll have to go on a huge bender one of these weekends just to reassure Samuel that I'm not a hopeless alcoholic."

She sipped at the water delicately and drummed her pretty nails against the glass. I wondered if she was having as much trouble sticking to her abstinence resolution as I was.

"When did you stop?"

"Most recently, this morning. How far behind on the rent is she? Whatever her name is. Eight months, a year?"

"Oh, no," I said, reassured by the overstatement. "Only three or four months. Plus a little money I loaned her."

"Let's make a plan of action for you," she said. "They're big on making plans in the confidence book. It helps you imagine a positive outcome."

As I went into the pantry to get a notepad, she called out, "This is going to work, William. Samuel and I got to you just in time."

something

I felt virtuous and hopeful for having taken notes on Charlotte's plan of action. So virtuous, in fact, that I was sure it would be easy to spend the evening propped up on my short chaise longue and finally get past the introduction so I could begin reading *The Mandarins* itself.

After dinner that night, in the glare of the reading light, I found where I'd left off a couple weeks earlier and read to the end of Rosemary Boyle's commentary. She concluded her introductory rant in an expansive mood, congratulating the reader. "Those who bought this book are to be applauded for their good intentions. You've undertaken a daunting task. You will not regret beginning this novel even if, like the vast majority of unpaid readers, you don't make it past the first chapter. Those in search of greener pastures should bear in mind that de Beauvoir was wildly prolific. And that this is her most readable work. Good luck."

An hour later, I was driving along a suburban parkway to an arranged meeting with a supposedly married man who was supposedly named Rick. Rick owned a van. Vans—the kind with few windows—are extremely popular, for obvious reasons, with married men who have secret lives. I was quickly coming to the conclusion that everyone had a secret life. After all, if I had a secret life, no one was above suspicion. My own father had had a secret life with his receptionist.

It would be nice, I thought, scanning the parking area off the side of the road for the green van, if Samuel and Charlotte turned out not to have secret lives, if both of them were content with their marriage and with each other, just as they appeared to be. It would lend balance and a sense of proportion to the confusing world of human relations. Surely one happy, uncomplicated marriage wasn't too much to hope for. And clearly, there was something to learn from them, even if I wasn't certain what it was.

As soon as I spotted the van pulled over in the agreed upon spot, surrounded by low-hanging trees, my mouth went dry with excitement and regret. It was unforgivable that I hadn't stayed home and read past the introduction to *The Mandarins*. I should have begun reading the book itself. A couple of chapters. Was that too much to expect of myself? I yanked up the parking brake and got out, hitched up my pants, and headed toward the van. I spotted Rick in the driver's seat, his window rolled down. Like many people I ran into in these settings, he had a pleasant, ordinary face, with the overfed, pampered look of marriage that's made up of equal parts contentment and defeat. He was nervous, always a reassuring sign, and one that stifled any mass-murderer concerns.

I could have read one chapter of de Beauvoir. Two pages. One page. It wouldn't have been much, but it would at least have been *something*. I had to promise myself I'd get to it tomorrow. No matter what.

"Hey," I said, using the gruff tone that always screams bad acting to me. "You Rick?"

"Everett? You're taller than I expected."

"Well." I loved the way people felt you were obliged to meet their private expectations and fantasies. The engine of the van was turned off, but the radio was on, tuned to a talk show where a commentator was rambling ungrammatically about Saddam Hussein's plot to blow up the U.S. with a "megabomb."

Rick looked at me suspiciously. Everyone was suspicious. "You're not a cop, are you?" he asked.

I assured him I wasn't, but I couldn't tell if he was relieved or disappointed.

drying out

From my bedroom window, I could see Kumiko Rothberg laying out her laundry on the grass in the yard behind the house. It was a hot, bright morning. Too bright. I felt slightly hungover from a lack of sleep and assaulted by all that optimistic sunshine.

Kumiko's laundry routine was another of the peasant affectations she'd picked up somewhere in her travels, although not, presumably, in Scarsdale, where she'd grown up. She shook out a white smock and spread it on the grass. There was a dryer in the basement of the house and a laundry line attached to her back porch, but when I'd pointed these out to her, she'd gone into a long story about having learned this superior method of clothes drying decades earlier from her "Guatemalan family," a mythic group of people she'd exploited for six months while studying Spanish in Central America.

She straightened out the smock, tossed one of her long gray braids over her shoulder, and looked directly at my window. I withdrew. Oddly enough, the more behind she got in the rent, the more embarrassed and concerned I felt when I spotted her, as if she were the landlord and I the tenant months behind on the rent.

real estate

Despite having worked in real estate for a decade, I'd resisted buying a piece of property until three years earlier. The ostensible reason for the delay was a vague political objection to ownership of property and government subsidies of same in the form of tax breaks. For years, even before buying my house, I had trouble remembering the specifics, probably because the whole thing was just self-righteous frosting on what was essentially a fear of settling down, not entirely dissimilar to Sylvia's problems. As a result of my delays, I'd been priced out of the downtown Boston neighborhood, not far from Edward, where I'd been renting for years, and had been priced into Somerville. Despite its density of population and abundance of vinyl siding, Somerville was most notable for its diverse population. The city was crawling with people of all shapes, colors, sexual orientations, and religions, from varied class and ethnic backgrounds, speaking dozens of languages, living more or less harmoniously, all drawn together by the fervent desire to move someplace better.

The outstanding virtue of my two-family house was its location. The sweeping views created the illusion that I was floating above the crowded streets, about to take off for a journey to a neighborhood where you could find artisan bread. Financially, the outstanding virtue was the commodious rental unit on the first floor of the house. Or so it had seemed when I bought the place.

All the rain had freshened the lawn, and the grass was a bright green, nearly artificial looking, making a nice contrast with Kumiko's bright white smocks. The sky in front of me and the houses down below looked bleached. It was time to deliver the complicated schedule of payments—a spreadsheet, in fact—I'd drawn up for Kumiko, following Charlotte's advice.

Song to a Seagull

I stood on the back porch of the house, where the mournful sounds of a Buffy Sainte-Marie tape were coming through the open window of Kumiko's apartment. Kumiko had a fondness for mournful sopranos.

"Morning," I said, trying to inject as much optimism into the greeting as possible.

She spun around, alarmed. "You frightened me," she accused.

"Lovely day." I squinted at the blinding sunlight.

She shook out a pillowcase and laid it on the ground. "I suppose it depends upon your definition of lovely."

"The sun is out," I said. "It must make everything dry more quickly."

She had droopy, sorrowful eyes, and when she looked at me, it was often with the pity a believer feels for the unenlightened. "It's interesting how speed is considered such a virtue in our culture, even for laundry."

I stepped down onto the lawn, a little square of grass bordered by lilac bushes and evergreens Edward had helped me plant shortly after I bought the place. "I think I used to own this album," I said. "I haven't heard it in years."

"If the music is bothering you, William, you just have to tell me. I'll turn it down."

"I didn't say it was too loud." Although the truth was, it was a little early in the day for that melancholy tremolo and all that yearning.

She gave me another of her pitying smiles. "As soon as I'm finished here, I'll go in and turn it off. I promise I won't play music unless I know you're out of the house. Unless the neighbors have been complaining, too. But I suspect they'd take my side. They're very supportive."

A threat was buried in the comment. Perhaps she was organizing the neighbors to throw up a picket line around the house if I tried to evict her.

I had the schedule neatly folded into an envelope, all very professional. I handed it to her.

"I took a long time drawing that up and I'd appreciate it if you'd read it carefully. There are about two dozen dates with exact figures next to each. If you follow it to the letter, you'll be entirely caught up on what you owe me within eight months. I'd like you to take a look and make sure it's clear." And then, because I was desperate to change the subject, I said: "How's the yoga going?"

"It's the center of my spiritual life. Forgive me if I'm not comfortable discussing my spirituality with my *landlord*."

She took the schedule out of the envelope and unfolded it, put on a pair of tiny black reading glasses, and peering over the tops of them, said to me, in a tone of reconciliation, "I hope you know how much I appreciate this."

The paper she was holding was covered with a list of dates and amounts and times of the day. Seeing it in her hands, I realized I should have used a much larger font. It was the kind of overly detailed timetable, tiny print and all, that could be used as Exhibit A to prove an unstable state of mind.

She devoted ten seconds to the schedule. "I have to go to a wedding on November twenty-sixth," she said. "Can we change that date to the twenty-ninth?"

The specificity of this one objection cheered me up. "Certainly," I said. "That shouldn't be a problem. I'll tell you what, you can skip that payment altogether so it doesn't throw everything else off. The rest looks fine?"

"I appreciate this, William. More than you'll ever know. Kindness is an undervalued quality in our age."

"I agree."

"I don't think that friend of yours, the woman you're trying to rent my apartment to, understands kindness in the same way you do."

Despite my better instincts, I was pleased by the flattering comparison. "I'm not trying to rent your apartment to her. I thought I'd made that clear."

"I felt as if she was looking right through me."

As I was stepping back into the house, feeling as if, all things considered, the conversation had gone reasonably well, she said, "I have a show lined up at an important gallery in December."

"That's wonderful. Congratulations."

"It's a breakthrough for my career. At the end, I should have enough for a down payment on a house, and I'm hoping you'll agree to work with me, despite your feelings about me."

"I'd be happy to help out."

"Good. And I'd be honored if you came to the opening. It would mean a great, great deal to me."

"I'd love to."

"It's in New Mexico."

"Ah. Well."

"I'm meeting the gallery owner in Boston tomorrow afternoon. Could we change tomorrow's payment, too? Or maybe I'll just skip that one instead of the one at the end of November, and then toss in something else in December."

trapped

"And I suppose you agreed?" Edward asked me.

"It's only for a day or two. I have a good feeling about this plan working. Charlotte, the woman I was telling you about, was very clear."

"You take her advice, some alcoholic stranger, but you won't take mine. You just invited me over to exploit me. Hand me the bucket."

I'd invited Edward to my apartment to tell him about Sylvia and to try and settle on an asking price for his apartment. But before we got to that, I asked him to help me with the kitchen sink, which had been draining slowly for a couple of months. He'd asked for towels, wrenches, a metal bucket I used to mop the floors, and a few household items, and had climbed into the cabinet under the sink with simian agility. I was sitting on the floor looking in, marveling at the flexibility of his compact body and the efficient way he worked.

"You should take Marty's seminar," he said. "She'd tell you what to do, and it wouldn't be to spend hours drawing up some hopeless schedule. You might as well watch what I'm doing down here so you can do it yourself next time. I'm not flying three thousand miles to fix your sink, and a plumber would take you for a couple of hundred bucks. Get your head under here."

I lay down on the floor and slid my head and shoulders under the sink, so that they were practically resting on his thighs. After years of wearing a military haircut in a failed attempt to appear more "masculine," he was letting his hair get longer. His hair was a pretty dirty blond and was growing in in ringlets. I grinned at him and watched as he explained about the trap and grease in his hoarse, cranky voice. He had a way of dressing up all of his instructions with a reprimand. He'd tell me how to do it, but I should have known how all along.

"You don't have to pretend to be annoyed all the time," I said. "It wouldn't make you too vulnerable to drop your guard every once in a while. Especially with me."

"I'm doing the lecturing, William." He unbolted the trap on the sink, and filthy water poured into the pail. "You should be using a drain opener more often. Don't let this build up again. Is that clear?"

"It is," I said. I loved his firm, impotent commands that seemed to be directly and mysteriously connected to his need to be dominated. There was something about the proximity of his curled up little body that I found unexpectedly arousing, and I shifted my legs and cast a lascivious glance in his direction. "I have some news for you," I said. "I think it's going to make you happy."

"Absence of news is generally what makes me happy these days."

"I have a buyer for your apartment."

He continued working on the sink, cleaning out the pipe and applying a sealant to the joint. When he was satisfied that everything was secure, he tossed all of the tools into the canvas bag I kept them in, mostly unused until he visited and repaired something. Without saying a word, he crawled out over me and turned on the faucet.

When I'd hauled my own body out from the cabinet, I said, "You don't look very pleased, Edward."

"There, you see, the drain is fine." He shut off the water and turned to face me with a look of disbelief. "How can you have a buyer when we haven't discussed price?"

"That's what you're here to do tonight. I've been working with this customer for a while, and as long as we come up with something fair, she'll go for it."

"In that case, I suppose I'd better start packing."

"Come on," I said. I went to him, turned him around, and brushed off the seat of his pants with my hand. "Just pretend you're happy and grateful."

"Don't touch me like that. Of course I'm happy you're helping me leave town. Finally there's a project involving me you can find time for. I'm sure the commission has nothing to do with it."

"I agreed to a one percent commission, remember? The rest will go straight into your pocket."

"You'll get credit for the sale and the office will make a few grand."

"True."

"On top of that, I've talked Marty into letting you list her condo. She's been trying to sell it on her Web site for two months now, but she hasn't had a single offer. I told her you'd save her time and ultimately make her more money. So please deliver on both counts. Now it's your turn to be happy and grateful."

I assured him that I was both, although really, it was a mixed blessing. True, I needed to bring new listings into the office, but without question, Marty would want a few hundred grand more than the place was worth. Everyone who tries to sell a piece of real estate himself asks for much more than it's worth. Even the ones who don't boast about their beastly natures.

"Let me take you out to dinner," I said. "We'll celebrate." Although judging from the sour look on his face, he was not in the mood for celebration.

"I can't. You have to drive me home in a few minutes. I have a date with a pilot, and he's landing in half an hour. I have to go clean up."

"A pilot?" He hadn't mentioned a word of this before, and the alleged date had about it the faint smell of fantasy. Typically, Edward was nervous about dates and took hours to get ready. He often canceled at the last minute. "Married, I suppose."

"Of course. All pilots are married, and they're all bisexual. Everyone knows that."

"I must have forgotten," I said. "You realize you're the one who told me you wanted to sell your apartment. It's you who decided to move."

"I do realize that, William. I'm not completely insane. I guess I just hadn't realized it would happen so quickly. Not that I'm not grateful."

As I was driving him home, more slowly than I ordinarily drive, I struggled to try and find something to talk about but couldn't come up with anything. It wouldn't do to assure him that the person interested in his condo had a solid track record of backing out of deals at the last minute and that it was nearly inconceivable she'd go through with the purchase. Finally, I told him that Charlotte had invited me to a cocktail party at their house next month. "If you're in town," I said, "I'd love to have you join me."

"I'm p-paralyzed with pleasure." Edward had recently read *The Great Gatsby,* and this line of Daisy Buchanan's, affected stutter and all, had become one of his new catchphrases. "You've wasted no time replacing me, have you?"

"It's hardly that. Anyway, it's mostly business. They're clients."

"It's such an obvious attempt to bond with Mommy and Daddy all over again."

We were stopped at a traffic light, and without saying anything, he undid his seat belt and opened the door. "I'll walk from here," he said. "I need the exercise."

"Let me know how the date goes," I said.

He dodged the traffic and disappeared down the sidewalk.

Well, I thought as I was driving home, two could play that game. I dialed the pedicurist grad student and set up an appointment for later that night. It certainly wasn't the way I'd been planning to spend my evening, but it was more appealing than the chaise longue.

rose

A few days later, I had a lunch date with Rose Forrest, the eighty-year-old woman who'd been my father's receptionist and mistress. She still lived in the Connecticut town where I'd grown up, but she took the train to Boston a few times a year to visit her brother, a decrepit bachelor who lived in a studio apartment in Back Bay.

She usually called me when she came to town, and usually I took her out to lunch at an overpriced restaurant, where she drank a lot, ate very little, and reminisced in a careful, evasive way about my father and their working relationship.

I'd made arrangements to meet her that day in the lobby of the Ritz. I didn't like the Ritz, with its ossified Boston ambiance and unimaginative food, but it was close to Rose's brother's apartment and was, I imagined, the kind of place my father would have approved of. Earlier in the week, I'd had a big score at the consignment shop—a pair of gray Helmut Lang pants that weren't exactly flattering but needed no alterations and a cashmere Yves Saint Laurent jacket—and I wore both, even though the jacket was probably out of season. In her younger days, Rose had made her own clothes, knock-offs of designer dresses and suits, and her brother, undoubtedly gay, had been a salesman in the men's department at Filene's.

Rose was folded into an armchair in the lobby of the hotel looking shockingly older than the last time I'd seen her, a little more than a year earlier. She'd always been a tall, slim woman with a delicate body that belied her strong will and commanding—though possibly wasted—intelligence. (Making appointments for my father's dental practice couldn't have been an intellectual challenge.) Today, she looked, for the first time in my experience, frail.

She held out her cold, bony hands to me, and I pulled her up from her chair and kissed her cheek.

"You're late, William," she said. "I've been here nearly half an hour."

I checked my watch. "I'm awfully sorry. But we said one. It's quarter of. Do you think you got here too early?"

"Oh? That's a possibility I hadn't considered. I'm slipping when it comes to dates and times and those sorts of things. Trevor insisted I get here whenever it was I got here. He's more vague with details than I am." She and her brother, whom I'd met only twice, both had odd pronunciation, reaching in a sweet, unconvincing way for an upper-class accent. De*tails*. She scrutinized me for a moment, and I grinned, hoping for a compliment on the jacket. "You're going gray," she said.

"Ah." It was one of the signs of aging that didn't concern me, at least not yet. "Only a few strands here and there."

"Yes, but that's how it begins. You should start putting something in it now, before it becomes too obvious. Your father dyed his hair, you know."

"I didn't know. I suppose I should have figured it out, now that you mention it." I wasn't about to tell her that my image of my father was so ill-defined I couldn't remember exactly what color his hair or his eyes had been. She took my arm, and I led her into the dining room. Frail as she was, she still had perfect posture and a dignified gait, both of which seemed connected in some way to the affected pronunciation. "How old was he when he died? Seventy-five?"

"Seventy-three. And no gray. I insisted he have it done right," she said. "Professionally. Not the ink you get in a drugstore."

"I'm sure he appreciated the advice."

"I don't know whether he did or not, but I'm sure someone appreciated the results."

I'd noticed over the years that Rose took pride in these small, insignificant ways in which she'd been a good influence in my father's life. I suppose they were the only things about her relationship with my father she was comfortable discussing with me, and probably they balanced out, in her own mind, her role as other woman. It wasn't for his sake she'd insisted on the professional dye job, or for her own, but for my mother's; she was the one who got the benefit of Rose's grooming tips. Thus, her relationship with my father hadn't compromised my parents' marriage but had made it better. For all I knew, it had.

I pushed in her chair. Her body seemed weightless.

"Do you want to start off with your usual?" I asked. "We can worry about the food later."

"I've stopped drinking wine," she said. "Doctor's orders, unfortunately."

"Nothing serious, I hope."

"I'm trying not to focus on it. I had that surgery six months ago, so I've had to make some adjustments."

I nodded and signaled for the waiter, slightly panicked. I had a vague memory of her telling me, in a phone conversation, about a hospitalization, but I wasn't sure if she'd told me the exact nature of the illness or any of the details of the treatment. I met with Rose for these lunches and sat through the conversation, at times strained, because doing so made me feel closer to my father than I ever had during his life, as if he and I were in collusion on an important secret, as if he trusted and confided in me in a way he never had. But it occurred to me, as I scanned the menu, that I didn't know Rose herself very well at all; she was a medium, through whom I was communicating with my father, not a real, three-dimensional person. Undoubtedly, she thought of me in a similar way, no matter how carefully I dressed for her and how diligent I was about pushing in her chair.

"How's your business?" she asked me. "Selling a lot, I suppose. I keep hearing about prices in Boston and Cambridge."

"Business is all right. I have a few promising things in the works. A friend selling a condo, a professor desperate to buy, a nice married couple moving in from the suburbs."

"That's happening a lot, married couples moving in from the suburbs. It's important to make changes when you've been together a long time." When you've *bean* together.

"I'm sure you're right."

"I hope you're able to help them out."

She often talked about marriage in an authoritative way, as if her role of mistress had given her special insight into the institution. She had her hands folded on top of the menu, not even feigning interest in food, and when the waiter came, she asked him to bring her a small salad, "Something I can push around on the plate."

"Do you ever regret not marrying?" I asked her. According to family gossip, she'd been engaged more than once and had backed out at the last minute.

"Not at all. I wasn't meant for motherhood and housewife duties. I would have felt boxed in by the whole business."

"I see what you mean," I said. Hearing her put it that way, I couldn't imagine her, with her affected way of speaking and her brittle posture, dealing with the sloppiness of children and a live-in husband.

She did as she'd promised and pushed the salad around on her plate without making much effort at eating it, and I began to think she might be a lot sicker than she was letting on. We talked about the weather and a few uncontroversial current events. She was a woman who was used to placating men like my father by rarely expressing an opinion. When the plates had been cleared and I sat nursing a coffee I'd ordered only to prolong the lunch, she told me she had a favor to ask.

"Please," I said. "If there's anything I can help you with."

"It's nothing like that. You see, I have, in my possession, some things that belonged to your father. And I'd like to send them to you."

"Of course. What kinds of things?"

She sighed and smiled in a fond, proud way. "They're gifts I gave him over the years. Personal things, mostly, but also some books, a few records he especially liked."

"Records?" I'd never known my father to listen to music or

express any opinions on the subject, and the idea that he might have musical favorites was a shock.

"I enjoyed giving him things—very nice things—but we agreed it wouldn't look right for him to bring them home. So I kept them for him. I probably should have thrown them out years ago, but I haven't been able to. Some things might fit you. He never had an opportunity to wear a lot of them. There's not more than a couple of boxes. I can have them shipped to you, if that's all right."

"Please do," I said. "I'd be honored." I was trying not to picture her shopping trips, buying clothes she knew would never be worn, or to think about where she'd kept everything, year after year, in her small apartment. I offered to walk her back to her brother's place, but she said she had an appointment with a hairdresser later that afternoon and would just wait in the lobby. It was fun to see people coming and going, she said, trying to guess where they were from and what they were doing there. I led her back to the chair she'd been sitting in earlier, and kissed her goodbye, saddened and unexpectedly relieved by the thought that this might be the last time I saw her.

getting my story straight

There was one thing about the forgettable, impersonal, and ultimately depressing forty-minute sexual encounter that I loved: I got to meet a lot of people I otherwise would never have met. The fact that it turned out, in many cases, I wouldn't otherwise want to meet them was irrelevant.

Despite a pretty steep level of disillusionment with the whole process, I loved knowing that all over the city, at every hour of the day and night, there were people—men and women of all ages and preferences and physical proportions—opening their doors to strangers and getting right down to carnal business. You could easily think of this as total depravity, as end-of-civilization decadence. Given the assorted risks involved, you could think of it as stupid or suicidal. On the other hand, if everyone were having as much sexual activity as he'd like, adhering to the rules of protection, and avoiding guilt and self-hatred, there'd be no such thing as road rage, and no one would ever have voted for George W. Bush. Life, on the whole, would be better.

My problem was that I'd let an activity become a habit, a habit become a distraction, and a distraction become an obsession. After a while, it had become like eating vast portions of flavorless food at every meal, simply because it's on the plate or because there's nothing good on television. Oh, one more bite, you think. Why not?

Thus, with an abundance of rationalizations and an absence of hunger, I went to meet Francis at yet another suburban hotel. It was a Monday night, I was exhausted, I was supposed to be going to Marty Gordon's apartment to give her an opinion of value and negotiate listing prices. But a message had appeared in my e-mailbox, I wasn't dying to wrangle with Marty about money, and I do enjoy visiting hotels.

I called Marty from my cell phone as I drove on the Mass Pike. "We'll have to do it another time," I said. "I have an emergency I have to attend to."

"What is this?" she asked. "You're testing my limits, seeing how much crap I'll let you get away with before we've even established a professional relationship?"

"Of course not," I said. "A problem I didn't foresee, that's all."

"Thirty seconds ago, it was an emergency. Now it's been downgraded to a problem. If we're on for another two minutes it'll be an 'issue.' Get your story straight, William. It's one of the rules I give in my first seminar. Get Your Story Straight."

"What about tomorrow night?" I asked.

"Okay, so now we're changing the subject. Hey, whatever. I can rearrange my schedule and my career around your emergency issues. I have no *life*, William. Be here at eight o'clock. One more 'problem' and I'm calling Century 21."

atmospheric

Francis had described himself as thirty-two and blond. His age was hard to judge in the dim light of the hotel room. He'd personalized the place with votive candles burning in small blue globes on the desk across from the bed.

"Atmospheric," I said.

"Vanilla. Aromatherapy. It's clarifying."

"Ah."

He was dressed for the occasion—naked, in other words—and on the whole, looked thoroughly done in, as if he'd be happy to crawl under the covers on the king-sized bed and go to sleep. He had thin, reddish blond hair, light eyebrows, and the kind of pale features that seem to disappear the longer you look at them. He sat at the desk chair and gazed at me with weary intensity.

"You're hot," he drawled, unconvincingly.

"Oh. Thanks." In a moment of architectural insanity, the hotel had been built directly above the Mass Pike, with traffic whizzing beneath it. Through the translucent curtains, I could see headlights zooming toward the room as if the cars were about to crash through the wall. "You, too," I said. "Hot." Having uttered that meaningless word, I needed to reorganize my thoughts about this meeting. "Mind if I use the bathroom?"

There were more candles burning on the counter around the sink, mixed in with antiseptic cleaners for inside and outside the body. I suppose the attention to cleanliness should have been re-assuring, but it all seemed so carefully planned and organized, it struck me as unwholesome, and the antithesis of sexual. I lifted the toilet seat with my foot and took a piss. I had a strong urge to leave, but I'd already canceled my meeting with Marty and I knew I'd end up at home arranging something else similar to this anyway.

As I took a seat on the edge of the wide bed, my eyes adjusted to the light and I saw, laid out on a low table near the window, a col-lection of nearly a dozen sex toys. They were lined up in an orderly way, according to size and color. Behind them was an assortment of lubricants in tubes and bottles, arranged by height. The bedside table had a big plastic bowl filled to the top with condoms; there was a stack of neatly folded towels and facecloths at the foot of the bed. Draped over the easy chair were thongs, bikinis, rubber shorts, and what appeared to be a pleated plaid skirt, like Catholic school-girls wear.

The way he'd set out the whole display reminded me of one of those Hong Kong tailors who used to set up shop in hotel rooms for a week, taking orders for custom-made suits. For a moment, I wasn't sure if I was expected to admire his collection or shop.

"You travel light," I said.

He shrugged. "Not really. I'm leaving tomorrow morning and I'm half packed."

"There's more, in other words?"

"If you don't see anything that interests you here, you can look in there." He pointed to a black duffel bag near my feet. His cock and balls were bunched up on the seat of the chair, like a family of mice huddled together for warmth. Maybe I could say I'd left some of my own accouterments out in the car and make a cowardly, be-right-back exit that way.

"They must love going through your carry-on at the airport," I said.

"They don't qualify as weapons."

A matter of opinion.

There was something grim about the seriousness of his attitude, as if he was lugging around this boatload of props out of need and didn't get much pleasure out of it. Taking in the candles, the display, the bowl of condoms, and his state of exhaustion, you'd have to conclude he'd done a couple of shows already that day, possibly that very evening.

"You look a little wiped out," I said. "Maybe I shouldn't stick around."

"Hey, come on," he said. "I'm all worked up." I looked back at the mice, sleeping soundly, begging not to be disturbed. "You said you would."

I sighed and gazed out at the traffic again. "Where are you from, anyway?"

"What difference does it make?"

"It makes no difference, I'm just interested. An unofficial poll."

"Atlanta," he said.

"Everyone's from Atlanta these days. Why is that? Based on my very unscientific study, half the people you run into on any given day are here from Atlanta. At least the naked ones in hotel rooms."

I could see that his patience, assuming that's what it was, was about to harden into contempt. His pale, nearly invisible eyes blazed for a moment in the unbaked dough of his face. "I turned down a couple of other guys." And then, sweetly, like a child, "You promised."

I was beginning to feel as if I'd seen a car pulled over on the highway, had stopped to help, and was now obliged to change the tire. All against my better judgment and my own desires. The truth was, I hadn't felt any sexual interest or enthusiasm all night and had arranged this whole meeting out of habit and to avoid dealing with Marty. I was as exhausted as he looked, and it occurred to me that, pleas to stay or not, he probably found my attitude and enervation as depressing as I found his.

But recognizing that we were in a similar state of restless ennui made me more sympathetic to him, even if no more attracted. I had made an implicit promise, and I felt obliged to deliver in some way.

"Look, I'll help you out," I said. "But I'll only get off on this if I stay fully dressed the whole time and you understand that I'm not going to get off."

"That's cool," he said. He stood up wearily, like someone who'd run a few too many miles that afternoon, and bent over the desk. "Start off with that red one in the middle there." He looked over his shoulder. "It's okay about not getting off. I won't get off either."

crutches

Like most people who are obsessed with fitness and advertise their superior health and physical condition, Marty Gordon lived in intense, unrelenting pain. It traveled from one region of her body to another and usually required a crutch or an elastic bandage, an elaborate brace, or some combination of the above. She offered the fact that she was able to live and function with this pain as proof of her stamina and courage and the effectiveness of her assertiveness training and exercise routines. The reasons for the pain were never mentioned.

When I got to her apartment the following night, she was carrying a metal walking stick with a pink rubber tip. She hobbled through the rooms, using the stick to point out to me the improvements she'd made over the years and the ways in which they ought to up the asking price. Her dog, a fat Rottweiler named Charlaine, was trailing behind her, occasionally nudging the fanny pack Marty had strapped around her waist. Charlaine was discussed at length on ReleaseTheBeast.com as the superior creature from whom Marty had learned many of her aggressive techniques. Based on my personal observations, she was a quiet and relatively docile animal who was casually possessive of Marty, mainly because she viewed her owner as a short, muscular can opener.

Their relationship seemed to follow the basic folie-à-deux pattern of most dog/owner, parent/child, husband/wife arrangements: Charlaine was plagued by many of the same physical ailments as Marty; the two shared a lot of the same steroid-based medications; Marty took Charlaine to her masseur for treatments. The dog looked at me with scornful dismissal that was eerily similar to Marty's.

"Walk-in closet," Marty said, shoving open a door in the hallway with her cane. "I had it built two years ago."

I peered in. The shelves and hooks against the walls were all spilling over with straps and crutches and back braces, making it look like a shrine at Lourdes. "If I need medical supplies," I said, "I know where to come."

She slammed the door shut. "It cost me twelve hundred dollars to have that closet built. New shelves, built-in cabinets. How come you're not writing it down?"

I flipped a page on the pad I was carrying and scribbled a note. *Big closet. Big deal.*

"Edward offered to help build the closet, but *I*"—full stop, to let the obvious point sink in—"don't believe in taking advantage of friends."

"No."

She opened her fanny pack and pulled out what looked like a lamb chop. Charlaine snatched it out of her hand and practically swallowed it whole. "So let's see, we're up to about eighty thousand in home improvements I've made, right? And I haven't even shown you the bedroom."

Because there was no love lost between Marty and me, we didn't see each other all that often. When I did see her, I was always struck by how petite she was. Her diminutive height was exacerbated by her stocky, muscular build. No matter what the season, she dressed in black, knee-length bicycle shorts and an assortment of baggy sweatshirts with her Web site and a close-up of Charlaine's mouth printed on the front and back. For all of her macho posturing, Marty had a surprisingly soft face, made to look more tender by large amber eyes. Even when she was barking orders at you, there was something vulnerable, even pleading, in her eyes, and I sometimes wondered if the underlying goal of all her bravado wasn't simply to bully you into loving her.

Most of Marty's apartment was decorated with exercise equipment, military memorabilia, and big boxes of brochures for her business. There was a frat house atmosphere throughout, as if the place was lived in by an overworked person who spent most of her time elsewhere.

Marty's bedroom, however, could easily have belonged to a ten-year-old girl. The walls were painted a flushed, florid shade of pink, there were white frilly curtains over the one window, and the bed—a narrow single with a white headboard—was covered with a flowered spread, a dozen or more toss pillows, and a collection of stuffed animals.

"This is obviously your private refuge," I said, trying to contain my surprise. I'd been in the apartment twice before, but had never been given a tour and certainly had never entered the inner sanctum.

"What's that supposed to mean?"

"It looks as if you come here to . . . I don't know, relax and unwind, get away from your obligations and responsibilities."

"Not really. I usually fall asleep out on the sofa in the living room. I paid nine hundred dollars to have the ceiling and the walls plastered. Plus I had the floor sanded and stained. That was another five hundred. Write it down."

I picked up a photo of a handsome man in uniform from the top of her bureau. "Is this your brother?" I asked.

"Why do you think he's my brother? Because he's black? Is that it?"

"Edward told me you have a brother who's in the military."

"True, but I don't have pictures of that asshole lying around here. That was my fiancé. He was killed in a helicopter accident in Kosovo."

"I'm sorry, Marty. I had no idea. Edward told me you'd been engaged, but—"

"Shit happens, William. When you're trying to serve your country and make the world a better place, shit happens. Some risks are worth taking. That's how I see it. I decided I could let his death kill me or make me stronger. Figure out which option I chose. Let's go into the kitchen."

Blowing Smoke

She pulled a chair out from her kitchen table and said, "Sit." Charlaine and I both sat at the same time. "I'll make you some green tea. I'm big on green tea. You should drink at least four cups of green tea a day. Green tea is full of antioxidants. I'll bet you didn't know that."

"You're right. I keep hearing about antioxidants, but I have no idea what they're good for."

"Your health, obviously."

"I know, but I meant specifically."

She turned from her tea preparations at the counter and put her hands on her hips. "In my seminars, I call that Kicking the Gift Horse. I tell you it's healthy, I offer you a cup of good health, something that might save your life, or at least make your death a little less painful, and you doubt it. You question it. You Kick the Gift Horse."

"You have the wrong idea," I said. "I'm not doubting it, I was wondering what specifically it was good for, what part of the body?"

"Why? Because if it's good for your heart you'll drink it, but if it's good for your liver you won't? Because you only want one part of your body to be healthy?"

"No, I was—"

"You were Kicking the Gift Horse, William. And you know what? I'm not buying into it." She clicked off the stove and the gas flame died with a gasp. "Go to Starbucks and pay for poison. I'm doing what I call Kicking Back."

"Tough love."

"That's what I'm paid for, baby." She tugged a chair out from the table with her good foot and sat down leaning toward me with her elbows on her knees. "I want six hundred grand for this place, and if you can't get it for me, I'm calling Century 21."

I was prepared for this, or something like it, and had done my homework. "The thing is, Marty—"

"Stop right there. I don't give a fuck about 'the thing,'

William. The only 'thing' I'm interested in is the bottom line. I paid seventy-five grand for this place and I've put over a hundred into it and I want to triple my investment. That's 'the thing.' A crappy place two doors down sold for five fifty. That was two months ago. No reason I shouldn't get six hundred."

I took out a sheet of comparables I'd prepared back at the office. "That place had an additional seven hundred square feet."

"Yeah? Well, it had no new kitchen, no refinished floors, and no walk-in closet. Six hundred. Take it or leave it."

Her doorbell rang. She gave me a hard, disapproving look, silently demanding I think it over, and then pushed herself up from the table. Charlaine had a moment of confusion, trying to decide between following Marty and guarding me. She growled and trailed after the hand that fed her. I could overhear a muffled exchange at the door, Marty dismissively saying, "Yeah, in the *kitchen,*" and then she and Charlaine returned with Edward in tow. He was cradling a large carton in his arms, and I leapt up from the table to help him.

"He made it in here on his own," Marty said, pulling out her chair. "I don't think he needs you at this point. Put it down out in the back hallway, Eddie. We're almost done. He picked up some brochures for me and brought them over. He likes helping out his friends."

"He doesn't drive," I said. "How did he get that over here?"

"Ever hear of taxis?" She pulled a ten-dollar bill out of the pack around her waist and slapped it down on the kitchen table. "Satisfied? He won't take it, but don't say I didn't try."

"I wouldn't dream of it. I did want to point out that that condo you mentioned before had two and a half baths. That's a big selling point."

"I don't care about a half bath, William. I don't care about a whole bath. You know my terms."

Edward sat at the table between us, his face flushed and sweating, and I had to fight off the urge to push his hair off his forehead. Marty told him to take the money for the taxi, and as he thanked her and pocketed it, Marty glared at me angrily.

"I can't stay," Edward said. "The cab's waiting downstairs. I thought you were coming last night."

"William had a last-minute emergency. Or was it a problem?"

"William has a lot of those. How are the negotiations coming along?"

I restated some of the facts and figures I'd presented to Marty, trying to impress Edward with my professionalism and how reasonable I was being. I could see Marty getting more restless and impatient. Edward saw it, too, and laid his hand on Marty's arm until I'd finished making my case. When I'd once asked Edward about the basis of his friendship with Marty, he'd told me, without hesitating, that she made him feel safe. He admired her strength and her determination. I interpreted this to mean she was a mother figure, but I suppose father was closer to the truth. Oddly enough, though, it seemed to be Edward who always took the role of protector and security adviser, telling Marty when to pull back, when to soften her image, when to give in. Poor little Edward, longing for submission, was destined to forever be the person in control, even of a bully like Marty.

"These numbers are no more convincing than the first time you gave them to me," Marty said.

"What you have to remember," Edward told her, "is that William's on your side. He wants you to get the most for this apartment you can. It's in his interest, too. If the place stays on the market too long, it begins to look bad."

"He's right," I said. "And in a market this hot, two weeks is a long time."

"You stay out of this, William. This is between Edward and

me. Did you check to make sure the printer spelled Charlaine's name right this time?"

"It's perfect. And I made them double the credit, too."

"Good man. You see, William, this is a friend. He's bringing something to the table."

"Hopefully," I said, "I'm bringing professional expertise to the table, a certain amount of experience."

Marty sighed with disgust and Charlaine craned her neck around and gave me a look of contempt. I could tell from the way Edward put his hand against his face my comment had been a blunder.

"You bring nothing to the table," Marty said. "It's my apartment, my improvements, my decision. You're taking something away from the table, namely seven percent of my money. I'm giving this to you as a favor to Edward. Period. So let's not talk about what you're bringing to the damned table. In my seminars, that's what I call Blowing Smoke." She unzipped the pack around her waist and tossed another massive treat to Charlaine. "I've done a little research myself, and I happen to know that your sales figures for the past six months stink. So don't try to Blow Smoke up my ass, okay?"

I assured her that I wouldn't dream of it and came close to asking her to rethink her offer of tea. It was hard to know what kind of research she was talking about having done, but it seems that even a child can use the Internet to discover the most personal details of your life.

Edward tactfully changed the subject, mentioned a few million-dollar condos I'd sold without specifying that the sales had been several years earlier, and then stood up. "I should go. The meter's still running. Walk me out, William. I don't want Marty to have to go up and down stairs again."

"You take care of yourself," Marty said as Edward hugged her. "I pray for you every day. And don't worry about the change from that twenty. We can figure it out later."

When I was sure we were out of earshot, I said, "She gave you a ten."

"You're so petty, William. How can you think I'd care about something like that? And you have no idea how to handle her. You're telling her she's got her numbers wrong instead of assuring her you're going to work with her. It's a good thing I showed up."

I followed him down the stairs to the street. "How was your date the other night? With the pilot."

"It was promising. Now go back upstairs, and please be sensible. I'll call you next week."

"Not sooner?" I asked. But he was stepping into the back of the taxi and didn't hear me.

likes and dislikes

"I don't like you," Marty said. "I never have. The way I see it, you're just dancing around Edward, fucking with his head, and ruining his life. You have been for three years now." She reached into her fanny pack and pulled out a box of cigarettes. She lit one and tossed the box onto the table.

"You smoke," I said.

"How'd you guess?"

"I thought, being a fitness instructor and all that . . ."

"Rule number one in my seminars is Assume Nothing. Does nobody any good at all. You could learn a lot from me, William. Rule number two, by the way, is Keep It Between Us. Where was I?"

"Something about not liking me."

"Exactly. I don't. But the funny thing is, I've got people tearing at me day and night, people who want something from me, people I feel obliged to help because I *like* them. Edward, for example. So when I come across somebody like you, somebody I don't give a shit about, somebody I actively *dis*like, the weird thing is, I start to like them. Why? Because I don't owe them anything, because I don't have to bullshit with them. That's my Achilles' heel. If I dislike you enough, I start to like you."

The whole nonsensical rant left me feeling flattered and defenseless. On top of that, I wanted the apartment listing. "I'll tell you what," I said. "I'll agree to list it at five eighty-five. If we don't get any serious offers in three weeks, we'll renegotiate."

Marty leaned forward in her chair and stubbed out the cigarette in the bottom of a coffee cup. "Nah, I'll tell *you* what, William, when I like someone, I like them. List it at five twenty-five."

"Five sixty-five," I said. I could tell from her look this was going nowhere. "All right. Five twenty-five."

We shook on it, and she led me to the door with Charlaine trailing behind.

"Another thing," I said. "From now on, you should go outside to smoke. People smell smoke in a place these days and they act like it's cat urine or some other odor they'll never get out."

"Good tip. See, you're earning your keep already."

I handed her a card for a house cleaner I'd met years earlier in a discussion group for people with obsessive cleaning behavioral problems, problems this guy had conquered by indulging in them professionally. "Call him. He'll come and spend a whole day scrubbing the place. You won't believe what a difference it will make. I'd volunteer to do it myself, but I don't have the time."

"Is he white?"

"He appears to be."

"All right. I only hire white people to do shit work for me. How much?"

"Don't worry about it. He'll bill me. He's got a diagnosed problem with obsessive compulsion, so he'll do a thorough job."

"Good man." She reached up and grabbed my biceps and squeezed. "Not bad. You been working out?"

"A few push-ups, a couple of times a month."

"You have to start somewhere."

She was closing the door when something else occurred to me, something I'd managed to skip over earlier. I reached up to prevent her from shutting the door. "How do you figure I'm ruining Edward's life?"

Charlaine was apparently put off by my gesture and made a lunge for me. Marty grabbed her collar, pulled her back into the apartment, and slammed the door. "He's in love with you," she called through the door. "He has been for years."

"Oh." I was about to defend myself—against what, I wasn't sure—but Charlaine was scratching at the door and growling, and I could hear a struggle going on. "He's dating a pilot now. It's promising."

"Yeah? Well don't get in the way of it. Keep out of it."

There was a loud boom, as if the dog had flung itself against the door. "Don't leave the dog here when people come to see the place," I said. "Take him out for a walk or something."

"Don't worry. And she's a girl, William. Get it right."

feelings

I'd met Edward more than three years earlier when I was dating a flight attendant named Trent. Like nuns, airline personnel seem to live, shop, and travel in small communities, and at the time, Edward and Trent were sharing the rent on a two-bedroom apartment on the wrong side of Beacon Hill.

I myself was on the wrong side of a failed LTR—not to mention the wrong side of forty—and I was using the excuse of having been dumped by my boyfriend of seventeen months to go out with elaborately inappropriate people. Trent fit neatly into that category, one of those bored, pretty narcissists who appear to live entirely for sex and, at the same time, consider themselves above all the sweat and messiness. As if he were dying to be ravaged by a Latin American soccer team, assuming they didn't muss up his hair. No matter what time we agreed to meet, he'd always arrive thirty minutes late. I'd show up half an hour late myself, and he'd still keep me waiting thirty minutes. Edward was often in the apartment while I waited, usually building a closet or putting up drywall, and I frequently ended up pressed against him, listening to the finer points of joint compound and proper sanding techniques. It did cross my mind that it would be a lot more fun having dinner with him than with coy, tardy Trent, but there was something about the shared, brotherly apartment and the homey renovation projects that made me resist the urge to invite him out. Perhaps I felt an element of shame connected to going out with Trent in the first place that made me consider myself unworthy of Edward.

By the time Edward had moved into his own condo, he and I had established a friendship, albeit one coated with a heavy layer of flirtation and push-pull tension. But love, as Marty had shouted through her door? Marty was often right about people, as if, with her bullying manner and incongruously large and soft eyes, she could push aside your defenses and look right into your heart. Or maybe, in the end, none of us is as hard to understand as we'd like to assume. In the end, most people just want to be left in peace to fuck, overeat, doze off watching the evening news, and sleep through the night without having to get up too often to piss.

Of course, Edward and I harbored "feelings" for each other. I was protective of my relationship with him, and it seemed to me that the best way to preserve it was to keep it at the level of complicated friendship. Friendships have a way of enduring while romantic relationships go quickly from a dreamy "I can't live without you" to a hopeful "Maybe he died in his sleep."

money

Gina was impressed that since she'd talked to me about my job performance, I'd brought in two new listings. Her only hesitation was in the asking price of Marty's condo. "I think you've under overpriced it," she said.

"Under overpriced it." I rattled the words around in my mouth for a minute while she watched me attentively from behind her desk. "Doesn't that mean I priced it just right?"

"There's no such thing as 'just right' in this game. That's how it is. You should be asking at least a hundred grand more."

"I wasn't going to tell you this," I said, "but this place was originally an FSBO."

"Oh? I didn't know that." She put the listing sheets I'd written up on the far corner of her desk, as if they were giving off an unpleasant odor, and picked up a different folder. "I suppose she was asking something ridiculous and no one looked at it."

Nothing raised more scorn and irritation than the mention of a property with a For Sale By Owner history. Conventional wisdom had it that the people who try selling their own houses and apartments are the same people who home-school their children, vacation in gigantic recreational vehicles, and do morris dancing.

"It was priced at about a hundred thousand more."

"In that case, I leave it up to you. I'm happy to see some motivation here, William. We're making progress. Next, I want to see some money."

I promised her she'd be seeing some very soon.

For most of my career in selling, I had been an effective real estate agent, and much to my surprise, I enjoyed the work. It wasn't the dollars-and-cents business end of things that appealed to me. It was the illusion, and perhaps even the reality, that I was helping people. Bricks and mortar, floors and ceilings and walls. A roof, a bathroom, and sometimes a basement. People open up and pour out their life stories with little more prompting than a question about whether they prefer gas or electric stoves. (For the record, everyone says gas, but hardly anyone really cares.) They begin by telling you how many bedrooms they need, and within a few sentences, they're revealing their childhood stories and regaling you with tales of failed relationships and hopes for the future. They claim they're looking for the perfect place to live, but really, they're shopping for the perfect life. And sometimes, I had the pleasant illusion of having delivered exactly that to my clients.

Money had never been of any particular interest to me, one of the luxuries of having done fairly well for most of my adult life. I'd gone into advertising because I considered it a creative field, not necessarily a lucrative one. I preferred to think of myself as an imaginative person, despite the fact that I'd never exhibited much artistic ability, aside from taking accordion lessons in high school. But most homosexual men are assumed to have an aura of nebulous creativity around them, and I took it on faith that I had a strand of imagination hardwired into my DNA. I'm sure the nervous collapse (to dramatize what had really been a brief love affair with Vicodin) that led to my career shift was mainly the result of discovering that I was swimming in the deep end of the tank with voracious capitalist sharks, not collaborating with a bunch of artistes.

In the late nineties, I'd sold a series of over overpriced condominiums, and on Edward's advice, I'd dumped some of my profits into tech stocks that he'd selected from the financial magazines he read in the back of airplanes. I bought the stocks because I wanted to stop his constant nagging about my refusal to manage my money in a responsible way. Secretly, I was hoping the stocks would collapse, thereby proving that I'd been right all along with my hide-it-in-the-mattress theory of investment. Alas, within months, the money had grown by an obscene percentage. When I realized how much I'd made and how rapidly the lump sum was continuing to grow, I sold all the stock in a fit of guilty panic and stuck my new resources into a savings account that earned almost no interest.

Six months later, the stock collapsed. If I'd waited to sell, I would have lost everything, a more appealing prospect than having to deal with my moral crisis over having made money simply because I had it to begin with.

I'd done the usual responsible, penitent things with it—given some to worthy causes, set up a small account for my brother's children. My brother was infuriated that I'd made a few hundred thousand in the stock market. "For doing *nothing,*" he kept reminding me, exacerbating my own complicated response to the situation.

the cousins

My mother called me at my office to see if I'd made contact with my rich cousins. I assured her that I had, and that, following her advice, my sales pitch had not been too hard or too humiliating. "I made my case and then asked them about their kids."

"They don't have children, William."

"Ah. Well, that explains their vague answer." I realize that being a parent is no easy task, but trying to keep track of the children of friends and relatives is not a simple matter either. "They're interested in oceanfront property, which isn't my specialty. How exactly are we related, anyway? It's never been clear to me."

"I'm not sure either. The children of cousins of mine, maybe? That's a guess." It pleased me that she wasn't particularly sentimental about family ties and connections. I've always lumped people obsessed with genealogy and family trees with conspiracy theorists and Civil War enthusiasts. "Oh look," she said, in a louder, lighter tone. "There's Betty Boop. Hi, Betty, you look adorable today . . . She's got about a week to live, if she's lucky."

As she strolled around the retirement village with her cell phone, my mother encountered vast numbers of fellow residents, all of whom referred to one another by cute, randomly chosen nicknames that changed from one sentence to the next. It was an inventive solution to the plague of memory slips that appeared to be affecting everyone, regardless of age. Everyone was so overloaded with news, information, terror alerts, threats of war, and nerve-jangling advertisements, no one could remember anything. All circuits were jammed. People were always accusing one another of forgetfulness the way, once upon a time, they'd accused one another of alcoholism, having an eating disorder, or having been sexually abused as a child. Half the conversation of most couples involved who'd forgotten what and which had the better memory for important information. Fortunately, genuine senility would render all the accusations of senility meaningless.

"Did they mention me?" my mother asked. "The cousins. Whoever they are."

"Your name came up. I told them you were dating."

"That's none of their business, William. I wish you hadn't done that. I suppose they were interested and wanted to know about him."

"I couldn't tell them much. How is all that going?"

"Jerry has a thyroid condition, so he has odd eating habits. We have dinner together almost every night. I'm trying to be a good influence."

Despite his unusual eyes and weathered face, her beau was handsome, based on the photo of him she'd sent me. As I got older, I was able to see and appreciate the appeal, and even the beauty, of people in their sixties, seventies, and eighties in a way that had previously eluded me, as if an evolutionary coping mechanism associated with age was kicking in. Less productively, I was finding men in their twenties more attractive, too.

"How serious is this?" I asked.

"At this age? Everything's serious. Two weeks is a long-term relationship. He's a very gentle man. He's interested in me, asks me questions all the time. It honestly never occurred to me that a man might do that. I'm trying to resist the temptation to meet him."

It took me a few seconds to register on this last comment, and when I did, I asked for clarification. "Are you saying you haven't met yet?"

"Our relationship has all been online and over the phone. I'm becoming quite the typist."

"I thought you said you've been having dinner together every night."

"We get dinner ready, he calls me, and we sit there with the phone. Talk, eat. On his phone plan, long distance is free, so we sometimes stay on for hours. I'll tell you one thing, it's a lot more relaxing than being face-to-face and worrying about the food stuck in your teeth."

"Virtual dating. I suppose you could do the same thing at the movies. Concerts. Lectures."

"Lectures? Please. There's no point in trying to absorb a lot of new information at this age. I don't suppose you've made any progress with *your* personal life."

I wasn't sure if that was a question or a statement. Some tense middle ground, more likely, born of the desire both to know and not know. About five years earlier, my mother had begun to discuss her own life with much more interest than she could muster when she discussed either mine or my brother's. I'd viewed it as a rite of passage, in which she was relinquishing her role of adult and letting me and my brother know that it was now our turn to take care of her. It was a shift in roles that pleased me, especially since minimal care had been required. In this case, she seemed to be approaching me less as a mother than as an equal, and I was saddened to think that there were very few particulars of my personal life I cared to share with her. I changed the subject.

"You'll never guess who I bumped into on the street the other day," I said.

"Rose Forrest."

"Good guess."

"We don't know all that many of the same people, and she has that brother in Boston, and there was something in your voice. I hope you at least took her out for a drink."

"She's not drinking. We had lunch. Although, frankly, she doesn't seem to be eating much either."

"You made the effort, that's what matters. A good restaurant? I always felt bad for her; she had half a life." True, but I wasn't about to point out who had the other half. "There's a lesson in there somewhere, William."

"I'm sure there is," I said, but it wasn't until after I'd hung up that I realized she meant a lesson for me.

focusing on the future

Charlotte and Samuel arrived in my office late on a Saturday morning when the air was warm and damp, a humid weather system left over from the summer. He held the door open for her again, always the gentleman, but this time, she strode in ahead of him, looking more addled than she had in the past, her hair in disarray and her face flushed pink, as if she'd just had an angry outburst. She was scowling, never an attractive expression. It was obvious they'd been arguing, and there was something in her determined gait that made me suspect they weren't talking to each other. I waved them to my desk and experienced a moment of confused pleasure as I watched them walk toward me. I had half a dozen places to show them, and by the end of the afternoon, they'd both be in better moods. *Happy couple,* I wrote in my notes. Not an observation but a goal.

"We've got a big day ahead of us," I said as they sat at my desk.

"Excellent," Samuel said. "But before we get to that, we have a little present for you." He handed me a coffee table book neatly wrapped in tissue paper. "Go ahead and open it now," he said, with the enthusiasm of a child. It was a pictorial history of Nahant with a sepia print of a rocky shoreline on the front. "We thought you might find it interesting."

"He thought you might find it interesting," Charlotte said. "I thought it might add some needed clutter to your apartment."

"You've seen his apartment?" Samuel asked. "When? You didn't tell me."

"I don't tell you everything," she said. "I fully expect you don't tell me everything either. Care to disagree? I didn't think so."

"It was a simple question, Charlotte." He bit her name.

"To which I gave a simple answer."

It can be excruciating and embarrassing to be in the company of a squabbling couple, but on the plus side, you can be reasonably certain they prefer your company to each other's.

Samuel shifted to the front of his seat. He'd replaced the business suit I'd first seen him in with a pair of blue jeans and a jersey. He looked less comfortable and relaxed in this casual wear than he had in the suit. The green polo shirt fit his lean torso snugly and emphasized his athletic build. Probably he was one of those men whose obsession with running and working out is a silent rebuke to his wife's fleshiness. I was guessing he chose to do his sit-ups in front of her, although they probably had ten empty rooms in their house.

"I'll show you the picture of our place," he said, sliding the book toward me.

"Oh, really," said Charlotte. "Can't we do this show-and-tell later? I mean, how is it relevant?"

"I'll take a quick look and then examine it more carefully later," I said.

"How shamelessly diplomatic you are, William."

Samuel turned to a photo of a rambling, shingled summer house that appeared to be perched on the edge of a rocky cliff. "Does it have some historical significance?" I asked. The photo took up an entire page of the book.

"The architect built a lot of grand old summer houses on the East Coast."

"And this," Charlotte said, closing the book, "was an early and relatively minor effort. Can we focus on the future, instead of dwelling on the glorious past?"

"I would *love* to do that," Samuel said. "I've been trying to do that all morning."

"Now that it's convenient for you to bury the hatchet. At long, long last."

"Oh, give it up, sweetheart, please. What have you got for us, William?"

"Lots of appointments," I told them. "I'll start out by taking you to see one or two that are respectable but unlikely, just to soften you up. Then we go to a couple of deeply flawed, and then, with your expectations lowered, I take you to the most likely candidate."

"We couldn't just start there?" Sam asked. "Obviously, we're not in the most lighthearted mood."

"Two people, two moods, Sam."

"Let's do it my way," I said, trying to steer them away from their argument. "You'll end up liking the likely candidate much more."

As I was leading them out to my car, Samuel assured me that the picture of their house was not a very good one, and that with the landscaping and the remodeling that had been done over the years, it was barely recognizable.

"I've invited him to the party," Charlotte said. "Assuming we still *have* the party. He can form his own opinion then."

Charlotte insisted Sam take the front seat of my spotless car for his long legs, and she sat in the back, adjusting her hair in the rearview mirror, and catching my eye. I pulled out of the parking space with an unusually clear sense of purpose, happy to be the calm center of this stormy weather system.

like marriage

The first apartment was a three-bedroom in a low-slung modern building along the river. The building was famous for its services and impressive views, but to my way of thinking, the apartments were little better than overgrown motel units, with a single-exposure fixation on the river that made me feel claustrophobic.

"The question is," I said, leading them through the rooms, "could you picture yourselves living here?"

"I could picture Samuel living here," Charlotte said. "Alone." The comment was so bluntly hostile, both she and Samuel laughed. She opened the sliding glass door, another motel fixture, and stepped onto the narrow balcony. A warm breeze carried in the smell of mud from the sluggish river and the sound of traffic, and lifted Charlotte's summery skirt above her knees. "Do people like having cars racing past them day and night?"

"Surprisingly, yes," I said. "Most people find it comforting, a hedge against the terrible reminder that, essentially, we're alone."

"Like marriage," Samuel said, and grinned, pleased with himself.

I took them to five more apartments, some that I'd visited, others that I'd only seen listings for. A sprawling three-bedroom in a run-down, castellated brick building outside of Harvard Square; a dark apartment that had been pieced together on one half of a Greek Revival house near the river; a loft that was daunting in size and far too open and sunny to imagine living in; a peculiar little converted carriage house buried under a chestnut tree; and to round out the trip to unlikely places, an expensive apartment in a bland building similar to the one we'd first visited that afternoon. None ridiculously inappropriate, but none right.

I could see Charlotte getting more depressed as the afternoon wore on. Most people get depressed when shuttling through the Goldilocks routine of visiting apartments that are wrong in small, specific ways and make the idea of moving seem pointless. Too big, too cramped, too dark, too chopped up, too expansive, too new. I sometimes wondered if people wouldn't be happier if housing were run more like an adoption. You put in an application with certain requests and requirements, and when something comes up, it's handed over to you, and you make it yours. It becomes the perfect place to live, not because it meets certain criteria, but because it's yours.

the one

The last apartment I had to show them was unquestionably the most promising—roomy, eccentric, and full of charm. It was on a pleasant side street lined with oak trees, not far from the river, walking distance to a few recklessly expensive food markets. I pulled up in front of the house slowly. It was an overgrown Queen Anne with a hipped roof, cross gable, two added-on towers, and a bunch of neoclassical porches that had been pasted onto unlikely corners of the house over the years. Somehow or other, they'd attached a sprawling Colonial Revival addition to the back. The house was painted a deep salmony color that everyone in the office found charming but that reminded me of undercooked meat.

I could tell by Charlotte's reverential silence she approved of the outside.

"There are eight units in the house," I said. "They're all different, each with its own porch or cupola."

"Really?" Sam said. "Cupola. I'd love one of those."

People are mad for cupola rooms, even though no one knows

what to do with them except use them for storage. Their unit had a porch instead, less glamorous but more practical.

I'd made an arrangement by telephone with the owners, a couple in their thirties. The wife had told me they'd be out doing errands for the better part of the day, but as I was fiddling with the keys, the husband opened the door. He stood there with a look of sullen discontent and pushed at his glasses.

"I'm William Collins. I'm from Cambridge Properties and we—"

"I know," he said. "We promised we'd be out of here, and I'm sorry, but things got hectic."

From somewhere inside, a woman called out, "Who *is* it?" in a tone that was not especially welcoming.

"It's them," the man called back.

"Who?"

"Them! The real estate people."

"Tell them I'll be right out," she called.

"I don't need to convey that message, do I?"

He led us into the living room, bright from a bay of rounded windows at one end. The apartment was on the top floor of the house, and the branches of the oak tree in front, just beginning to turn autumn colors, were tossing around in the warm breeze, and the afternoon sky peeking through the leaves was deep blue. I made introductions, and told Barry, the husband, I'd be happy to show my clients around myself. "Probably not a good idea," he said. Clearly, this was a reference to the voice from the other room.

It was a beautiful apartment, and the rich colors of the walls— dense shades of peach and burnt umber—the perfect placement of the furniture, the layers of drapes, the padded valances, the abundance of toss pillows all screamed interior decorator, which in turn screamed software millionaire. My brother, Kevin, was in software. His wife was in software. My rich cousins were or had been in software. Everyone on the news was in software. I had no idea what it meant to "be in software." I would never learn because "software" was one of those words, like "carbohydrates" and "Cher," that triggers an off switch in my brain.

Less attractive than the decor was a heavy smell of bacon that permeated the apartment. If the sellers had been my clients, I'd have told them to avoid cooking this particular food until the apartment sold. Everyone likes to eat bacon, but no one wants to be thought of as the kind of person who indulges. Much better to bake fresh bread, something no one does but everyone wants to picture themselves doing.

Barry, the husband, was a short man dressed in a pair of short pants and sandals. He wasn't plump, but there was a soft fleshiness to his pale face and something in the too-tight fit of his clothes that made me think he'd probably gained weight recently. Probably the result of marriage. Almost everyone I knew gained vast amounts of weight in the first years of married life, further support for a theory I have that people generally marry for love— of food.

He had the unhappy, confused expression a lot of recently married men get in their early thirties when they're wondering where their youth and freedom went, questions soon to be made irrelevant by the arrival of a child or the beginning of a messy love affair.

Vanessa, the voice from beyond, appeared in the living room, wiping her hands on a white bar towel she had looped through the belt of her pants. She looked alarmingly similar to her husband, in size, shape, coloring, and even hairstyle. "I'm sorry we weren't out as we promised, but we got busy all of a sudden."

"I told them," Barry said.

"Well, I'm telling them again." She jabbed this rebuke home with a grin and exposed a mouthful of braces. "Let's start in the kitchen and work our way forward." She introduced herself to Samuel and Charlotte with an exuberance that struck me as overdone, and

Barry, rendered insignificant, collapsed into a chair and picked up a magazine.

"This really is a wonderful apartment," Vanessa said, leading us down a long hallway. "We're sad about having to leave, but Barry got a fantastic job offer out in Columbus and I'm from there and we'll be closer to my mother, who isn't doing very well right now. Barry's being great about the whole thing. I'm sure I wouldn't be half as agreeable as he's being, if the tables were turned. Believe me, my mother is *not* easy to take. Like mother, like daughter, I'm afraid." She looked over her shoulder and smiled at us. "For the past year, I've felt a need to be closer to home. The job and my mother are convenient excuses."

Her tone was so convincingly warm and cheerful as she spoke about her husband, I couldn't connect it to the chilly scene that they'd played out in the living room. But then again, it's not uncommon to discover that people talk glowingly about a spouse whom they seem, in person, to dislike intensely, as if they have an idealized version they carry in their heads and then launch into angry disappointment when confronted with the genuine article.

"Let me show you the porch off the back," she said. "It's one of the nicer features. I figure it's best to start there since it's probably where you'll spend most of your time."

The day had turned into a breezy dream, with big dignified clouds sailing through a blue sky. Weather like this seemed to hold out the promise that if you were very good and played your cards right, your life would always be just this pleasant. It was real estate weather, the kind of atmospheric conditions that make any dwelling seem like the absolute best place on earth to live.

The porch was a square outdoor room with a teak floor and a surprisingly high ceiling held aloft at either end by white pillars. The shape of it and its position on the house made it feel like a gazebo floating in the trees. Not far off, we could see the rooftops of the Brattle Street mansions and a faint sparkle of sunlight on the river. Samuel stood off to one side of the porch, gazing out at the view, making a noble attempt at appearing interested. If his eyes were focused on the trees, his mind, it was obvious, was somewhere else. And when I looked back at Charlotte, she was watching her husband, not with anger or hostility, but with understanding and a weary kind of sorrow.

I started to follow Vanessa into the house, but Charlotte pulled me aside and waited until her husband was out of sight. "I want this apartment," she said.

"I knew you'd like it. Wait until you see the rest. There are a few oddities, but nothing seriously wrong."

"No. I mean I really want this place. I can see us living here, happily." Her tone was pleading, almost desperate, and although she was talking about happiness, she looked miserable. "Can you talk Samuel into it?"

"I don't think so. I think the two of you need to discuss it and come to a decision. That's how it usually works."

"Usually, yes, even for us. But not today. It's the right move for everyone. You'd benefit as well. You could try. You could try to help me out, all right?"

Vanessa reappeared at the end of the hallway and beckoned us. "There's a lot more to see," she said.

Charlotte touched my arm and tilted her head, a silent plea. "I'll see what I can do," I said.

People exhibit less interest in the specifics of a potential new home when they've decided, based on an intangible emotional response, that this is the place for them. When a customer starts asking for a lot of details about the boiler and the gutters, I can tell they're looking for an excuse to walk out without making an offer. As Vanessa led us through the maze of rooms, Samuel hauled out an impressive list of questions: What was the condition of the roof? How recently had the plumbing been updated? Had the basement been tested for radon gas? Were there, as far as they knew, any underground oil storage tanks anywhere on the property? Mildew? Mold?

Barry appeared in the bedroom with his hands jammed tightly into the pockets of his shorts, and offered to show Samuel his study. As often happened in these real estate transactions, the couples were forming alliances along gender lines, leaving me stranded gawkily in the middle.

I followed the guys. Barry's study was a tiny room off the hallway, a closet that had been expanded and brightened by way of a dinner-plate-sized window. It was tightly packed with computer equipment and bookshelves holding the usual assortment of discs, DVDs, and similar computer-related accouterments that had risen to importance since books had become irrelevant cultural artifacts. This room existed in nearly every living space occupied by a heterosexual couple, and it was always the exclusive domain of the man. At some point, the husband had retreated to a remote corner of the house and claimed it as his own. A basement, a workshop in a garage, a study behind the kitchen, a converted closet under the stairs. Inevitably, it was the location of the computer, and given my own computer habits, I couldn't help believing that not all of these men were spending all of their time comparing prices on automotive supplies and looking for the cheapest airfare to St. Louis.

Crammed into the little room, my head nearly brushing the ceiling, I felt a wave of sympathy for Charlotte and a sudden closeness to Sam. Barry left us alone in the study, and Sam took a seat at the narrow, built-in desk.

"What's your reaction so far?" I asked.

He shrugged and looked around the room. "Not very impressed. I was hoping for something more open, more space."

"Charlotte's quite taken with it."

"Oh? How do you know that? I suppose she told you. Well, wouldn't it be nice if she'd thought to tell me? It might be the more sensible way to go about it."

"I wasn't going to mention this because I don't want to put any pressure on you, but I just checked with the listing broker, and there's some very serious interest in the place. She's expecting an offer later this weekend." It was the kind of lie Jack was always telling his clients. I'd sit at my desk, listening to him spin out these imaginary scenarios, hoping the client would hang up on him. They seemed like such obvious fabrications, but they almost always worked.

"Is that so?" He sounded skeptical.

"A Harvard Business School professor and his wife. She didn't give me the name, of course, or too many details. It might be wise to make an offer this afternoon. I think it would please Charlotte a great deal."

"I'll take that into consideration," he said, and pushed himself up from the chair.

i doubt that's true

I took Samuel and Charlotte out for lunch. I chose a restaurant not far from my office where all natural light, and most artificial, was carefully blocked at all hours of the day. It seemed marginally less humiliating to give a heavy sales pitch, full of exaggerations and outright lies, in a place where I was only partly visible. The deep shadows appealed to my vanity as well. I'd tried to talk myself into believing the creasing and collapsing of my face came off as virile cragginess and was, thus, an asset, but then a mirror would suddenly pop up between me and my delusions of Paul Newman.

∧

We were shown to the darkest corner of the restaurant, and I sat opposite them, pulling out listing sheets and sales figures for the Cambridge market over the past several months, all in an attempt to convince Samuel that buying the condo was the best possible investment he could make. We worked our way through a stack of documents, passing around a little votive candle and holding it up to the pages. Charlotte was strangely quiet, as if she didn't want to spoil my work by appearing too eager. I could sense Samuel was still unconvinced, unless he was simply trying to annoy his wife by holding out.

"I'm not going to leap into anything," Samuel said in a flat, final tone. "It's a nice place, not great, but nice. I'm not saying no, but I'm not jumping." He turned around. "The service isn't very good here, is it?"

Later, when we'd nearly finished our meal and had sunk to the level of discussing the merits of a couple of new restaurants none of us had been to, Andrew Scali swam into my peripheral vision. I could see his bald pate and his wide, healthy grin approaching, even in the dim light of the restaurant.

"Well, well, well," he said, in his hearty, jocular way. "Look at this. Three of my favorite people in the world, together at one table. Don't get up. Who's doing what to whom?"

He pulled up a chair and straddled it with the back facing the table, grinning and assuming dominance over the party, as if he were responsible for bringing us all together.

"You know Andrew?" Charlotte asked me.

"Everyone does," I said, and then, trying to be provocative, I added, "But few know him as well as I do."

Andy chuckled at this comment. He liked to categorize people, probably as a way of keeping his thousands of acquaintances clear in his mind. He seemed, in recent years, to have moved me in his mental filing cabinet from "Helpful Friend" to "Amusing Acquaintance" and had the annoying habit of acting as if most of what I said was a joke. He was an accountant, but that was merely the title on his door. Most of his time and energy went into a stunning variety of real estate investments and creative entrepreneurial endeavors that had earned him, judging from the way he lived, vast sums of money.

He was fifty-three years old and up until twelve years ago had been a happily married husband and father living in a leafy suburb outside of Boston. Now he lived in a spectacular four-story town house on Beacon Hill with Sean, a vain (justifiably, considering his looks) perfumer.

"William's helping us find an apartment," Samuel said. He had, I noticed, sat up straighter in his chair as soon as Andy approached. Andy, who tended to convey an air of passionate organization and competence, sometimes had this effect on people, men especially. You saw him and you wanted to be, or at least appear to be, more capable and efficient than you ordinarily were. If you didn't, Andy would lay his strong, stubby fingers on you and start offering help. Let me put you in touch with so and so, all right? Would you let me make some inquiries on your behalf regarding that matter?

I'd met Andrew when he was in the very earliest stages of his sexual awakening, when he knew he was interested in men but hadn't yet figured out what he wanted to do with them. For the sake of convenience and conviviality, we pretended we'd had a brief relationship, but that was recklessly overstating a single, unenthusiastic mutual masturbation episode followed by months of me coaching him on how he could negotiate a more open and honest life. I was genuinely pleased that he'd worked out an agreeable arrangement for himself, but I occasionally resented that he'd blossomed so strongly so quickly and was now in a position to give me advice about my addled existence.

"Samuel and I have worked on a couple of projects together," Andy said to me. "We might even be working on a couple of projects now." He nodded toward Samuel and winked, bonding the two of them in a manly conspiracy overlaid with flirtation.

Not that there was a question of anything going on between the two of them. It was doubtful Samuel was bisexual, and more important, Andrew had started to go out with much younger men about six years earlier; once you cross that bridge, there's no turning back.

Going out with significantly younger lovers does wonders for a man's confidence, physique, and complexion, but it's always a disaster for his wardrobe. Andy was decked out in a powder blue T-shirt and navy sports jacket and a pair of blue jeans that had been washed in a trendy combination of sand and acid. The shaved head was a fairly recent Sean-inspired attempt at masking the fact that he was going bald.

I showed him the papers on the condo, and made a number of exaggerated claims about its beauty and value. Andrew tried his best to appear impressed. Any real estate deal under a few million dollars was hardly worth his time.

"What are you doing on this side of the river?" I asked.

His hand descended to my shoulder. "Secret high-level luncheon meeting." He delivered this comment in a tone of self-effacing mockery, mostly, I suspected, to hide the fact that it was true.

He described a candy factory and low-income housing and the skeleton of a deal he was putting together with investors. Samuel listened with a faint smile that looked to me like jealousy disguised as bemusement. Andrew worked hard on all of his many deals, but they paid off so spectacularly, a lot of men resented his financial success the way I sometimes resented his personal triumphs. Charlotte's attempt at appearing interested in what he was saying was much less convincing than her husband's. After swirling her spoon around her coffee cup a few dozen times, she cut him off.

"How's Sean?" she asked. There was challenge in her tone; like most beautiful things, Sean required an exhausting amount of maintenance.

"He's great, and the store's really taking off. He appreciates your business. Charlotte's one of his regular customers. More than we can say for you, William."

"I'm not the perfume type," I said.

"I doubt that's true," Andy said, clapping me on the back.

Andrew checked his watch, rose from the table, and began adjusting his sports jacket and straightening out his T-shirt. "Take care of these folks, William. They're good people. And William won't steer you wrong. He's honest. You can take his advice." Having bestowed his blessings, he left.

They *could* take my advice, but so far, Samuel didn't seem to be interested in doing so, and I had a slightly panicked feeling that if I didn't convince him to make an offer on the apartment, I would have failed Charlotte and missed my goal of sending them off to Nahant happily reunited. It seemed entirely possible that if they passed up this place, I might never see them again. I excused myself and cornered Andrew near the entrance where he was waiting for his clients.

"You're a cozy little trio," he said. "You aren't fucking Samuel, are you?"

"Certainly not." I paused and looked back at our table. They still weren't talking to each other. "I didn't know it was an option."

"I'm sure it isn't, but you know me, I suspect everyone. Frankly, I'd rather fuck her, anyway. She's the brains of the outfit. What's with you, Collins? You're all agitated and sweaty. Everything okay?"

"I need you to do me a favor," I said.

"How much?"

"Nothing like that. Just come back to the table. Say you've been thinking about their condo and that it seems like a great investment.

Say you're interested in taking a look at it, if they don't make an offer. I'm trying to get Samuel to move on it today. This afternoon if possible. I can tell he's a little bit in awe of you."

He laughed. "In awe. Come on."

Prompted to deliver another compliment, I did: "Absolutely. Your success, on all fronts."

He ran his hand back across his bald head and checked his watch again. "You desperate for the sale? Bills to pay?"

"Big bills," I said. "Like you wouldn't believe."

It was a lot less humiliating than confessing my real motives.

done

Mission accomplished, I wrote in my notes for the Thompson-O'Malley file later that afternoon. *Solid offer on condo. Thnks to manipulation and lies. Charlotte happy. About apt or just because victory over Samuel? Does it matter? Call Andrew to thank for playing alng. C & S turned down my offer of dinner. Boo hoo.*

getting around

A few days after I put in the offer on the apartment for Charlotte and Sam, I stopped by Veronica's pet grooming shop on my way to work.

What amused me most about Veronica, the owner, was the disjunction between the care she brought to styling her canine customers and the haphazard way she approached her own appearance. Although it was easy to spot the raw beauty in her face, she rarely brushed her gray hair, and usually draped her large body in bulky sweaters covered with animal fur. She'd grown up in a wealthy New England family and had rebelled at a young age by taking drugs, becoming obese, and volunteering for a radical animal rights organization. Now in her late fifties, she had the casual sloppiness of the aging hippie, and the gentle, disorganized demeanor and conversational style of a lifelong pothead.

I had convinced myself that I liked helping her out because doing so involved cleaning, and cleaning a living thing was at least as satisfying as cleaning the floor under a bed. I don't go for the gooey sentimentality that people use to mask the pleasure of owning a living creature over which you have complete control. But being around Veronica's animals, forgiving, kind, and nonjudgmental, provided me with a form of attention that I crave and hadn't yet found in the basement apartments where I'd been spending my time.

I was helping bathe a wiry, hyperactive Jack Russell terrier when she told me she'd been giving serious consideration to buying an apartment.

"I figure I should own something before they start that war in Iraq," she said.

The dog was nervously looking from me to Veronica and back again, and I bent down and kissed its nose.

"Okay," I said. "A very good idea." I didn't see the connection between the two things, but there were a lot of missing pieces in Veronica's conversations, and I'd learned not to question anyone's motives for buying or selling.

"That's what they're cooking up, you know. Justification for finishing off the last unfinished mess. It's all over the news now. They can get away with it because everyone's so confused. No one knows what the hell is going on and everyone feels obliged to go along with anything the little leader proposes. How'd I get onto that?"

"Something about a condominium."

"I figure I'll care a little less somehow. Shut the door, pay the mortgage, and be another selfish home owner. You think you can help me?"

"I'd love to," I said. "We can go next door and look at a couple of listings if you want."

"Let's finish up with this guy first."

The dog, whose name was Spirou, was trembling even though we'd bathed him in warm water. I wrapped him in a towel and picked him up.

"Careful," Veronica said. "The owner claims he bites."

The dog began chewing on my earlobe in an affectionate way. Despite my activities of the night before with a longhaired man who claimed to be called Julian, it felt like the most intimate thing that had been done to me in a very long time.

"I don't think he bites," I said. "I think he's a little pushover."

Veronica observed our make-out session and shrugged. "You're probably right. The owner's a beautiful, talkative lawyer. Maybe she was trying to warn me that *she* bites. Although I doubt that, too. Most people take on their dog's personality."

"I thought it was the other way around."

"No. Dogs begin to look like their owners, but the owners act like their dogs. Which is a good thing since dogs have better personalities than people."

"Can we take him back to the office with us? Give him a walk?"

"I don't see why not. Let's loop around the block a couple times so I can smoke a joint."

We walked back to my office with the dog pulling frantically on the leash and leaping into the air as if his legs were spring-loaded. Since buying my house, I'd considered getting a dog a number of times, but I alternated between fearing slobbering dependence upon me and the possibility that the dog might not like me. "Don't let him get the best of you," Veronica rasped, holding in a lungful of smoke. "Take control. Here." She yanked on the leash and Spirou coughed.

"Careful," I said. "You'll choke him."

"They like to be controlled," she bellowed. "You don't get it. They love it."

The more pot she smoked, the louder her voice got, so that by the time we entered the office, she was practically shouting. Spirou ran over to Jack's desk and started chewing on his shoelaces. "Nice manners," he said.

"So what's your price range?" I asked Veronica. "We should start there." I retrieved the dog and put him on my lap, and he sat there, nervously staring into my eyes.

"Oh, I don't know," she brayed. "I inherited money from a crazy aunt who didn't have any children. I always thought she considered me evil incarnate, but apparently not. She lived in Minneapolis, that area, somewhere out there. I think I met her a couple of times, but I can't remember her name, not that I can remember anything. What was I saying?"

"Your price range."

"Right. Nice but not too nice. I don't care about the neighborhood or public schools or any of that. Someplace where you can imagine human beings living, not little robots with perfect bodies and big jobs. You know what I want. I hate shopping. You think I should look before I buy?"

"I would say yes. Absolutely."

"Shit, that's what I was afraid of." She watched me squirm as Spirou chewed on my ear again. "You need a dog," she shouted. "That'd straighten you out in short order."

"What does that mean?" I asked. "Straighten me out?"

"I've got a lot of friends. Word gets around. So do you, apparently."

"I guess you have to get back to work," I said. "I'll call."

"A friend of mine who knows I know you said he saw you in a hotel room thing a few weeks ago. He was impressed with your energy." She roared at this. I didn't have a clue about her sexuality, but she was completely nonjudgmental about everyone else's. "I didn't press him for details, although you best believe I was tempted."

I put Spirou down on the floor again, hoping he'd run back to Jack and put Veronica's rant to an end. Instead, he leapt back onto my lap. "If this dog were available," I told her, "I'd take him home in a minute."

"You're only saying that because you know he's spoken for. You're that type. Hotel rooms. Jesus. See if you can find me an apartment with a fireplace. Not that I'll ever use it."

Simply buy it

I'd instructed Sylvia to wait for me in front of Edward's building so we could arrive at his front door together. "It's better if I go in with you. Makes the whole thing more professional. And be sure to give yourself at least twenty extra minutes to find a parking space. Parking is hell down there."

After waiting for a long time on Edward's front stoop, I concluded with relief that Sylvia had changed her mind and backed out of the deal already. I rang his bell and was buzzed into the building. Sylvia opened the door to his apartment. She looked at me over the tops of her turquoise glasses and shook her head slowly from side to side, either in disgust or delight. Finally, she threw her arms around me.

"It's perfect," she said. "It's perfection."

I reminded her that we'd agreed to meet on the stoop.

"I gave myself twenty minutes, as instructed, but there was a parking space directly in front of the door, so I figured I might as well come in."

"Believe me," I said, "that will never happen again. Call it beginner's luck. Where's Edward?"

"He went out to get some wine or cookies or something. Celebration is in order. We've already settled on a price and agreed on the closing date." She hooked her arm through mine and led me into the galley kitchen that Edward had outfitted with salvage from railroad cars. "Look at what he's done in here," she said. "It's brilliant, isn't it?"

"I've spent vast amounts of time here. I'm familiar with every corner. I told you you'd like it," I said. "You should have waited for me to start negotiating."

"When you see the right thing, William, you must leap. You must seize it." She folded her arms over her thin chest and said very calmly, "You must simply buy it."

I'd heard her utter these words of wisdom at least half a dozen times before, but there was a new note of resolve in her voice. It was not comforting. If someone is going to behave as erratically as Sylvia, she at least owes you the courtesy of being consistent.

"You should know," I said, "that he gets almost no afternoon sunlight in here."

"I hate afternoon sunlight. By three in the afternoon, all sunlight is redundant. I never understood the attraction."

"There's also a problem with the dishwasher." I went over to the cleverly concealed unit and opened it. "It's never worked right, and it seems to be beyond repair. Cute exterior, but you can't count on it to do what it's supposed to do."

Sylvia closed it. "I don't eat. Why would a dishwasher interest me? Don't get practical on me. This time, I'm going through with the purchase, so there's no point in hauling out the problems. I welcome them, each and every one. Show me more so I can get really excited. Hopefully the windows don't open. And I'd be in despair if there was central heating."

"I have a moral obligation to disclose everything, that's all."

"You're in the wrong business for moral obligations. And speaking of disclosure, you should have told me that you and Edward are buddies."

"Buddies," I said. "What a ridiculous way to describe our relationship."

"How would you describe it?"

"I have no idea. That's probably why I didn't mention it."

Sold

Edward showed up about fifteen minutes later, carrying a bag from the bakery around the corner and a bottle of wine. He handed the latter to Sylvia. She peered at the label over the top of her big eyeglasses and complimented his choice. "This is the best year for this wine," she said, tapping the bottle with one of her long, unpainted fingernails. "We must have read the same review."

Edward had a vast storehouse of knowledge about wine—years, vineyards, and countries of origin. He studied wines the way he studied mutual funds and the scorecards in *Consumer Reports*. I never understood how he sustained this particular interest; he rarely drank.

Since the last time I'd seen him, his light hair had grown even longer and curlier. He had the faint glow of a suntan that brought out the boyish clarity of his eyes, and he was wearing a pair of slim gray flannel pants and a striped dress shirt, buttoned to the chin.

The outfit, tidy and age-appropriate, combined with the hair and the tan made him look as if some internal gear had clicked into place and brought into alignment all the bits and pieces of his personality. For a minute, I felt my face flush with a shameful combination of envy and angst: he was pulling his life together and moving it elsewhere. Perhaps the airline pilot was coaching him on his wardrobe.

"What's wrong?" he asked. "That horrible look you're giving me."

"I was just thinking about how nice you look."

"Oh, why aren't I a man?" Sylvia cooed. "A woman would never say that to another woman unless she didn't mean it."

"I wouldn't waste too much envy," Edward said. He spilled the bag of cookies onto a plate, a thoughtful but wasted effort since no one would eat them. "William doesn't mean it either."

"I do mean it," I said. "Why can't you accept a simple compliment from me? I'm trying to be kind and sincere and you're turning it into something else. It's ridiculous. Now I'm angry at you. I retract the compliment."

"I'm glad we cleared that up," Sylvia said.

These two new best friends had agreed upon a price that was only slightly lower than the one I had suggested Edward ask for his place. Their negotiations, although brief, had been mature and productive. As for a closing date, they'd settled on something in early December.

I couldn't have asked for a more amiable or happy outcome. In addition to that, my involvement had been minimal, thus making the whole thing incredibly easy. And in addition to *that*, Sylvia generously and unnecessarily agreed to pay a couple percentage points more in a broker's fee than I was expecting, largely because she felt guilty about the amount of time I'd spent with her over the years.

Still, the closing date made the sale seem real, and there was something in the general tone of Sylvia's voice and questions about the building that made me think she was going to go through with the deal this time. As I sat watching them chatting about the apartment and the neighborhood, encouraging each other to nibble at the cookies, I realized that by getting Sylvia involved in the deal, I might have made Edward's plans for leaving easier, not more complicated.

"You might want to think about moving the closing date to January," I said. "That will give you more time to get everything together."

"I'm not going to move in the heart of winter," Edward said.

"You're right to move to San Diego," Sylvia said. "If I didn't have that god-awful tenure, I'd move there myself. For you, at this stage, it's the perfect city. It's a balm to the senses. On top of that, it's full of homosexuals."

"Yes," I pointed out. "In fact, there are hardly any heterosexuals in the whole city and no straight men whatsoever. In short, Edward will never get a date."

"That is utterly untrue," Sylvia pointed out. "Don't you remember the chapter in my book about southern California?" I had a vague memory of something entitled "The Earth Moves." "I had the most shattering orgasm of my life there and it was most definitely *not* with a gay man. You should look him up, Edward. He wrote me a letter after the book came out, furious that I hadn't used his real name, threatening a lawsuit if I didn't have it included in the next edition. Fortunately, there wasn't one."

It was late in the afternoon, and I had an appointment I had to get to in fifteen minutes. I didn't like the idea of leaving the two of them in the apartment alone, but I had no choice.

I asked Edward to see me out, and he walked down to the street with me. The air was suddenly cool; the wind had changed direction and brought in a strong smell of the ocean, and the tops of the brick town houses along Edward's street were painted with the deep gold of afternoon sun. It was the dog-walking hour, and the sidewalks were alive with the howling of dogs and the happy reproaches of their owners, trying to sound irritated by their wayward behavior. I thought of Spirou with a pang.

"I almost got a dog the other day," I said. "Well, what I mean is, I wanted one. Getting him wasn't exactly an option, since he belonged to someone else." I was dithering. "Edward, are you sure you want to sell?"

"I'm not interested in being a landlord, I'll eventually want to buy something out there. Of course I want to sell."

"How is it practical? Working with Marty? I don't see it."

"You don't have to see it. I see it. It's not for the rest of my life, that's obvious. I'm learning a few skills, how to use a computer. I want out—out of the airlines, out of Boston. Think of it as a convenient excuse."

At that moment, he sounded depressingly practical. "You'll miss this neighborhood."

"What you really mean," he said, "is that you'll miss it, once I'm not here for you to visit. Unfortunately, I'm the one who has to point that out."

accepted

C & S offer accepted, I wrote in my notes. *Samuel plsed—dinner w/ happy couple at Indian restaurant—Charlotte radiant—grn blouse, NOT silk—food mediocre—sag paneer—heartburn—bring champagne (and Edward) to Nahant cocktail party.*

monogamy

I called Andrew Scali a number of times to thank him for helping me convince Samuel and Charlotte, but he was never at home, and on principle—what principle he couldn't articulate—he never answered his cell phone. I finally got through one night as I was driving back from a visit to a man supposedly named Cory.

It turned out that Cory was not thirty-seven, not a swimmer, did not weigh 150 pounds, and was not, by most objective standards, "vry gdlkng." He was, he explained while I was getting dressed, in a "monogamous" relationship with a sixty-three-year-old man named Bob. Cory, like a lot of men who have considerably older lovers, thought of himself as perennially young, and despite graying hair and some slackening in the triceps, he had a boyish quality in his exaggerated gestures and grin.

"Monogamous," I said, buckling my belt. "Really. That's rare these days."

"I can't answer for everyone."

"No." I doubted he could answer for himself, but I tried anyway. "And just out of curiosity, you define monogamous as . . ."

He shrugged, as if it should be obvious. "We never fool around with other people. No threesomes, no group things. It's just the two of us. When we're together."

At least, I thought as I was driving home along the river, he had a definition. Maybe my problem in sticking to my celibacy resolution was not that I was continuing to have meaningless, semi-anonymous sex on a regular basis, but that I hadn't defined my terms properly. Maybe that was what I needed to work on.

I called Andrew's house again, and Sean answered.

"William Collins," he said. "It's been months. How are you?"

"I'm fine," I said. "And you?"

"Not terrible," he said. "Exhausted, but that's not new." Sean was thirty-two, and was perpetually exhausted. This seemed to be the case for a lot of pretty people, as if there was something wearying about lugging around the burden of beauty and always being the object of admiration and envy. Sean had the kind of dramatic, slightly exaggerated looks that arouse a great number of second glances, comments, and blunt advances, and there undoubtedly *was* something tiring about the barrage of attention he received, no matter how flattering it was and how addicted to it he'd become.

"You must be working too hard, Sean."

"I was hoping the store would be a flop so I could retire, but it's doing better all the time. All of a sudden, everyone wants to buy expensive little things. Designer soap, expensive body lotion, my bottles of specially made perfume." He yawned. "You've never been in. Come to the shop and take me out for lunch."

"I'd love to. I'll call and make a date."

Of course I never would. Sean had a languid manner that made me feel like a lecherous uncle around him. Spending time with him and Andrew was complicated because you were required to lavish vast amounts of inappropriate attention on Sean and squeeze his ass every once in a while. If you didn't, Andrew would be insulted and Sean would get bored. But there was a fine line of decorum that you couldn't cross, so you always had to be on your toes.

"Where are you?" he asked. "It sounds as if you're driving."

"I'm driving along the river, up past Harvard."

"Describe it to me, William. I'm stuck on Beacon Hill."

"In a three-million-dollar town house. Poor boy. Well, there's a full moon tonight, and the trees along the riverbank have all turned yellow and red. It's windy and the air is full of leaves."

"You're full of longing. I can hear it in your voice. Are you coming from a date?"

A date. "Not exactly."

"I see," he said, and from those two syllables, it was clear that he saw correctly.

Sean was Brazilian by birth but had spent the majority of his life around Boston. It seemed rude to ask him where he got his name. He had a faint accent that added a note of lubricious glamour to his enervated speech. Despite the fact that he colored his hair an unnatural shade of blond, I suspected him of enormous integrity. It was tempting to think of him as a hustler, using Andrew for his money, but when you saw the two of them together, you realized that Sean did most of the caretaking, and it was easy to imagine him sticking by Andy forever, no matter how wide the age difference. I'd always suspected them of being monogamous, in the Webster's sense of the word.

Andrew had "found" Sean (to quote Andy's Dickensian way of putting it) working in a body care shop in Lawrence, one of the blighted mill towns outside of Boston. There had been a nineteenth-century-style courtship involving Sunday dinners with Sean's large extended family—cousins and the aunts who'd raised him—followed by Andy setting Sean up in his own business on Newbury Street.

"I'm sure you're calling for Andrew," he said. "You never call for me, William."

"I'm intimidated by your youth and beauty." It was always a forgivable excuse. "Is he there?"

"He's out having dinner with some clients. At least that's what he tells me."

"I'm sure it's true. He's completely loyal. Tell him I called. I wanted to thank him for helping me out with some customers. Charlotte O'Malley and Samuel Thompson."

"Oh, those two," he said, yawning. "She buys perfume from me. She's unhappy, but I'm doing my best to change that."

"Funny," I said, "but I thought I was doing the same thing."

"Just don't make her too happy. I need her business. And if you ever want to work on your own happiness, come and see me. In the meantime, you'd better hang up. Pay attention to the road and the moonlight on the water. Enjoy the longing."

II.d.

"What's happening with the condo you have listed in Jamaica Plain, the one owned by the marine?" Gina asked. She flipped through a stack of papers until she found the relevant one. "'Dreamy One-Bedroom Retreat,'" she read.

"Before we go there," Mildred said, "I have an issue with the description."

We were in the middle of one of our weekly staff meetings, and all eyes turned toward Mildred. She, the psychologist dabbling in real estate for the fun of it, was the only person in the office who seemed to love these meetings. She was a stickler for honesty in the description of apartments, something that was completely counterproductive.

"I was over there the other day. For one thing, there's nothing dreamy about it. It's subordinary. And since it faces Centre Street, I don't see how it qualifies as a retreat."

"To be honest," I said, "I had trouble finding a flattering way to describe it. I thought dreamy sounded innocuous enough, and I'm sure some people dream of living in characterless places. As for the retreat part, the bedroom's on the back and has one tiny window, so it's quiet."

Mildred persisted. "It isn't helpful, William. People are expecting something romantic and unusual. They walk into a storage space with a bed tossed in the corner."

"Look," Jack said, "the whole point of an ad is to misrepresent a place. You give people a false impression and hope it sticks, even once they've seen the apartment itself. William happens to be very good at giving false impressions. Better than I realized."

I thanked Jack. Since overhearing Veronica braying about my hotel escapades, he had, much to my surprise, been considerably more deferential toward me than he usually was. I'm not sure what he imagined had gone on, but maybe he was relieved to have confirmation that I had a personal life, even if the details of it were sketchy.

"Any nibbles?" Gina asked.

"A few, nothing too serious."

"It's overpriced," Mildred said.

Gina tossed the paper on the table. "Not by enough, I told you that at the start, William. How many open houses have you had?"

"I'm having them weekly."

"What about the marine, is she being helpful? I know she's one of those do-it-yourselfers."

There was a communal groan.

"She's been surprisingly helpful. She stays out of the way, keeps the place clean, if not exactly tidy. We've had two offers, but they were both way below asking, and she was right to turn them down."

Marty had been shockingly understanding about the offers, and hadn't blamed me for the fact that the place hadn't yet sold. "Let me tell you how it is, William," she'd said. "All these people making these lousy offers are going through life Shopping in the Bargain Basement. I tell people: When you Shop in the Bargain Basement, you save a few bucks, but you don't wear Armani." She'd been so considerate and reasonable, I'd started to feel as if I'd failed her. I'd begun calling the people I'd worked with in the past, sending out bulk e-mails touting the apartment, and had scheduled an open house for every Sunday afternoon at 1 P.M. until the place sold.

"Tell her to get rid of those boxes and papers," Deirdre said. "It's like walking into a dreamy one-bedroom filing cabinet."

"She's pushed a lot of that around," I said. "As much as she can. She has a bad back, plus problems with her knees, hips, shoulders, neck, wrists, tendons, and arches."

"I have a major U.D. on my hands, and both parties are getting desperate. The problem is, I have to sell each something the other one wants. That way they both end up feeling they've won. If you have her clear the place out some, I could drag both of them around. They're newscasters."

U.D. was Deirdre's code for Ugly Divorce. If you played your cards right, a U.D. was a dream come true. In the best-case scenario, you sold the property the couple owned jointly, and then got each of them into a new living space. You had to deal with a lot of acrimony, anger, and attorneys, but you might end up with three closings in one week. Despite her aversion to unhappy couples, and her feeling that all of these miserable people considered her shallow for being so blissfully married, Deirdre was the queen of the U.D. in our office.

Deirdre's dull husband, Raymond, had an especially good reputation among local newscasters, a pseudocelebrity subculture that seemed to marry and divorce and remarry within their own club with astonishing frequency. Their breakups were always ugly and usually involved cut-rate, tacky variations on the standard celebrity divorce details: vacations with mistresses, but to dreary destinations; plastic surgery bills, but from doctors on the fringes of Miami; squabbles over three and four cars, but usually old Toyotas.

"I'll get right on it," I said. "Are you thinking of the place for the husband, or the wife?"

"Either. It just has to be kept secret because they'd be mortified if word got out they were looking at such cheap places. They're on one of those local stations no one watches, and I don't think they've got two million if you put everything together. Fortunately, there's no 'child' involved." Everyone paid lip service to the joys of children, but no one in the office liked working with the mess and clutter of big happy families. "My one fear is that they're going to realize they're made for each other before the divorce goes through."

"Get them over there," Jack said. "I'd love to see William score on this one."

thinking about it

I called Marty to arrange a time when I could come by and help hide some of her papers. She'd become amazingly agreeable on the subject of letting people in and organizing her schedule around my requests. Charlaine and all canine traces were kept carefully out of sight when people came to look at the place. There was never a whiff of cigarette smoke in the air, and finally she confessed to me ("Strictly on a Between Us Basis, William") that she'd made major strides toward kicking the habit. "I'm down to one pack a day," she told me.

"That's . . . great," I said. "What had you been up to?"

"OK, William, let me tell you something. That's what I call Stepping in Someone's Shit. Someone tells you they've practically stopped smoking, what you're supposed to do is, you pat them on the back, you tell them congratulations, you take them out to dinner, you buy them a new stove. What you *don't* do is turn judgmental and Step in Their Shit. OK?"

We arranged a time for me to come by and help her, and she

even agreed to let me rent her a small storage space not far from her building.

"What do these people do?" she asked. She was keeping a detailed list of everyone who walked into the place, including ages, professions, income levels. When I told her they were newscasters, she perked up. "Maybe I could get a spot on their broadcast. I'd make excellent TV."

"It's extremely local. Since you're about to move west," I reminded her, "it wouldn't do you much good."

She sighed again with what sounded like disgust. "Look down at your feet, William. Are you looking? OK, you see that Shit right there, well, you're doing it again. You're Stepping in It."

"Sorry. Not to change the subject, but I assume you heard the good news about Edward's apartment. It was one person who came by to look at it, and she took it right there and then. Amazing, isn't it?"

"If you're trying to tell me that it's not your fault my place hasn't sold, save your breath. Number one, I know it's not your fault, and number two, it *is* your fault. So let's just drop the comparisons."

"Fair enough. How's he doing with that airline pilot romance?"

"I don't have time to sit around gossiping about my friends. If you're so interested, ask him yourself. He told me he agreed to go to some cocktail party with you even though he hates the idea of going. Talk up my apartment out there. You never know."

breathing exercises

To reach the fresh breezes and pounding surf of Nahant, you had to drive through some of the grittiest industrial areas surrounding Boston and cross the rusting hulk of the Tobin Bridge, site of notorious traffic problems and a number of high-profile suicide leaps. It was six o'clock when I drove onto the bridge with Edward in the passenger seat beside me. The sky was a light shade of purple, the day just beginning its slide into the pretty melancholy of twilight. Behind us, the city was glowing in that last hour of clear, fine-tuned sunshine, and off to our right, the smokestacks of a brick power station were belching white clouds of steam.

We were running late; Edward's bathroom preparations had taken even longer than usual. I'd expressed annoyance, but I was in no particular hurry to get to Charlotte and Samuel's house. If I'd ever had a taste for large parties, I'd lost it years ago. Now I was more comfortable at small, muted gatherings at which people who know one another too well drink in moderation, feign interest in one another, discuss real estate, and go home early.

It was a cool evening, and the chilled air blowing in the open windows of the car made it feel appropriately autumnal. We were halfway across the bridge and suspended above the inner reaches of Boston harbor when traffic came to a dead stop. Maybe there was an accident ahead or another of the construction projects that had been creating havoc in the city for more than a decade. Edward pushed back his seat so that he was nearly recumbent, closed his eyes, and made a sound that was close to a whimper.

"Tell me when we get to the other side," he croaked.

"Nap time?"

"You know I hate bridges. How did you talk me into coming on this excursion? If I'd known we'd be driving over this thing I could have done some mental preparation. Or stayed at home."

"Try to relax. I had no idea you're phobic about bridges. You spend half your life at thirty-five thousand feet. We're much closer to firm ground now."

"I didn't say I enjoy flying, either. Why do you think I'm getting out of the business? I never did enjoy it, that's the funny part.

But at first I liked the idea of being nowhere most of the time, above traffic jams and lines at the supermarket and people trying to sell you something over the phone. It was always boring, obviously, but in a dependable, reassuring way. I'd imagine a happy relationship would be like that—dependable boredom is the whole point. It's what makes it so nice."

He sighed, mourning his losses, and I reached out and took his hand. "We'll be on the other side in a few minutes."

"And what's over there? Used car dealerships and people I don't know."

"Maybe you should do some deep breathing. I've heard it's good for anxiety."

"Yes, especially if you've taken ten milligrams of Xanax before you start."

It had been pointed out to me—by Andrew Scali, once divorce had made him an expert on the human psyche—that on the whole, I was more sympathetic to women than to men. I'd been insulted by this observation: I preferred to think of myself as universally empathic, even though I knew he was right. In the case of Andy, for example, I'd listened to his woes for years, taken some pleasure in helping him, but a great deal more in watching him reveal his vulnerabilities. Undoubtedly, it was all about dominance and competition. But I felt surprisingly little of this with Edward. I just wanted to take care of him. His hand was cool and damp in mine, his fingers were twitching nervously, and I had a strong urge to take him in my arms and comfort him, stroke his curly hair. He looked small and beautiful lying back with his eyes closed, a threat to no one except, possibly, himself. But holding him was impossible, given the arrangement of the seats and the stick shift and the years of friendship.

"I'm sorry," I told him, "but I'm fresh out of Xanax. Let's give the breathing thing a try. I'll do it with you."

He squeezed my hand and without opening his eyes, he said, "For someone else, that might help, but we're both too ironic to start a meditation group."

The honeymoon period of any relationship, whether romantic or sexual or merely amiable, is a brief vacation from ironic detachment and sarcastic undercutting. Edward and I were long past that.

"Maybe," I said, "you're anxious about leaving town, about moving, about being connected in some professional way with Marty. There must be some significance to the fact that you have an anxiety attack half an hour after I bring you Sylvia's deposit and signed papers."

"Don't try to coddle me," Edward said. "I'd much rather you try to distract me. Tell me what you did last night."

The wind picked up, and I leaned across Edward's body and rolled up his window. The water below us was ruffled with white-caps and the pretty, oily mystery of pollution.

"I'm afraid that wouldn't offer much of a distraction. I stayed home and did a little housecleaning, read for a few hours, then went to bed."

"You live the life of a monk, don't you? Thomas Merton on his best day. If you're going to lie about what you did, at least toss in a few details of regrettable behavior. Give me an hour of television, a few beers and a bag of potato chips, a desperate midnight call to that Belgian obsession of yours."

"Didier's left town. And I don't like beer."

"They don't have to be plausible details."

"All right," I said, "if it will make you happy." There was no reason to think he'd believe the truth any more readily than he'd believe lies.

thomas merton on his best day

"I met someone online. In a chat room. Do you know what those are? Chat rooms? Have your computer lessons advanced that far?"

"As far as I can tell, it's a virtual place where strangers from different parts of the world gather and lie to each other. Who did you meet?"

"He claimed to be called Alberto."

"How mellifluous. And you were who, Michelangelo?"

"Everett." I realized, for the first time, the similarity to my friend's name, and hoped he didn't notice it. "Anyway, he invited me to his place."

"How impulsive. Just like that."

"I'd sent him my picture."

"High school yearbook?"

"Slightly more recent. He lived out in the suburbs, maybe twenty minutes from me. I wasn't sure why I was driving all that way, and when I got there, it turned out to be a little ranch plopped into the middle of a cluster of similar houses."

"Depressing. This is why I'm against gay marriage and raising children and all of that. You start out wanting health care benefits and you end up living in a suburban ranch house with plastic toys on the front lawn."

It hadn't been a depressing house. In fact, Alberto's taste wasn't far from mine—clean lines and sleek modern furniture, with the added attraction of playful colors and an appealing degree of clutter: magazines and books, some clothes tossed onto chairs, the kinds of things I couldn't bear to see in my own house. There were older trees and immense, carefully sculpted bushes on either side of the property, giving the place the restful illusion of privacy. But I didn't feel any special need to praise the decor to Edward or, for that matter, to talk too truthfully about Alberto himself. He'd looked amazingly similar to his photo, only more handsome in a lean, dark way. I even had the impression that his name truly was Alberto.

"Give me a type," Edward said.

"Oh, French movie star of a certain era."

"Let's make it specific. The young Alain Delon?"

"Yes, if you like."

"Who wouldn't like? Go on."

Upon walking into the house, I was thrown off balance by Alberto's unexpected beauty, and by a wistful melancholy in his eyes. Seeing him, I had the same feeling of happy disorientation I'd had one year when my tax accountant told me I was getting a huge return from the IRS. I was so confused by his appearance and the contrast to the sorts of men I was used to meeting that, without going through the nice-place or can-I-have-a-glass-of-water charade, I took him in my arms, pulled his slim body against mine, and began kissing his mouth hungrily. I was even more disoriented when I realized that he was kissing back with greedy ardor, rising up on his toes so he could reach my mouth more easily.

We were standing in the entry hall of the house. There was a mirror in front of us, and in it, I saw that my arms were wrapped around his back so tightly I appeared to be trying to squeeze the breath out of him. The house felt hermetically sealed off from the outside world, with the resonant silence of a vault. The only sound was the steady ticking of a clock in another room and an occasional sigh (from him or me, I wasn't sure which) that in a different context might have been a cry of discomfort. Eventually, I reached down and grabbed his thighs in my hands. He leapt up and wrapped his legs around my hips, and I carried him into the living room and gently spilled him onto a big armless sofa. The room was dark except for the bluish muddle of a streetlight oozing in through the floor-to-ceiling curtains over an immense picture window. In that diffused light, Alberto looked even more handsome than before, his lips red and slightly swollen, his black eyes shining. He reached up from below me and started to unbuckle my belt, but I pushed his hands away. "Not yet," I told him.

I had his body pinned beneath mine and was cupping his face in my hands. I could see that he wasn't young—there were a few streaks of gray in his hair—and for some reason, I was moved by this and wanted to possess him even more.

He made another attempt at unbuckling my pants and then his own, but I pulled his hands away. Finally, he pushed himself from me, and sank down into the cushions. In a breathy slur, he said, "I want you to fuck me."

"Yes," I said. "But first, this."

At some point I glanced at the clock, loudly ticking on the mantelpiece, and realized that I'd been in the house for nearly an hour and hadn't advanced past second base, or whatever the appropriate sports metaphor was. I wanted this to go on for much longer, and even had a confused hope that we would eventually wander into his bedroom, fall asleep on his bed, and wake throughout the night, starting up and breaking off, prolonging the entire event until well past dawn. I mumbled compliments about his smell and the warm softness of his skin.

"Don't," I said, moving his hand. "I want to make you wait."

Bay rum; that, I realized, was what he smelled like. "I know," he said. "But my boyfriend gets home in an hour, and I need time to shower and put my clothes in the washing machine."

in theory, yes

"You must have approved of the laundry business," Edward said.

"In theory, yes. But at that moment, it was like being doused with cold water."

"Of course, you must have realized he wasn't single. Living in the suburbs and all."

"I must have."

"And then what? The time constraint stoked the flames of your passion and there was a volcanic eruption of ecstasy?"

"Yes, something along those lines," I told him, and then added, to cut off all further sarcasm and comebacks, "End of story."

He turned toward me and opened his eyes. "I suppose it beat staying at home and scrubbing the bathtub."

In the end, that might have been preferable. The news about the boyfriend had come as such a disappointment that I got up from the sofa and went to the bathroom. Suddenly, the entire house took on the aura of hostile territory or at least territory in which I had no place. The casual domesticity of shampoo bottles lined up along the edge of the bathtub, a ceramic mug holding two razors and two toothbrushes, and a pair of green towels draped over the shower curtain made me feel like an unwelcome intruder. Someone very well might wake up in the middle of the night and start making love to Alberto, but it was never going to be me.

Half an hour later, I looked at Alberto's pretty face, flushed with private passion, and was disappointed to realize that he was having sex with only one part of me. As for the rest, I was a third wheel—fourth if you count the absent boyfriend—and saying anything to remind him that I was in the room would only spoil his fun. Of course this was the whole point of most of these encounters, sexual congress efficiently reduced to its most essential compo-nents. I was breaking the rules by wanting more, and in addition to disappointment, I felt humiliated by my own desire. I came, I went, and as I was pulling out of the driveway, I realized I'd left behind a white sleeveless T-shirt that was, at that very moment, probably being crammed into the bottom of a wastebasket, under-neath coffee grounds and cat litter.

I hadn't told Edward the whole story, and for his sake, I'd left out the most embarrassing and salient details, one being that lying on the sofa, holding Alberto's face in my hands, I'd said, "I love you," over and over in a feverish, mortifying whisper.

Now, sitting in the car on the bridge, I heard Edward calling my name, as if he were trying to rouse me from sleep. He was sit-ting up, and it was me who had his eyes closed. I was breathing deeply, as if trying to fend off my own anxiety attack.

"Time to get out of neutral," he told me. "The traffic's moving."

Nahant

We drove for another thirty minutes through a landscape that had been insulted with fast-food joints and injured with car dealerships, and then arrived at a rotary with signs pointing to the causeway that connected Nahant to the mainland. There was a deserted ten-nis court on one side of the road, and on the other, a lonesome bathhouse that looked as if it hadn't been in use for several decades. The causeway itself curved slightly so that for the entire two-mile stretch of road, it was impossible to see more than a few feet in front of you at a time. This created the illusion that you could be driving along this road forever or, a reasonable alternative, that you were about to drop off into the open water. Suddenly, all traces of the city and scarred industrial landscape seemed to have been washed out by the tide.

There was one main road that circled the perimeter of the island. A sandy lowlands planted with windswept grasses, a ball field, a deserted coast guard station, and then a cluster of newly constructed monstrosities jumbled together with summer cottages that had been winterized and looked as if they were about to topple over under the weight of their renovations. For several years now, Nahant had been plagued by mysterious, unseasonable storms, related, almost certainly, to global climate change. There was always footage on the local news of the National Guard fishing people out of these expensive residential mistakes. The sky-high insurance rates on the island and the thrill of natural disaster had increased real estate prices over the past decade or so, and now houses here went for more than they did in the city. The boom was helped by Nahant's reputation for being a safe place to raise children, never mind the fact that the entire landmass was nearly swept out to sea by storms at least twice a year.

We followed the main road around the coast until we started to climb up out of the lowlands to higher, rockier ground. The houses were older, grander, surrounded by wide lawns and gnarled trees.

"I hope they live up here," Edward said. "These people look as if they could afford to hire decent caterers."

pampered and expensive

Edward read aloud from complicated directions that Charlotte had sent me, and soon we were pulling into their driveway. The sprawling shingled house wouldn't have looked out of place in one of the nicer neighborhoods of a lesser Hampton. According to the book Samuel had given me, it had been built in the 1910s as a summer cottage. There was a history of storm damage and renovations, insulation projects and improvements, and as Samuel had said, it was barely recognizable from the photo in the book. Still, it exuded the charm of old money, of generations gathered under one roof for vacations, of long, dull dinners, and furtive pleasures in the darker corners of the garden.

I parked under a pine tree on one side of the lawn, and we walked, as instructed, along a flagstone path that cut through a dense hedge of rhododendrons. The backyard sloped down from the house like a plush carpet to a rocky ledge that dropped into the ocean. It was dark now, but it was a clear, windy night, and shadows from the swaying trees and bushes encircling the yard were swimming on the moonlit lawn. Across the open water, the skyline of Boston was glittering like an expensive toy.

"I'm impressed with your new crowd," Edward said. "I'm a big advocate of making friends outside your class."

"It's the lighting," I said. "It makes everything look pampered and expensive. Even you, I might add. This new look of yours, with the dress shirts and the flannel pants, is very becoming."

"It's emotional maturity, also known as the grim acceptance of the aging process."

A wide porch stretched across the entire back of the house. It was lined with chairs, like the deck of a ship, and some of them were rocking in the wind. A woman was standing against the railing, smoking, her arms wrapped around her chest. I'd developed sympathy for smokers, whose once-glamorous addiction had turned them into social pariahs almost overnight. You saw them huddled in doorways outside of office buildings, restaurants, bars, trying to look dignified, their cigarette-ad gestures graceful anachronisms.

"In exile?" I asked.

The wind blew her thick, dark hair into her face, another indignity, and she reached up to disentangle it from her nose and clear it out of her eyes, the cigarette an impediment.

"I'm . . . afraid so," she finally got out. She laughed nervously, a dry ha ha ha that sounded close to a wheeze. "Pretty picture, isn't it? Woman in a gale, joylessly trying to get some nicotine into her system. Ha ha. The smoke isn't bothering you, is it?" Given the wind, it was a silly question, but she was attractive enough to get away with it without sounding obsequious. She lifted one foot and ground out the cigarette against the sole of her shoe. "I shouldn't be doing it anyway. I set rules for myself—no smoking at parties—and then I can't stick to even the tiniest ones." She looked around for a place to toss the butt, and finding none, dropped it over the railing. "Don't tell anyone. Friends of him, or her?"

"I've never met either of them," Edward said. "William is their real estate agent, which doesn't exactly explain why we're here."

"Oh, that's you. I've heard all about you. And the new place. I work with Sam. In the accounting department, I'm sorry to say." She frowned and shrugged.

She was standing with her arms folded protectively across her chest, and even though she was being self-deprecating about her work, she gave off the casual confidence you often find in people who know they're beautiful. She looked young, which is to say younger than me, probably by close to a decade. There was something remotely familiar about her; then I realized I'd seen her picture on the Web site for Beacon Hill Solutions, wearing a lot of makeup, with her hair pulled back severely. She was prettier in person, but in a more wholesome, athletic way. She was probably very good at soccer and volleyball.

"I think we're arriving late," I said. "How's the party?"

"People I mostly don't know talking about other people I

don't know. I shouldn't have come, but I wanted to see the house. I don't belong here."

"Neither do we," I said. "And I'm guessing you know more people here than we do."

She took a cigarette out of a pack of Marlboros and passed me the box. "Could you toss these out for me? I don't have the heart to do it. One more and then I'll meander back inside and try to find you. We'll be the misfits, all huddled together."

Entering the house meant letting in a blast of ocean air, sending curtains billowing and causing an unfortunate number of people to look in our direction. A dozen or so guests turned toward Edward and me, gave a boozy who-the-hell-are-you glance, and then, apparently deciding that we were insignificant supporting players in their lives, quickly turned away.

"Oh, God," Edward said. "Why am I here? Why did I let you talk me into coming? Why are *you* here?"

"Relax. We can pay our respects, have something to drink, and then slip out."

Not that I was eager to admit it to him, but he had a valid point. There were, undoubtedly, lots of lively, interesting, smart, and psychologically wounded people here, but I immediately felt as if Edward and I were creatures from another planet, imitating normalcy while trying unsuccessfully to hide the antennae sticking out of our heads.

It was a long, wide room with a fireplace blazing in the center of one wall and an enormous number of windows that looked directly out to the ocean. The room smelled of the fire, and it was much too warm. This was one of those spectacular rooms that makes potential buyers swoon and ultimately ends up unused.

We maneuvered through the crowd to a deserted alcove with bookcases and a little furniture vignette that comprised an overstuffed chair and a reading lamp. Another lovely, lifeless spot. I reached for a bowl of peanuts on a round table, but Edward moved it to a bookshelf behind him. "I don't want to have to listen to your regrets about having gorged on these all the way home. You have to keep yourself fit for Alberto."

"I knew I shouldn't have told you about all that."

"Don't worry," he said. "We both know there's a lot about all that you didn't tell me."

Ten minutes later, when it was approaching time to leave our safe haven and hunt down the hosts, a tall, dark-haired young man lumbered into our corner. He stuck out his hand like a gracious CEO greeting a few of his lesser employees. "Hi guys," he said. "How's it going? I'm Daniel. You probably must be friends of my parents."

I introduced the two of us and told him I'd helped his parents find their apartment in the city.

"Right, right," he said. He was scanning the room, as if he'd already lost interest in us and was hunting for more promising grazing grounds. "They're all excited about that. Or Charlotte is anyway. Hey, whatever keeps them happy, right?"

Clearly, he considered himself beyond this; he'd moved on in his own life and was trying to be supportive of their irrelevant, geriatric venture. He had his father's lanky athleticism and long face, but Samuel's striking good looks had been diluted in this younger edition. Daniel's eyes lacked depth, like one of those handsome actors who can't convincingly portray intellectual acuity. I couldn't see anything of Charlotte in his appearance. How lonely she must have felt, isolated out here with her twin boys.

"I thought you were off at college," I said.

"Yeah, well, I had a long weekend, and some friends were driving to Boston. My girlfriend's still in high school down here, so the whole trip seemed like a great idea. Plus I got to please the parents."

"I've forgotten where you're going to school."

He warmed to this safe, reliable topic, and mentioned a mid-sized school in northern Vermont named after a saint, another of those Catholic colleges known for heavy drinking and clandestine promiscuity.

"I've heard it's hard to get in there, these days," I said. I hadn't. As long as you're mildly complimentary, you can get away with saying anything.

"Yeah, it's got an excellent reputation. Being half an hour from great skiing and all."

This explanation was uttered without irony. Most decisions about colleges seemed to lean heavily on the quality of the health club facilities or the ease of getting into a junior-year-in-Australia program. I wasn't in a strong position to argue for intellectual rigor, but the current attitude toward education confused me. All of my peers invested vast amounts of time and money in educating their offspring, but if one of their kids got a bad grade on a paper or was criticized by a teacher for disrupting a class or not doing the required assignment, they rushed to school to throw their twenty-grand-a-year weight around. Children were being raised to believe that everything they said and did and thought was interesting and valuable, but since learning is essentially an admission that there's something you don't yet know, most were stuck with the misconceptions and faulty information they'd picked up at age five.

Edward was staring at Daniel with a mixture of admiration and envy, undoubtedly trying to tamp down his resentment that Daniel's young life was so much more blessed than his own had been. Edward had had one of those happy, cheerful childhoods that turned ugly and psychologically violent overnight. It was impressive that he'd survived it with so much dignity and so few outward signs of damage. What was most incredible to me was that he'd forgiven his parents enough to fly into Cincinnati monthly to tend to them and even pay a few of their bills. His parents held Edward—representative of moral decay and godlessness—personally responsible for the events of September 11. I was fascinated by the ways in which people who claimed to be religious blamed homosexuality and abortion and oral sex for the terrorist attacks when it was so blatantly apparent that one of the main causes had been religion.

"Don't let us keep you," I said. "There must be a lot of people who want to talk with you."

"Not really." He shoved his hands into the pockets of his baggy khakis and began rattling loose change. "I've known almost everyone here my whole life. We don't have anything new to say to each other."

"Like me and William," Edward said.

"You've been together a long time?"

He tossed this question off so casually, and with such automatic acceptance, I was ashamed of myself for having passed any harsh judgments on him. Neither Edward nor I said anything, each waiting for the other to utter the disavowal. A lot of people assumed we were a couple, and as long as we weren't one, the assumption pleased me, especially there in that roomful of strangers.

We were saved from further conversation by the approach of a small round woman with the mottled complexion of a drinker. She put her arm around Daniel's waist and leaned against him in a way that was probably intended to be maternal, but looked lascivious. The top of her curly head came up to Daniel's armpit. "I can't believe you're in college already," she cooed. "I remember when you were running across the lawn in your diapers. And now you're taller than me and Ned put together. With a stomach like a drum." She tapped it, making a hollow sound, and then lifted up his jersey to reveal a taut abdomen split by a thin line of hair.

I was amazed by the lewd way women flirt with their friends' teenaged sons and the equally lewd way teenaged girls flirt with male friends of their parents. Probably I was annoyed that they could get away with behavior that, had it come from me, would have resulted in an arrest warrant.

"I haven't seen a stomach like that in twenty years." She dropped the jersey down over Exhibit A and turned her attention to Edward and me. "Are you the antique dealers?"

A gay couple that had recently opened up a shop somewhere in town? "No," I said. "We're the other ones."

"Oh? Do I know about you?"

I explained about the apartment in Cambridge.

"Charlotte's been talking about that for years," she said. "She's always been restless. Me, I'm content to sit home and get fat. It's funny she wants to get out now, now that everyone else is trying to find a place out here where it's safe. There's nothing more important than safety these days." She patted Daniel's stomach again. "I hope this finally makes her happy."

When she'd dragged Daniel to the other side of the room, Edward took a handful of peanuts and said, "I'll bet you anything that kid is hung like a horse."

"An irrelevant wager since neither one of us will ever know."

I was convinced that Edward liked well-endowed men partly because he felt intellectually superior to someone with the genitalia of a farm animal.

"Let's go find the hosts," I said. "Then we can sneak out."

"You go ahead. I'm going to get a huge gin and tonic."

"You don't drink," I reminded him.

"I'm feeling reckless. It'll help me get across the bridge on the way home."

the major leagues

Left to my own devices, I tried to do what I usually do at parties, scan the crowd and divide it into three neat groups: My League, Out of My League, and A League of Their Own. Into the first group I ordinarily dump anyone with a bad haircut, the slumped posture of self-doubt, and an inappropriately loud laugh. Out of My Leaguers include all women over five ten and any man with a barbed-wire tattoo encircling his biceps. The folks in A League of Their Own are the ones talking to themselves while examining the cheese selection or drinking anything other than beer directly out of a bottle.

This group was hard to read. They were a reasonably ordinary looking bunch of exclusively heterosexual couples who were probably more than ordinarily successful. Mixed in were a few of the disheveled, sun-weathered types in corduroy you often see in seaside communities, artists or drunks with money and sailboats. Older crowd, I thought, before realizing that few were older than me. My League, for the most part, but the smell of money in the air—not vast sums, but significant amounts spent with competitive vigor—bumped them Out of My League entirely. No one, I was distressed to note, was behaving inappropriately enough to be a likely candidate for A League of Their Own, but the night was young.

There was no sign of Charlotte or Samuel. The door to the porch banged open too loudly, and the windblown woman who'd been smoking entered. I watched her make her way across the room, with a graceful, self-conscious gait, like a teenager who knows or expects that she's being observed at every moment. Another misfit maybe, but it seemed unlikely that she, like me, was wearing secondhand clothes.

how embarrassing

Charlotte was in the kitchen, seated on a stool at a counter, talking or listening to a man who was propped up against the sink. The man's face looked as if it had been pumped up with air. "Because she doesn't *know* me," he was saying. "You think she knows me, but she doesn't have a *clue.*"

"I don't think she knows you," Charlotte said. Her voice was weary and flirtatious. "I don't have any opinion on the matter. For Christ's sake, Richard, she's your wife. Of course she doesn't know you. Count your blessings."

The man, who'd latched on to this theme with what was clearly drunken tenacity, kept at it. "She doesn't *know* me, that's what I'm trying to tell you."

"Well, I don't really know you either. Maybe, this is just a thought, you don't know yourself."

"Ah, cruel," he said. He turned to me. "She's cruel, this woman."

"I was afraid you weren't coming," Charlotte told me. "I've been counting on you to rescue me from Richard. I once made the mistake of encouraging him."

"Once," he said. "It's been a very long once." He went to her and touched her neck tenderly, but without any heat. "Too bad we're such good neighbors."

When Richard had made a drunken, cheerful departure, Charlotte sat up on her stool a little straighter and gazed at me with a look of melancholy bemusement. "Why is it that the sloppy attention of someone you find overbearing, unattractive, and ridiculous can make you feel better about yourself than the devotion of your unnervingly handsome husband? Rhetorical question. Even your attention makes me feel better, William.

Your chivalrous intervention on my behalf at the restaurant. Making sure Samuel put in the offer."

"I just wanted to make the sale."

She wagged a finger at me. "No, not just. Who else have you met?"

"Most significantly, Daniel. In addition, a little woman who appears to be devoted to him, or his abdomen anyway, and a tall woman smoking a cigarette on the porch. She works with Sam. A volleyball player is my guess."

"Not volleyball. Horses. That's Kate. Raised with money and horses and now dangerously single after a failed marriage to a homosexual. No offense." She went to the refrigerator, poured a glass of orange juice, and handed it to me. "I'm guessing you don't want a real drink."

The combination of salt air and suburban ennui made me long for something alcoholic, but for the sake of solidarity with her sobriety, I felt I shouldn't ask for one.

"Where is Samuel?" I asked.

"Probably giving someone a tour of the house. He loves to give tours of the house and show off new gadgets and tiny improvements. They're horribly uninteresting. Tell him you've already seen everything if he offers." She looked at me with narrowed, exhausted eyes and played with the hair hanging against her neck. "You're thinking I've had too much to drink," she said.

"Not at all. It never crossed my mind."

"I'm having another minor sobriety setback."

"I understand completely." And then, realizing that I'd been aching to tell someone for a long time, I said, "I've been having minor celibacy setbacks for weeks and weeks now."

"Really!" she said. "I'm shocked. Not to mention trumped. What form do the setbacks take?"

"Assignations." There was something polite and even romantic about the word. I didn't need to mention parked vans and terry-cloth window treatments. But she was gazing at me closely, as if trying to read between the lines.

"Surely not in that spotless apartment of yours."

"No, never. What brought on your setback?"

"Daniel, I suppose. It was hard sending him off to college, but it's been worse having him back this weekend. He's so composed, perpetually unfazed. We never clicked. Almost from the minute he started talking, it seemed as if we didn't have anything in common. It just hit me when he returned yesterday that he's gone. Probably for good. The best I can hope for is the occasional birthday visit and, somewhere down the line, a grandchild who'll stitch us together a tiny bit more closely, unless he and a future wife can afford a nanny."

People will tell you almost anything, but it's rare they'll be so blunt about their relationship with their kids. I found her confession almost too poignant, and I wanted to look away from her. I'd been emotionally tenderized by my meeting with Alberto the night before, and by talking about it, or some of it, with Edward. I not only heard the longing in her voice, I felt it deep inside me.

"I'd guess you're being much too harsh on yourself. I can tell you're a wonderful mother."

"You're only saying that because I'm fat. If I were one of those thin volleyball equestrian types, you'd have seen the problem immediately."

She'd spoken with her usual arch delivery, but I could see that her eyes were filling up. "Despite all of that," I said, "you look lovely tonight." I set down the juice glass and put my arms around her. I could smell the same strong, earthy perfume I'd smelled on her once before. "And for what it's worth, I have a feeling it's all going to be fine."

"You wouldn't understand," she said. "That's why I told you."

Without thinking about what I was doing, I leaned down and kissed her on the lips. "How embarrassing," she said, but didn't pull away.

The kitchen door swung open, and Edward came in, making the moment even more awkward.

all her shameful secrets

People in various stages of inebriation wandered in and out of the kitchen, clutching little plates of food and assuring Charlotte that they were having a wonderful time. A couple of young, grumpy caterers kept showing up in tandem to replenish their trays and complain to each other about the heat in the living room and the rudeness of the guests, all with no apparent concern for offending Charlotte. Charlotte didn't introduce us to anyone, and it seemed to me she enjoyed being holed up in the kitchen with two men no one else at the party recognized.

"I'd love to see the rest of the house," Edward said. "And if you give us a tour, William can write off the trip as a professional expense."

"It's amazing to me you two are such good friends."

"Do we seem so different?" I asked.

"No, I just didn't realize men have friendships."

"I didn't realize we were men," Edward said.

She led us up a staircase off the kitchen in a narrow wainscoted hallway. "The servants' quarters," she said. "Their dark little rooms up under the eaves, and then this cramped passageway down to the kitchen to feed the Thompson family. This is where my ancestry would have lived—sweating and praying—in case you were thinking I take any of this for granted. This is where I do my sewing and darning," she said, waving vaguely at a few completely empty rooms.

Charlotte's tour of the rest of the upstairs was equally perfunctory. She carelessly indicated a few doors as we walked down the long hallway. "Linen closet, guest room, bathroom, more closets. Small room with peculiar shape. Daniel's room. Probably best not to open that one. He has a military love of order. Never a sock out of place."

"Something he and William share," Edward said. He was carrying his tall glass with him, sipping occasionally at the icy mix of gin and tonic.

At the end of the hallway, she pointed to a narrow door. "Former attic, currently my office. We can go up if you're interested and promise not to look at anything too closely. All my shameful secrets."

As she was opening the door, Daniel emerged from his bedroom, holding the hand of a very small and remarkably pale girl. The girl was dressed in skintight Capri pants with a halter top arrangement above that exposed a lot of soft stomach, but her expression had the calm superiority of virginity, proudly and meticulously preserved. She couldn't have been five feet tall, but she carried her head as if she were looking down on the rest of the world. Virtue, I suppose, can give you that edge. Despite the way they were holding hands, it was impossible to imagine they'd been doing anything in Daniel's bedroom other than folding laundry.

"Mom. There you are." Daniel said this with the same tone you'd use to scold a child who'd just missed dinner. "People are asking for you downstairs. You disappeared."

Charlotte introduced us to the girl, whose name turned out to be something along the lines of Heather, although, when I said, "Nice to meet you, Heather," she corrected me in an incomprehensible way. She had the same confident look as Daniel, and the two of them, standing side by side, seemed to be waiting patiently for the rest of us to step aside and let them rule the world.

"I guess I'm obliged to reappear downstairs," Charlotte said. "The view from the balcony is the best in the house, should you want to go explore on your own."

The staircase leading up was so tight and steep, I felt as if we were climbing a ladder. When we were halfway up, Charlotte stuck her head through the doorway and said, "There's a bag of books next to my desk. Things I've worked on in the past. Feel free to take it with you, William, if you're curious about how I spend my days. They might keep your mind off other things."

At the top of the staircase, we emerged into a surprisingly large room with a high ceiling and sloping walls. I was disappointed to see that someone, doubtlessly Charlotte and Samuel, had outfitted the place with skylights, an architectural feature that fills me with the same pessimism about the future as the hot tub. Little high-tech spotlights suspended from a track of wires illuminated the desk. The office was furnished with a couple of comfortable easy chairs slipcovered with flowery chintz and a bulky old sofa that demanded you lie down on it and take a nap. Edward went to it immediately and sprawled out, his hands behind his head. There were French doors off to one side, presumably opening up to the balcony Charlotte had mentioned, although the light was reflecting off them and I couldn't see the view.

"I'm drunk," Edward said.

"That was quick. Half a glass?"

I went to the desk in the corner and pretended to study Charlotte's computer, a sleek thing with a flat screen. The desk was covered with neat stacks of paper, calendars, and schedules she'd made for herself regarding deadlines and appointments with her dentist. I quietly slid open the drawers, looking for a shameful secret or two. Inside the deep second drawer was a tattered manuscript held together with an elastic band. The title page read: "*So You Said* by Charlotte O'Malley."

"You and *she* certainly seem to be hitting it off," Edward yawned.

"Jealous?" I asked. I took out the manuscript and flipped through a few pages.

"Yes, as a matter of fact, I am. I felt completely abandoned by you when I walked into the kitchen and saw the two of you making out."

"Making out? I don't think that's the right term. And why abandoned? What did it have to do with you?" Judging from the lines of dialogue, the pages appeared to be a novel or a collection of stories. I slipped it into the bag of books beside the desk as discreetly as I could.

"Why invite me all the way out here if you're just going to leave me to the drink cart and get cozy with the hostess in the kitchen? You didn't need me here to do that."

"I know, but it was more fun knowing you're here. And if anyone should feel abandoned, it's me. You're the one leaving town, you're the one dating a pilot."

He had his eyes closed and his hands behind his head, and his face was touched by moonlight and the deep shadows of the desk lamp. Seeing him on that puffy sofa, here at the top of the house, far from the crowd of strangers down below, knowing that in less than two months he was moving to the other side of the country, I felt closer to him than I'd felt in many years, as if the two of us were connected by a strong, intangible bond I'd taken entirely for granted and just now realized was mutable. More alarming still, I felt a sudden flush of desire and longing for him that reminded me of what I'd felt the night before with Alberto. Except now the whole tumble of events of the past twenty-four hours was a confusion of details—what had really happened, what I'd imagined, the version I'd told Edward.

He opened his eyes and caught me looking at him. He always knew what I was thinking, and I felt miserably found out.

"What do you want from me, William?" he said, part question, part accusation.

"The thing is," I began, with no idea where I could take the sentence. I moved toward the sofa. But just that slight repositioning of my body gave me a better view through the French doors out to the balcony, and more specifically, a better view of Samuel, standing in a corner with his arm around the waist of Kate, his coworker from the porch. She had her head resting on Samuel's shoulder in a calm, familiar way that was unmistakably more than friendly. As usually happens in situations like this, I felt like the guilty party for having spotted them. I moved away from the door and onto the arm of the sofa as quickly as I could. I said nothing to Edward, the doors swung open, and Samuel and Kate entered—laughing, as if they'd been blown in by the wind.

With amazing dexterity, Samuel took in Edward's position on the sofa and me sitting near his feet and made the best of his own bad situation.

"I'm sorry," he said, as if embarrassed for my sake, not his own. "I didn't mean to interrupt."

"Not at all," I said. I stood and shook his hand. He tried to introduce Kate, but that deteriorated into a series of clumsy interruptions and broken fragments about the three of us having met down below. Kate was standing next to Samuel, arms folded across her chest. She looked unhappy and slightly bored, as if she was already anticipating the inevitable, tedious discussion of guilt and discretion that she and Samuel would have.

"You must have come up here for the view," she said.

"Exactly," I said. "And to collect a bag of books Charlotte put aside for me."

If Kate was irritated with me for having come upon her with

her lover, I felt betrayed by her for turning out to be more of an insider here than she'd portrayed herself on the porch.

There was more talk of the view and then an unnecessary explanation of how Samuel had brought his coworker up here to show her how clearly you could see, from the balcony, the building in which they both had offices. When that explanation went nowhere, Samuel ushered us all down the little staircase and cautioned us about hitting our heads on the low ceiling. Halfway down, I quietly passed Kate the pack of cigarettes she'd handed me outside, and she accepted it gratefully.

In the second-floor hallway, Samuel let Kate and Edward get ahead of us while he fidgeted with the latch on the door. "I've been meaning to call you for a few days now," he said to me in a low voice. The door swung open again. "I hate this door. There's something wrong with the hinges, or maybe the door frame is crooked. I'm not sure which. I'm not the least bit handy. I always thought I'd learn one day, how to do things, but it just never happened."

"Funny," I said. "I figured you'd be the Mr. Fix-It type." I didn't. Men who are handsome as Samuel are rarely capable even of calling the right people to do their work for them. "Not having second thoughts about the apartment, are you?"

"Oh, no." He put his arm around my shoulder. "Nothing like that. Just a few details to go over, things that wouldn't interest Charlotte. Call me. Come down to my office, and I'll take you out for lunch. The two of us. And we won't mention anything about that." He nodded in the direction of the attic, but it was unclear if he was asking for a favor or suggesting he was doing one for me.

mr. collins?

The drive home was a lot faster, and in the cool dark, the blighted industrial landscape took on a look of garish beauty, with lights sparkling and the tops of smokestacks blinking. Edward slept most of the way, his seat reclined, the gin and tonic having its way with him. It was peaceful with him sleeping there in the passenger seat. Occasionally, he'd wake up and make a comment as if we'd been in the middle of a conversation, then drift back to sleep.

The street in front of Edward's building was shadowy and the old trees lining the sidewalk were shedding their leaves in the wind. I tugged on Edward's earlobe to wake him.

"I've been to worse parties," he said. "Although not many."

"You should get out more often."

He sat in his seat for a minute, silently waiting for something. But whatever had passed between us briefly in Charlotte's study had disappeared. There was a sudden, loud clatter on the roof of the car, and then it began to pour, so hard it was almost impossible to see out the windows. After a minute or two, it subsided to a steady rain. Edward opened his door and waved from the sidewalk without turning around. I watched him climb the steps to his building, drop his keys, fumble for a moment in the wet, velvety shadows, and then slip inside. I wasn't ready to leave yet; I had no good reason to go home. I had a lot of bad reasons to go home, and some of them had a sticky, persistent appeal. By now, all the fleeting physical pleasures of my erotic adventures were blended in with the feelings of disappointment and regret, so they'd all become part of the same experience. Even the wearying rituals I'd go through upon arrival at home as a stall tactic—the late-night tidying, scrubbing the sink with Tang, straightening out the towels—pushed against me with tender inevitability. It wasn't yet ten o'clock.

I watched as the lights went on in Edward's apartment. I've always tried to be patient and forgiving when friends make obvious mistakes. Even lots of obvious mistakes. But it's intolerable to watch them make the exact same mistake over and over. I'd sat in my car on this street looking up at the lights going on in Edward's apartment dozens of times over the years. Maybe I was making the same mistake over and over. Maybe it was time to make a new one.

I turned off the engine and put on the emergency flashers. I was illegally parked, but what was the worst that could happen? Towed? I could face that later, maybe in the morning.

At the bottom of his steps, I heard someone call my name with a familiar, mocking tone.

"Mr. Collins?"

Oh, don't let it be, I thought, hoping it was.

"What brings you into this neighborhood tonight, Mr. Collins?"

Didier, the last person I wanted to see just then, was standing in the shadows under a tree, a cigarette dangling from his skinny fingers, the branches protecting him from the soft rain. I couldn't see his face clearly, but I could hear his smirk.

"You're out of the country," I said. "You don't live here any longer. Therefore, Mr. Didier, I do not see you."

"You're mean, Mr. Collins. And lying on top of it. I'm thirsty. Come buy me a drink."

hypotheticals

"What have you done about cleaning up the marine's apartment?" Deirdre asked me. She was sitting at her desk shopping online for beds. Despite her claims of having a marriage of unprecedented happiness, she'd spent days hunting down a company in Norway that made something called a Royal Family Super Deluxe–sized mattress. This miracle of construction appeared to have the same dimensions as a few of the studio apartments I'd sold in Cambridge over the years. I'd noticed that the beds of an awful lot of married couples grew in direct proportion to the number of years they'd been together. I suppose increasing the bed size was cheaper than getting separate apartments and had some of the same advantages.

"She's agreed to let me rent her a storage unit until the place sells," I told her. "But given her health problems, I'm going to have to move everything myself."

"The newscasters are dithering, so there's no great rush, but I'd like to get them out of my life as soon as possible. Endless boasting about how miserable they are, flaunting their divorce as if it were a badge of intelligence. I'm going to have to order the sheets for this bed separately from a company in Canada. I hope my washing machine can handle them."

"I should warn you," I said, "that Marty wants to pitch her company to the newscasters for a profile on their show."

She waved off this comment. "Let her. They love being flattered. It's tough being a celebrity no one's ever heard of."

I watched her punching her keyboard for a few more minutes, buying distance from her perfect husband. "I have a personal question to ask you," I said. "But I'm afraid you might be insulted by it."

Her face lit up at this, as if she was delighted by the assumption that anything in her personal life could be controversial. "Ask away, please."

"If Raymond were having an affair, which I know absolutely would never happen, would you want to know about it?"

"Oh, this is one of those hypothetical personal questions which isn't a personal question at all. I suppose it's really about that married couple you're working with, the ones with the big house. I could tell they were in trouble the minute I saw them way back when in their little raincoats. That's why I passed them along to you." She paused for a moment, waiting for me to confirm or deny this, and looking at her wholesome, handsome face, I found I couldn't do either. She nodded, as if my silence was good enough for her. "In theory, everyone wants to know, William, but in reality, no one does. In reality, we all go through massive, uncomfortable contortions to hang on to the ridiculous belief that we're the only truly happily married couple in the universe. I hope you realize that's more of an answer than you were looking for. And don't worry. I won't breathe a word of this to Jack. Your secret is safe with me."

"What secret is that?"

"When it comes to other people, William, we all, in theory, want to know nothing. But in reality, everyone wants every gritty detail. But I'm not asking. It's just nice to know you have more going on than I imagined. I think we're all relieved."

so it seems

Deirdre assumes I'm sleeping with Sam? Or Charlt? So it seems. Both? Call Ken O'Leary to set up inspection on apartmnt. Bring board of trustees docs to Samuel. Lunch w/ him? And his mistress? Outdated term, "mistress"? Deirdre: We're all relieved? What were they assuming? Get list of painters for Charlt. I have more going on than they imagined? What if I have less going on?

after the fact

Later that afternoon, Sylvia Blanchard came to my office to coordinate a time for an inspection of Edward's apartment. In the past, she'd let these details drift while she wallowed in regret and ambivalence and hunted down excuses to back out of the purchase. I found myself doing with her the exact opposite of what I usually did: I advised her to slow down and not get tangled up in formalities. Naturally, she didn't take my advice. She crowed about her love of formalities, her fondness for details, and her newfound determination to move forward at full speed.

"You see," she said, "I've decided to become quite American in my behavior. Give me, give me, give me. I want to buy everything, I want to ingest as much as I can, I want to own and possess and control. I'm dining at the all-you-can-eat luncheon buffet. I want it all and I want it *now*." Her long, thin legs were wound around each other, and she was leaning forward in her seat with her elbows digging into her knee. She was all angles, sharp and insistent, vibrating with determination. "Call little Edward and let's make some plans. At very least I'd love to go over there with a tape measure and a pad of paper so I can figure out the dimensions of all the disposable *junk* I'm going to load into the place."

"He's out of town," I told her, "but I'll leave a message and have him get back to you."

"I don't know whether to believe you or not, but I don't have time to argue. Purchasing the apartment has given me the focus for my next project—an analysis of the spiritual soul of America in the wake of September eleventh. I'm going to call it *After the Fact*. I've been looking down my very long nose at American consumerism for years, but now that I've embraced it, I understand it completely. It's always been marvelous, but it needed a rationale.

Now it has one: shop your way to a feeling of safety and security."
She unwound herself and stood up, her body once again taking a
recognizable human shape. "Struck from above by a dastardly
enemy and the response is an encouragement to visit Disneyland,
buy bigger cars, and then launch an attack on a country unrelated
to the problem. It's all brilliantly Fall of the Roman Empire. I'm so
happy to be living here during the final days."

"That attitude wounds me to the core of my patriotism and
cultural identity."

"Yes," she said. "And how else can a dull academic get a little
attention?"

I was happy to have an excuse to call Edward. It had been close
to a week since the party, and because I hadn't done as I'd intended
and knocked on his door in the rain, I'd hesitated about getting in
touch. When he answered, I felt an uncharacteristic and immediate
urge to confess.

"I almost came up to your apartment after I dropped you off,"
I said.

"You almost do a lot of things, William. I'm not sure why
you're telling me about what you almost did but then, ultimately,
did not do. Am I supposed to applaud your good intentions?
Why not tell me why you didn't come in instead of how you almost did."

"It was the parking situation, as always."

He offered no response to this.

"And as I was heading to your door, I bumped into Didier.
He's back in town."

"Yes, I know."

"How do you know?"

"That's an irrelevant question. I suppose that means your
pointless little obsession is back in full flower."

"No, not exactly. Not at all, in fact. He's helping me with

something." Against the odds, this seemed to be true. I had seen him three times since meeting him on the street, and for the first time since making my resolution about celibacy, I was sticking to it.

"Helping you? Good for him. Is that what you called to tell me?"

"Edward," I said. "I had a few thoughts about your apartment. Sylvia wants to move on it quickly, but I wonder if it wouldn't make more sense for you to rent it out for a while, see how you like San Diego, if the business with Marty works out. Why not leave yourself the option of coming back? If you keep it furnished, I could find a businessman who'd pay a fortune every month. You'd be making a huge profit, and you could do the whole move west with a few suitcases instead of dismantling your entire life. Just get on the plane and go."

"I get on the plane and go three times a day. I'm looking forward to dismantling my life and reassembling it somewhere else. I've committed to a plan and I'm following through on it. I have no intention of renting."

I hung up the phone, realizing that my plans for the sale of this condo were not going as I'd envisioned; it was going to happen.

Scents

Charlotte had called me a few days after the party to complain that I'd left the house abruptly—as I saw it, the only sensible thing to do under the circumstances—and insisted that I meet her at an address she gave me on Newbury Street in downtown Boston. It was the first truly cold day of the fall, and she was dressed in a big gray sweater and a pair of sunglasses. Despite her claims of being fat, she looked fit, even wrapped in layers of heavy wool. I smiled at her as I approached, but it was the first time I'd seen her alone since stumbling over Samuel and Kate, and I couldn't look at her without factoring in the sad, guilty fact that I knew more about her life than she knew. Even if, as Deirdre had said, it was information she wouldn't want to know. I kissed her on both cheeks, in a showy, friendly way, hoping to wipe out the embarrassment of the kiss in her kitchen.

"I didn't know if you were planning on lunch," I said, "so I brought my appetite just in case."

"We might get to that," she told me. "But first I want to take you over there."

She pointed across the street to a storefront that turned out to be Sean's perfume boutique. "I've never been in," I told her.

"I know. He mentioned that when I called to place an order. I made an appointment for us. He's going to compose something for you."

"Compose? Really? That's thoughtful, but I don't wear cologne."

"On principle?"

"No, no. I don't have principles."

"You can give it to someone else," she said. "One of the people you're not being celibate with. Just tell Sean exactly who you're giving it to and he'll know what to do. I think you'll find the whole experience helpful."

You had to make an appointment with Sean, she explained, so that he could devote a full hour to mixing oils and balancing base and heart and top notes, giving you exactly the right blend for your personality, the occasion, or the psychology of the person you were giving it to. The creation of his perfumes was all very scientific yet, at the same time, born of mysterious ancient arts.

"I didn't imagine you'd be the type to get caught up in alchemy," I said.

"I let my cynicism drop once or twice a year," she said. "It's nice to believe in something, especially if it's harmless and non-habit-forming."

Entering the store was like entering an igloo, not that I'd know. Everything was white, glass, or shining metal, and the temperature was surprisingly low. I'd expected to be bombarded with the smell of flowers and musk, but there wasn't a hint of fragrance, almost as if the air had been scrubbed clean. The decor, Charlotte whispered, had something to do with clearing your palate and your olfactory expectations. Andy must have spent a fortune having the place decorated for his young lover; nothing costs more than making an interior look empty.

Sean was seated on a tall stool behind the counter, an elegantly transparent piece of Lucite lit from within. He was dressed in white pants and a white cotton turtleneck. He wasn't thin, and given his perpetual state of exhaustion, it was impossible to imagine him working out or exercising. He had a lazy, sensual fleshiness that was ridiculously attractive. He might only have been thirty-two as he claimed, but he had the appealing world-weariness that a lot of beautiful Brazilian men have, and it made him seem wise.

"So it took Charlotte to get you to come visit me," he said.

"I wouldn't trust myself to be alone with you," I said.

"Oh, I won't be bought off that easily, William."

He slithered off his stool and came around the counter clutching a small blue bottle. He handed Charlotte the bottle and gave her a lascivious embrace that she returned, while rolling her eyes at me.

"Is that the perfume you sometimes wear?" I asked.

"We made it for Samuel," Sean explained. "But Charlotte wears it so she can always have him with her. Smart, isn't it?"

"Yes, very." Although it might have been smarter to have

Samuel wearing her perfume as a reminder. "I don't wear perfume, so mine will be for someone else, too."

Sean went back behind the counter, pulled out a pad of unlined white paper and a slim silver pen that looked like a small icicle, and we got down to business.

"It helps to know something about the person you're giving it to. We'll start with the easy things. Man or woman? Age. Name. Eye color."

Sean wrote down my answers in small, careful handwriting.

"Didier," Charlotte said. "French, in other words."

"Belgian. Assuming he's telling me the truth about where he's from."

"If you were going to lie, you wouldn't claim Belgium," Sean said. "Switzerland, maybe. What you're saying is, you're giving an expensive bottle of scent to someone you don't trust." He tapped his silver pen against his lips. He had beautiful lips, plump and red, and he was always, understandably, drawing attention to them in subtle ways. "Do you think this is wise, William?"

"It's a complicated situation."

"This is what everyone tells me who has a stupid situation. 'It's complicated.' You can't believe how much people tell me about themselves when they come in to buy some perfume. I should hang out a shingle."

"You have a shingle," Charlotte reminded him. "A sign, in fact."

The whole country had become accustomed to watching television shows in which people reveal their darkest secrets to millions of strangers, open up all their closets, and display filthy laundry for the sake of entertainment. As a result, people had begun to haul out their hidden selves to anyone who'd listen, from their real estate agent to their shoe salesman. The only time people didn't reveal their darkest secrets was in psychotherapy. There, they just asked for pills to blunt the symptoms so they could go on with their unbalanced but familiar behavior.

"What does this Belgian Didier do for work? What kind of music does he like to listen to? What color scarves does he wear on winter afternoons? Is he a good dancer? How long is his hair? What are his hobbies?"

"He likes to smoke," I said, offering the one thing I knew about him for certain. "I've only known him for a couple of years. Off and on."

He sighed and put down his pen. "Give me an image. The first thing that comes to mind when you think of him. And please, nothing pornographic because I'm basically a shy person."

"A smoky apartment with heavy curtains in a damp European city. Does that help?"

Sean began selecting flasks of oil from the lighted shelves behind him. He slid open several drawers and pulled out beakers, pipettes, and other chemistry lab accouterments. His movements were smooth and graceful, almost as if he'd choreographed the whole performance. He swirled the oil in the flasks before setting them down on the counter. There, under carefully positioned lights from above, they shimmered as if they were emitting rays of energy. "I'll start out with a dark foundation," he said. "Civet, an animal secretion, but dirtier than musk. Do you think I'm on the right track?"

"It sounds about right. I think he once told me he plays chess," I said. "If that's any use."

"I'll try to work with it. But ultimately, I'm just going to go with my own instincts."

"That's what he did with Samuel, and he got him exactly right," Charlotte said.

mr. didier

Didier's appearance on the street outside of Edward's apartment had been unexpected, but not entirely. He was a stray, and like all strays, he had a way of turning up and disappearing at unpredictable times. Originally, I'd thought he was just irresponsible, but after a while, I began to think that he understood the limits of his charms and didn't want to wear out his welcome.

For the sake of my own dignity, I wish I could say that I had developed a full-scale erotic obsession with Didier because he was intelligent and kind. Sweet. Needy. I wish I could say I was drawn to his manners and sophisticated wit. I wish I could say he had an endearing lost-soul or bedraggled-puppy-dog quality that made me want to take care of him. Barring all of that—and all of that had to be barred because none of it was true—I wish I could say I was attracted to his beauty, in a Platonic-ideal sort of way. But Didier was not a beauty by even the most lenient standards. He barely came up to my shoulder and was skinnier than I was; he had a dark, pointy, I-am-insane face that he further disfigured with a little patch of fuzzy hair under his thin lower lip. He was the incomprehensibly proud owner of a frail, hyperactive penis I found annoying, and his head was covered in a mop of tight curls that he sometimes had highlighted with orange. His body smelled faintly but distinctly of cigarettes at all hours of the day and night. I didn't have more than a clue about his age; in the time I'd known him, it had bounced back and forth between an impossible twenty-four and an improbable thirty-two. My guess was forty, but what difference did it really make?

He had, at some point in his jumbled history, discovered the only infallible method of making himself erotically irresistible and indispensable: he figured out, with his tiny, piercing eyes and his eerily sensitive body, exactly what you most wanted—and then he withheld it. As a tool of seduction, you can't do better.

I had sworn off Didier and banned him from getting in touch with me, because I had grown tired of his evasions and deceptions, the way he made plans and then broke them at the last minute or simply didn't show up, the humiliating way he tossed off lies without even trying to make them plausible. But seeing him on the street outside of Edward's building, I'd felt the same irresistible urge a drunk feels for a drink he knows will lead to ruin. If, a minute earlier, I'd felt that walking into Edward's apartment would save me from a lifetime of Didiers, I'd suddenly felt as if Didier would save me from caring so much about Edward.

I walked down the steps in the soft rain and joined him under the protection of the trees. "It's been too long," I told him.

"You said not to talk to you anymore, Mr. Collins, and so I stop talking to you. I do always what you tell me to do." Didier, of course, never did what you told him to do, one of the secrets of his success. "I was out of the country for a while, and now I am back."

"I see." He took out a fresh cigarette, and I lit it for him. "And where were you?"

"I went back to Brussels on business. From there, I was everywhere."

"Brussels is lovely in the winter."

"You're teasing me, Mr. Collins. Brussels is awful in the winter. Summer, too. Everywhere else was better."

"I love everywhere else," I said. "So much character."

"You are teasing me again, Mr. Collins."

He supposedly worked for a shoe manufacturing company, but sometimes he referred to it as a leather company and sometimes as a vaguely defined import/export business. In one of my bleaker moments, I'd gone online to search the name of the company he had given me and had come up with a Web site written in a language I'd never seen before. When I made the mistake of mentioning this fact to him, he turned it around and said, "You don't trust me. You hurt my feelings. Nothing I can say can convince you, so why would I try? Americans love to be spies, like James Bond."

"He's British."

"It is the same thing to the rest of the world, Mr. Collins."

In the two years I'd known him, I'd seen him surprisingly few times, probably not more than a couple of dozen meetings, although some of those had lasted as long as three days. Despite that somewhat limited contact, I'd spent so many hours spinning out lurid fantasies of him, I'd wasted so many days waiting pointlessly for him to show up for dates he didn't have the decency to break, that I'd felt, almost from the start of the relationship, as if we were a real, live, long-term couple, minus the anger, resentment, and gnawing boredom.

"So how's the shoe business, Mr. Didier?" I asked.

"It isn't good, it isn't bad. What more do you want to know than that, Mr. Collins? You don't care about the shoe business anyway."

"That's true."

"Of course it's true. I know you, Mr. Collins. I know you better than you know yourself. I know, for example," he said, drawing on his cigarette as he eyed me, "that you are now just dying to invite me back to your little house on the hill."

"Dying is a bit strong."

"I can see it in your eyes, Mr. Collins. Even in the dark and the rain."

"Why don't you invite me to your apartment? You told me you live in this neighborhood, didn't you?"

"But I can tell by this question, Mr. Collins, that you don't believe me. So if I invited you there now, it would be trying to prove something to you. And why do that? Besides, my mother is visiting for two months."

the remote control

Sean had filled several small beakers with blends of oils. As he added a drop here or there, he made notes in his meticulous handwriting on an index card. He worked with intensity, but a kind of detached weariness, sighing from time to time. Then, as if he'd suddenly received a jolt of divine inspiration, he poured all the oils together in a deep beaker and swirled it around, with sharp snaps of his wrist, for at least a minute, staring at me with what I took to be disapproval. Without sniffing it himself, he passed the beaker to me. "This is preliminary," he said. "I have to add some orchestration and a few more colors. But this will tell you the general mood."

The fragrance took a while to find me, but when it did, it entered my nose and went to my head exactly like a shot of straight whiskey, and from there, spread down through the rest of my body with a strange warmth. There was an underlying sharpness to it, something bitter and citrusy that wasn't exactly pleasant, but was addictive. All the dark, musky tones, those animal secretions Sean had mentioned, were there, like faint, seductive music coming from another apartment.

"How am I doing?" Sean asked.

I reluctantly passed the beaker to Charlotte. She drew back from it as if she'd been stung. "Not my type at all."

"No," I said. "Not my type either, but that's how it goes. At the moment, we're just friends."

Sean gave me one of those fond, pitying looks you give a child who needs another twenty years of experience to understand the full import of what he's just said. "Forgive me if I'm dubious."

I was dubious, too, but something had clicked with Didier, in a completely unexpected way. When he proposed that I invite him back to my house, I had, of course, assumed that I'd be unable to resist. But even so, pride and vanity compelled me to make him think I wasn't going to.

"I would love to invite you to my house, Mr. Didier," I'd said, "but I think we both know where that would lead."

"No, I don't know. Maybe you should just tell me."

"The fact is, I am not having sex anymore. Not with you, not with anyone. I've taken a vow of celibacy."

"Celibacy?" he asked, with surprising reverence. He tossed his cigarette down to the wet earth under the tree. And then, without even a trace of accent, he said, "That is so *hot*, Mr. Collins."

"Oh, really? You think so?"

"Yes, I love that. Please. I want you to fuck me right now."

This was all so blunt, so direct, so completely out of character for him, so counter to his usual withholding, I felt, for the first time, power pass into my hands, as if he'd just given me the remote control to a television set with 350 fantastic channels.

"You're missing the point, Didier," I told him. "I can't fuck you because I can't fuck anyone. That's what celibate means."

"My priest, when I was sixteen, was celibate, and he fucked me."

I somehow managed to avoid shoving Didier into the backseat of my car, driving him to my house, and locking him in the attic for a few days. It was the first time I'd ever felt that I was irresistible to him, and I knew I could only sustain his interest by resisting him. But beyond that, I felt a surge of control over my own impulses that was even more intoxicating than Didier's nicotine-stained charms. So, I thought, this feeling is what I was after when, all those weeks earlier, I'd unsuccessfully sworn off sex.

happy

I could feel myself growing calm as I watched Sean work, the drops falling into the beaker, the quick flick of his wrist as he swirled the oils, his look of dreamy concentration. "Watching him," I said to Charlotte, "you'd have to assume Sean is happy in his work."

"I agree. It's one of the pleasures of coming in here. It's wonderful watching someone do something they love, no matter what it is."

Without looking up from his science project, Sean said, "What you're telling me, William, is that you're not happy. I'm trying to change that, but there's only so much you can do with oil and imagination."

Of all the many things you're not supposed to accuse people of, being unhappy is certainly the main one. Crazy, stupid, lazy, cowardly, these are all acceptable accusations among friends in polite society, but unhappy wounds on a deeper level.

"You're not going to get happy because of Didier," Sean said. "And not because of perfume. You need spiritual fulfillment. And that wouldn't really hurt you, either, Charlotte."

"I have marriage," Charlotte said. "Not the same thing?"

"No. Not even a good one."

alcohol instead

"That wasn't an insult," I assured Charlotte as we walked up New-bury Street, the wind blowing in our faces. "He was saying that even though you *do* have a good marriage, it isn't enough. You need—we both need—spiritual fulfillment. Whatever that is."

"Maybe instead I should have said I have alcohol. And you, apparently, have sex."

"I'm guessing the response would have been the same. I'm making great progress with abstinence, by the way."

"How virtuous. Maybe we should get competitive about our self-control. I haven't had a drink since the party. I haven't really wanted one." She stopped and adjusted her sweater; it was colder than it was when we went into Sean's store, possibly a harbinger of an early winter. I don't mind cold weather, but winter always makes me long for a settled life, at least for a few months. So far, this winter didn't look any more promising than any other in that respect.

"I'm a little confused on one point," she said. "Your friendship with Edward. Not that it's my business, but of course Samuel told me he and Kate stumbled upon you, and . . ." She shrugged. "It's just not the way you presented the relationship. And then you left so quickly. And now Didier. It's not that I really *need* to under-stand."

"Stumbled upon us, eh?"

"I'm sure it was more embarrassing for them than for you. Al-though as I recall, you hadn't even been at the party all that long at that point."

My responsibility seemed clear to me, and it wasn't to either Edward or to myself. "It sounds as if Samuel was exaggerating," I said. "Maybe we should just leave it at that, get some lunch, and discuss our spiritual quests."

the missing piece

For the most part, I'm baffled by spirituality. When people talk about their spiritual quests and the comfort they take in spiritual pursuits, I usually have no idea what they're talking about. Or to be honest, I often have the impression that they don't know what they're talking about.

Religion, spirituality's sturdier cousin, has its drawbacks, like, for example, being the cause of eighty-five percent of the violent conflict in the world. But at least religions have specificity, systems of punishments and rewards that are spelled out in detail. Religions have a narrative driving them, and they have, in some form or other, God, that main character to end all main characters. Omniscient and opinionated, good but demanding, just, even if, occasionally, prone to capricious behavior; the elusive, ever-unobtainable father / love object / benefactor all rolled into one tidy package of omnipotence.

Spirituality, in contrast, has eye pillows and green tea. It has unmelodic music. People often cite their spiritual quest as a desire to connect with something larger than themselves, but frequently, the journey crosses paths with Oprah Winfrey or someone selling a video on late night TV.

The big questions that seem to nag at so many people—What's it all about? Why are we here? What is the meaning of Life?—have never nagged me. When you operate on a premise of muted pessimism and don't expect great things of yourself, it doesn't come as a major shock or disappointment to discover that human life in general is lacking in purpose and that your life, in particular, is insignificant.

But after Sean told me that I was lacking a spiritual connection, I began to think that he might have a valid point. For a long time, I'd been aware that something was missing from my life, although I'd never paid too much attention to the feeling because the entire economy is based on making people believe something is missing from their lives—a new car, softer towels, God.

I was sitting in my living room, opening and closing the bottle of scent Sean had made for me and trying to decipher its spiritual meaning when I heard the door slam on the first floor. I went to the window and peered down at Kumiko Rothberg, standing on the sidewalk clutching a string bag filled with mats and straps and plastic bricks and a puffy round pillow. She'd told me once that practicing yoga had changed her life. When I asked her how, she'd given me her look of melancholy condescension and had said that it had helped her "understand." I'd dismissed her evasive language, although she certainly understood how to live a rent-free life. I chided myself for being so dismissive of her and put on a sweater. You can learn from anyone.

As soon as Kumiko saw me emerge from the house, she said, "I'm late." This was an obvious attempt to head off a rent discussion. In the past month, she'd tossed a few dollar bills in my direction and had asked, three days earlier, that I recalibrate my elaborate payment schedule to clarify what she now owed. I'd responded to her request with a lot of useless sarcasm that had dissolved into a little badminton game of traded, insincere compliments. Then, feeling guilty for having been too harsh and probably for charging her rent in the first place, I'd spent an hour on the computer at the office recalibrating as requested.

"I won't keep you," I said. "I just wanted to ask your advice about something." This unexpected comment caught her off guard, and she looked at me as if I were about to grab her bag of goodies and run off with it. "I've been thinking about taking a yoga class, and I hoped you might have some advice about a teacher or school or however it works."

She flipped one of her braids behind her shoulder. "You don't strike me as the yoga type, William."

Judging from the yoga types I routinely encountered on the streets bullying their way to classes, all posture and passive aggression, I was tempted to thank her for the compliment. But a part of me was wounded. "That hasn't been determined yet," I said.

"In other words, you haven't practiced before." She said the word "practiced" with a studied reverence that made it sound like a challenge.

"Not really," I said.

"I gather that means no."

"I've done a lot of stretching."

She sighed and shifted her weight from one leg to the other. She had on a pair of turquoise stretch pants and a big T-shirt artfully spattered with paint and tied jauntily into a knot at her waist. She was, I noticed for the first time, in very good shape—lean and strong. For some reason, this made me more upset about the rent. Fitness, for the most part, is an expensive luxury. "Tell me what you hope to get out of it, William."

"The usual, I guess. Flexibility, strength, a little fun. I was hoping it would improve my posture."

She checked her watch. "You could join a gym for that. What else are you looking for?"

It was a simple, fair question, but I felt myself blushing furiously, as if she had made a pointed inquiry into my sex life or my bathroom habits. "Clarity?" I asked. When she responded to this by looking down the street and raising her eyebrows slightly, as if announcing to the neighborhood that I was a sad case, I added, "I'm searching for some . . . spiritual connections in my life."

A cab rounded the corner and pulled up to the curb. "Call me later tonight," she said. "I'm not saying I can help you, but I'm willing to try."

"That's kind of you."

"You've been kind to me," she said. "It's only right that I return some of your kindness."

I stood in silence, cowed by her implicit admission of avoiding the rent, and watched the driver load her bag into the trunk. She got into the backseat with the easy comfort of someone who's used to being whisked off by paid drivers. "I'll treat you to a class. I might miss that day's payment, if you don't mind."

"Don't worry about it."

At that, the taxi drove off. I watched it disappear down the hill, feeling as if I had a plan.

Solutions

Beacon Hill Solutions, Samuel's consulting firm, had its offices on the thirty-ninth floor of a mirrored glass building in the antique financial district of downtown Boston. The building took up the bulk of an entire block and had several addresses, depending upon which entrance you used. Buildings like this, all dizzying height, glass skin, inlaid wood, and marble, were far less impressive than they'd been not long ago. All the expensive luxury built into the design didn't seem as reassuring and immutable as it once had. I suppose all the expensive luxuries of the entire country didn't seem as immutable and reassuring as they once had. As a hedge against disaster, they'd proven inadequate.

On the thirty-ninth floor, the elevator door opened into a reception area that looked like a men's club—gleaming dark wood on the walls, heavy furniture, and big abstract paintings that could call to mind either a splendid autumn afternoon or Armageddon, depending upon your mood. The receptionist assured me that Samuel would be with me soon and then, tossing out mixed signals, offered me coffee, espresso, several types of breakfast pastries, and three different newspapers.

I took out my Thompson-O'Malley folder to make sure I had all the papers in order. This serious office made me want to make a professional presentation of the information Samuel was looking for. But after waiting fifteen minutes, my professionalism melted into annoyance. *Keep me waiting,* I wrote in my notes. *Open hostility. Sacrifice me/Edwrd to hide affair with Kate. Where do they fuck? Need stdio apt / love nest? Ck listings in ovrprced waterfront building on Lewis Wharf?*

The windows went from the floor to the ceiling, and sitting in a leather armchair clutching a newspaper as if it were a life preserver, I could see the sparkle of Boston Harbor dizzyingly far below, and across the water, the runways at Logan Airport. From this angle, the planes seemed to be taking off in slow motion, with a definite lack of enthusiasm. They stayed patiently lined up on the tarmac in the bright morning sun, and then, one by one, lumbered down the runway and departed heavily.

The sight of two planes belonging to the airline Edward worked for made me realize I had no idea where he was or what his schedule was that week. For all I knew, he might be sitting in the back of one of those planes, poring over an instructional guide to mutual funds. As I was watching one of the planes lift its nose and rise into the air, I saw out of the corner of my eyes, a billow of black smoke and then a burst of bright orange flames. A plane on the side of the runway was on fire. A squadron of fire trucks and emergency vehicles appeared from behind a terminal and raced toward the blaze, all, from my vantage point, in calm silence. I let my papers fall to the floor as I stood and turned to the receptionist.

She covered the mouthpiece of her headset and said, "It's a training drill. It happens twice a month at exactly this time. Don't worry, everyone freaks out when they first see it. They should do it somewhere else."

I settled back into the soft luxury of the leather chair and picked up a phone on the table near me. Edward's voice mail clicked on immediately. "Where are you?" I asked no one. "I've been thinking about you, and wanted to make sure everything's OK. We have to talk. I don't want you to sell your apartment. I'm serious, Edward. I don't want you to move. Call me."

I'd been at home that morning, a little over a year earlier, vacuuming, of course, when my phone rang and my mother squawked at me to turn on my television and then hung up. I have a phobia about daytime television and turning on the set before sundown instantly fills me with despair. I assumed she was calling about another celebrity murder or sex scandal. When I got a second call from Deirdre giving me the same advice in the same tone of excited misery, I carefully put away the vacuum cleaner, got dressed, straightened out the towels in the bathroom, and dug out the remote control.

I called Edward immediately. I left a message. I called two of his airline buddies. The first knew nothing of his schedule, the second made a vague, ominous reference to an early morning transcontinental flight. I spent the next five hours of that day with its insipidly beautiful weather unsuccessfully trying to locate my friend. The phone lines were frequently dead, and even when I could get a dial tone, the airlines were impossible to get through to. Every minute I didn't hear from Edward seemed more proof of the fact that he'd vanished.

It was the late afternoon when I finally did talk to someone at his airline. I explained myself and was put on hold for twenty minutes, which I spent sitting at my kitchen table, ripping newspaper, and weeping in a violent way. I've always had a hard time crying, not because I consider it unbecoming behavior in a man, but because I consider it unbecoming behavior in a tall man.

When the person I'd spoken to came back on and told me that Edward was not listed on any of their manifests and was most likely safely stranded somewhere in the West, I cleaned up the newspaper, had a drink, and tried to drown my sorrows with someone named Huck. There was a message from Edward on my machine when I returned that night. "I'm in Salt Lake City. I'm fine. More or less. I really, really would rather not talk about it ever." Aside from his recent allusions and expressed fears, we never had talked about it.

something the matter

Samuel sauntered down a long, narrow hallway, pushed open a glass door, and shook my hand. I was slightly taller than him, but there was something about the way he walked here—his territory—that made me feel he was towering over me. With his dark business suit and his hair slicked back in that neat, rigid way, he looked more dashing than ever, although, in this setting, a little harsh and predatory. Maybe everyone looks predatory in office buildings of this sort. Or maybe it was just that seeing him here in these flashy surroundings touched off more resentment over what he'd told Charlotte about coming upon Edward and me. Why had he felt the need to say anything?

As he led me out of the waiting room and into the much less

impressive hallways of the offices where the work was actually done, he apologized for making me come all the way downtown.

"It's not as if it's far," I said. "Besides, I'm downtown often."

"Right, that friend you brought to the party lives down here, doesn't he?"

"For the time being."

"Right, right," he said, feigning interest.

Samuel's office gave few clues as to what he actually did in it, but judging from the clutter on the desk and the papers spread out across the bookcase under the window, there was a lot of whatever it was.

"So," he said, sitting behind his desk and folding his hands in front of him. "What have you got for me?"

I took out the papers and spread them across the blotter in front of him. What I had for him was the kind of information most buyers don't have the patience or interest to study in detail; generally, they leave it up to their lawyers to assure them, in broad blanket terms, that everything is all right. By the time they discover that everything isn't, they're ready to sell anyway and pass the problems on to the next person.

Samuel took out a pair of half eyeglasses and slipped them onto the end of his nose. He went down a column of figures, nodding and occasionally asking a question or two. Despite his thoroughness in looking it over, I had the impression that he was stalling for time.

"The association is conscientious," I said. "But the problems with the financing are due mostly to some irresponsible decisions that were made about ten years ago. Everyone who's looked at these has been impressed with their progress, but you might . . ." I broke off, too overcome with resentment toward him to continue.

He took off his glasses and put them on top of the papers. "Something the matter?"

"I hope you know I'm a very discreet person, Samuel."

"Of course I do. I trust you completely." Undoubtedly, he'd intended his words as complimentary, but here in this office, surrounded by all the trappings of his position, they made me feel like a lesser man, or at least someone who lacked enough ambition to be untrustworthy.

"Thanks to my job, I'm privy to a surprising amount of personal information, and I never discuss any of it with anyone."

"Ah," he said, as if a light had gone off. He pushed aside the papers I'd handed him, leaned back in his chair, and stared out the window, a showy move that looked staged.

"I'm devoted to her, William," he sighed. "Truthfully, I can't stand the thought of anything bad happening to her. She's my wife."

I was happy for the clarification, because prior to that, it wasn't clear to me which of the two women he was talking about. He said the word "wife" with the glowing, reverential tone men often use to describe a spouse they're betraying.

"We four appeared downstairs more or less at the same time, and then you vanished. Charlotte asked a lot of questions about why you'd left so suddenly. I had to say something." He spread out his hands, the universal gesture of innocence. "Marriages are complicated. We have a good one. I don't want to see her hurt in any way."

He was telling me that it was incumbent upon him, and now on me, to keep all information about whatever was going on between him and Kate from Charlotte. Letting her know would be cruel, possibly harmful. Secrecy had become the moral imperative; the affair with Kate itself was beside the point.

There was a picture of their family on a corner of his desk, taken on the beach, of course, since most people associate beaches with cameras as much as with swimming. Charlotte appeared slimmer, tidier, more youthful in a variety of small ways that meant nothing individually, but added up to quite a lot. Samuel looked exactly as he did today, give or take a few gray hairs. I felt a shudder of revulsion toward him.

back rubs

I've always believed that part of being a truly good person is the loud and mournful acknowledgment of your moral failings. For just as it's supposedly true that you can't be completely insane if you know you're crazy, then it stands to reason that you can't be one hundred percent bad if you acknowledge that you're a total shit. A couple of years earlier, I'd come across a battered copy of the original paperback of *The Godfather.* It had been decades since I'd read it, and I had started rereading thinking I'd kill half an hour before tossing it out. Like most things in life, it was both better and worse than I remembered. It falls into a surprisingly large subgenre of fiction in which burly men get back rubs and talk about "snatch." The novel is spectacularly crass, but so compelling I'd had to put my life on hold until I'd read every page. Ultimately, I found it deeply depressing. It wasn't that the characters kill one another off with impunity, destroy businesses and families the way most people do laundry, and lop the heads off innocent animals without a second thought. What depressed me so profoundly was that they'd constructed a twisted moral code that allowed them to behave horrendously while still believing they were doing good.

Samuel appeared sincere enough about protecting his wife, but he didn't seem to be taking into consideration the fact that he was protecting her against his own behavior. And wasn't the point, really, that he was trying to protect his affair with Kate?

"Kate," I said, feeling the least I could do to make a stand for myself was to drag her name into the conversation, "seems like a nice woman. We talked with her on the porch as we were coming in."

"I suppose she was outside smoking," he said, a frown of disapproval creasing his face. He swung his little glasses around in his hand. "Well, what can you do? We all have our vices. I got her the name of a Russian hypnotist who's helped a lot of people I know." He shrugged. "Of course, I can't force her to go. You can't force anyone to do anything."

"She's a grown-up," I said, trying to emphasize her youth.

"As a matter of fact, she's remarkably grown-up. She's taking care of her mother and a divorced sister. She bought a big house up in Ipswich, and the three of them live in it, don't ask me how. She has a little pied-à-terre in the city she sometimes uses when she gets stuck at work late."

That answered a lot of questions and killed the idea of earning some money off the affair. In the end, everything gets back to real estate.

"She has a couple of horses and they seem to be the center of her life. It's a whole world I know nothing about."

"Do you ride with her?"

He laughed at the idea. "It isn't like that. If it's all right with you, I'll have some copies made of these documents and go over them more closely later." He glanced at his watch, and taking the cue, I began to gather up my own things. "I broke it off," he said. He stood and stretched. "More than once. Then, last fall, after . . . everything . . . I just realized how short life is and how important it is to enjoy it. You never know, do you?"

endearing new traits

Something I'd recently learned about Didier that surprised me was that he cooked. Actually, I was also surprised to learn that he ate. I'd assumed he picked at the occasional meal under duress, but mostly lived on Export A's and moderately priced red wine. He had the piercing, distracted eyes of a man who is always thinking about sex and cigarettes, and I had a hard time imagining him sitting through the smoke-free, asexual tedium of an appetizer–main course–dessert ritual. But since our encounter on the street outside of Edward's apartment, he had been using food as a pretext for getting together on a nearly nightly basis. Sometimes he took me out to dinner, charging it to the expense account of his mysterious company, and sometimes he showed up at my house with a bag of groceries and cooked simple, delicious meals I could picture a French (or Belgian) housewife serving to her hungry family. Although the only spices he used were the ones I had on hand in the cabinets, nothing he cooked ever tasted even remotely like the dishes I made using the same herbs.

At first it was disconcerting to have him pursue me so diligently; part of his louche appeal had always been his elusiveness, and in the past, I'd had to leave several phone messages over the course of a few days before I'd even hear from him. It's hard to know how to deal with people who suddenly change their behavior in a radical way, especially if the change is positive. But I'd begun to find his eagerness to get together flattering and satisfying; so completely satisfying that I'd spent weeks blissfully free of the gnawing urge to retreat to my computer and line up an evening of lubricious disenchantment.

It was a perfectly balanced situation, but the tension had to be maintained. If I did what both of us wanted and had sex with him,

I knew he'd immediately lose interest in me, and I would once again become the beggar pounding at the gates.

A few days after my meeting with Samuel, he showed up at my door at seven o'clock, exactly as he'd indicated he would in a message. Promptness was one of his endearing new traits. He had a white plastic bag of groceries in each hand and a freshly lit cigarette dangling from his mouth. I hated the smell of smoke in the house, but I couldn't bear to listen to his rants about the hypocrisy of American attitudes toward tobacco, so I put up with it and opened all the windows for hours after he left, despite the increasingly chilly nights.

"Right on time," I said and followed him in to the kitchen.

"Don't act so surprised, Mr. Collins. I've been showing up on time for many days now. Plus I'm hungry and exhausted. I've had a very busy day."

"I won't ask for specifics, Mr. Didier."

"No, you won't. But I would supply them if you did even though you would not believe what I told you. You like to think I do nothing all day except fuck."

"Not *all* day, no." Although it did please me to imagine that he had an inexhaustible libido.

He began to unload the contents of his bags on my kitchen counter—a collection of root vegetables, large leafy things that looked ancient and overgrown, and a package of heartbreakingly small hens. I rarely had the patience for cooking, and I'd often felt a twinge of regret when I entered my underused, aggressively clean kitchen. I sat at the table across from him, pleased to watch him, in his slim sharkskin pants and his turtleneck, tossing food around, chopping and sautéing, and ripping open cabinet doors. I'd initially been upset at the splattered grease and the food that ended up on the floor or between cracks in the counter, but that had worn off almost as soon as I tasted the first meal he'd prepared. I suppose some things—the warm comfort of a home-cooked meal?—are worth a little mess, loss of control, and lowering of standards.

"You see, Mr. Collins, Americans do not know how to eat. They only think about quantity."

"Please," I said, "I'm not in the mood for one of your anti-American lectures. I'm going through a deeply patriotic phase."

"Ah, I have to listen to anti-Europe from the minute I wake up until I get into bed and pull my blankets to my chin, but you cannot stand a little criticism."

"Surely you don't expect me to believe you go to bed and sleep, like boring, average people do, Mr. Didier? And watch the ash on that cigarette; some just dropped into the frying pan."

"Oh yes, isn't this exactly what I'm talking about? Americans can fill their food with chemicals and radiation and antibiotics and genetic craziness, but a flake of cigarette ash and the world is coming to an end. And yes, I sleep several hours a night, like a real human being."

"Several? I'm shocked."

"Several. And please stop looking at my ass. It's not polite to stare unless you intend to grope. I can feel your eyes on me, even with my back turned. You're just teasing me and playing with my head, now that you've become the pope."

"I suppose that's why you keep coming around."

"It must be, right?"

I had intended to sit there and watch him prepare the entire feast, lewdly appreciating his skills and sleazy charm, but when he began trussing up the little birds with string, I decided to retreat to the living room to read. I'm one of those cowardly carnivores who prefers to stay as far as possible from the mayhem of stockyards, henhouses, and the poignancy of anything resembling a body or a face.

I settled onto the sofa in the living room with the bag of business books Charlotte had ghostwritten. The subject matter of these volumes was of so little interest to me, I could barely force myself to read the titles, and was unable to make it all the way through a single subtitle: *How to Wow Now: A Punchy New Management Approach to the; Who Poached My Salmon? A Radical New Style of Management; Miss Management: A Fresh Feminist Look at Corporate.*

Most of the books were designed with elaborate graphics— huge bold-faced headlines, aggressive bullet points, amusing illustrations—that seemed intended to assure the reader he didn't have to bother slogging through the actual text. Charlotte's name appeared nowhere on the title or copyright pages, but all of the putative authors thanked her profusely for her assistance in the copious acknowledgments.

I took out the manuscript I'd lifted from Charlotte's desk drawer. I'd been meaning to read it since I'd more or less stolen it, but I'd felt too guilty about having done so and too disillusioned about their marriage. But with time, the guilt had worn off, as guilt tends to do, and with Didier in the kitchen, slamming things around and filling the apartment with the smells of garlic and cigarettes, I began reading *So You Said.*

The book was a collection of stories, each in the form of a monologue delivered to a psychotherapist who never actually appears, but is occasionally complimented ("Nice bookshelves, doc") or insulted ("You don't really *do* anything, do you, doctor? Your job is just sitting there") by the speaker. The patients were all women, and they all had the same problem: being in love with a man who was genuinely (and thus blamelessly, if I was reading correctly) incapable of loving them back. It was written with brio and wit, and what the stories lacked in variety of theme, they made up for with a diversity of voices. As I sat reading them, I had the same pleasant shock I'd experienced when I heard a friend I didn't know to be a musician play a series of beautiful Chopin etudes. If the stories had one single, persistent flaw, it was that they all had happy, unearned endings.

But as I read on, I became more and more uncomfortable. I began to feel as if I was reading Charlotte's journal, and despite my voyeuristic tendencies, I had to stop. I'd suddenly peered a little too deeply into some hidden part of Charlotte's psyche, the part in which she longed for things she would never have. It wasn't only the content of the stories—the impossible longing for love, the patient mercy toward the men—but also the writing itself; it was good, but probably not quite good enough. Judging from the gratitude of the alleged authors of the business books, Charlotte's greatest talent might well have been doing a kind of writing she didn't enjoy, wasn't interested in, and had very little respect for.

As I put the manuscript away, I realized that I had a problem on my hands: how was I going to return it without revealing to Charlotte that I'd taken it?

Didier appeared in the doorway from the kitchen, cigarette in mouth, pointing at the ringing telephone on the coffee table. "I'm expecting a call," he said. "I gave them your number. So, if this is for me, tell them I'm not here."

It was Edward, finally returning the message I'd left from Samuel's office.

"Where are you?" I asked. "I've been worried about you."

"I'm in San Diego, looking at real estate."

"Alone?"

"At the moment, yes. I can get a lot more for my money out here, I'll tell you that. Possibly even a tiny house in an undesirable neighborhood. You and Didier can come visit me."

"I'm not making any travel plans, alone or with anyone else, certainly not Didier. There's some interest in Marty's apartment, by the way. It hasn't been the easiest sell in the world. We have one good prospect, assuming Marty doesn't squelch the deal by trying to exploit the buyers for publicity."

"Well, whatever you do, don't try to convince her to do anything. It's always a bad approach with Marty. You always have to make her think it's her idea."

"Can we make a plan to get together? We need to have a serious discussion."

"Serious? How serious? And what's that noise in the background? You're not cooking, are you?"

There was a door between Didier and me, and even though the door was open, I was amazed that Edward was able to hear the sounds of his cooking. Perhaps he responded to some internal vibrations that the rest of the world couldn't detect.

"No, I'm not cooking. I'm sitting in the living room. I'm alone, reading. At some point I'll probably wander into the kitchen and pop a frozen dinner in the microwave." I wasn't sure why I bothered lying to Edward about Didier since he seemed to suspect everything anyway, but I hated facing his disapproval, and I felt that talking about it would put me in a weaker position for the next subject I wanted to bring up. "You never responded to the message I left you a few days ago. You didn't even acknowledge receiving it."

"I was doing you a favor. You left it in a moment of sentimental weakness. I didn't take it seriously and I won't hold it against you."

"But I meant it seriously. I don't want you to move."

"Why not?"

"You won't be happy there. You won't be happy working for Marty. You'll miss your apartment, your friends, a few of the things you actually like about Boston, and everything you hate. I promise you."

"You're so selfless, William. You're always thinking of me and my needs, never about your own."

"But I am thinking about my own," I told him. "I'll miss you.

I miss you already, and you haven't even left." I had a strange feeling that I was being pulled along by a strong current, although the direction I was headed wasn't clear to me.

"And why is that?"

"We've got a lot of unresolved issues, you and I."

"Oh, really? What are you talking about? Your commission on the apartment? Books I borrowed from you that I haven't returned? That forty dollars you loaned me last year?"

"I'm talking about emotions, Edward. I'm talking about friendship. I'm talking about love."

Love is such a small, shapeless word, so easy to throw around, but it takes up an enormous amount of space in a conversation. I heard my voice becoming choked with feeling or, as Edward had called it, sentimental weakness. I heard Edward's long exhausted sigh. What I didn't hear was Didier picking up the phone in the next room.

"I always hate to interrupt, Mr. Collins," he said. "But your dinner is ready."

ulterior motives

"You ruin everything for me," I told Didier. "You rush in at the worst moment and make endless complications for me."

"I did not ruin the dinner," he said.

That was true. The food was a smashing success, even if his announcement of it had caused Edward to hang up his phone without saying good-bye.

"So who is this you were proclaiming love to on the phone?"

"It was my friend Edward. You've heard me mention him a few times."

"Yes, of course. He is the center of your life. And if you're so in love with him, why aren't you fucking him? Oh, I forgot, you aren't fucking anyone. You have become celibate for reasons that no one knows, especially you."

"I have something for you," I said. I pulled out of my pocket the little bottle of scent Sean had made and passed it to him across the dining room table. He took it out of its velvet sack, uncapped it, and waved it back and forth under his thin nose. "It was made especially for you, Mr. Didier. I told the perfumer a few of my impressions, a couple of the very few incontrovertible facts I know about your life, and this is what he came up with."

He passed the bottle under his nose once again, this time with greater interest and concentration. "If that is so, Mr. Collins, then you told the perfumer I'm a dirty person. My soul is soiled."

"Your soul?"

"It's all here in this bottle. Well, thank you for the compliment. But why give me a bottle of expensive perfume if you don't want to keep me coming back, if you don't want to be my lover?"

"It's a gesture of friendship," I said. "Can't someone give someone else a present without an ulterior motive, especially one involving sex?"

"There are always ulterior motives, Mr. Collins, and they always involve sex. There are no other ulterior motives."

I thought about this for a minute. "I disagree, Mr. Didier. There are all kinds of other ulterior motives. There's money, for example. There's real estate, which I suppose is the same thing. There's chicken. In some cases, there's love."

He recapped the bottle and slid it into the tight front pocket of his pants. "Yes, love. There is that. But not for me, Mr. Collins, and probably not for you, either. Wait here while I get dessert."

intentions

I insisted that I drive Kumiko to the yoga class to avoid the ridiculous expense of her taking a taxi, hoping she might pass the savings on to me. I also wanted to make sure we arrived at the studio together, since I also dreaded the idea of walking into such a place alone for the very first time. We met at the appointed hour in the driveway, and she spent several minutes arranging her props in the backseat, making sure I understood the favor she was doing me by loaning me some of her Styrofoam bricks and canvas straps. As soon as I closed the door on the driver's side of my car, she placed a disapproving hand on my arm and gave me a stern look. "What's that smell?" she asked.

"Smell? I don't know what you're talking about."

"I smell something. Cologne, aftershave, strong soap, hair spray, shampoo, scented laundry detergent, mouthwash, shaving cream; I can't tell exactly what it is."

"I don't wear perfume," I said. "Nor do I wear aftershave or cologne, or hair spray. If you're accusing me of shaving, showering, or washing my clothes, I'm guilty."

"You're coming from hostility, William." She stared at me with a look of wounded indignation. "I can't bring you into the class if you're wearing perfume. It invades other people's space. Some have allergies. People go to look inward, into themselves, and if someone's there gobbling up all the oxygen in the room with their chemical odor, it's a distraction and potential health hazard."

"Speaking of invading someone's space," I said, "I'd rather we didn't discuss the smell of my body right now." I revved the engine, put the car into gear, and backed out of the drive at a reckless speed.

"I don't feel comfortable paying for someone who's wearing perfume. It's against Dotty's rules. She owns the school."

"Don't pay for me," I said. "As a matter of fact, I'll pay for you, unless that would make you feel compromised, too."

"Dotty prefers we pay for the entire semester in advance, so that's what I did. But I appreciate the offer. I want you to know I feel terrible about missing the last payment or two."

Since Kumiko had missed the last fifteen or twenty payments, I didn't see any point in responding.

The yoga studio turned out to be less than a mile away from the house, a short pleasant walk, especially if you were on the way to an exercise class. Upon entering the place, I felt a new wave of resentment about the perfume conversation; the sweet smell of incense was so strong, it would have been impossible to detect anyone's body odor, no matter how many layers of scent they were wearing. Kumiko greeted several other students with clasped hands, a shallow bow, and a word that was undoubtedly meant to be Sanskrit. A simple hello was obviously inadequate here.

In its previous incarnation, the studio had been an insurance agency, and there was something recognizably corporate about the gray wall-to-wall carpeting and the vertical blinds over the windows. One aspect of my spiritual quest I had not considered was that I'd have to stand in a room with Kumiko and expose my long arms and legs. I don't know why it bothered me so much, since I had no compunction about entering a stranger's house and exposing my entire body within seconds of meeting, but partial nudity always makes me feel more vulnerable than full disclosure.

Kumiko spread a mat on the floor, neatly lined up some of the props, and ordered me to settle in by pointing her finger.

There were a couple of dozen other people in the room, an admirable assortment of ages and sizes, most of them folding themselves into peculiar shapes, staring into the distance with a look of studied calm, or doing some form of deep, sonorous breathing. I tried my best to achieve invisibility by closing my eyes and contemplating my reasons for being there. The reasons were related somehow to spirituality, I remembered that much, but the specifics had already grown dim. I was haunted by Didier's comments on love, which I felt were accurate but insulting, and related to the spiritual question, although the connection was again foggy.

I was saved from further contemplation by the sound of a gong and the sudden appearance of Dotty at the front of the room. She was a fleshy woman with a crestfallen expression, a rumpled face, and a mane of gray hair. Not the specimen of youthful physical perfection I had been expecting, but that made me feel more comfortable in her presence and certain that she had something profound to offer. She lit a small cone of incense and seated herself, Buddha-style, on a round pillow.

"Before we begin," she said, "I have a couple of brief, important announcements to make." She had a weary, heartbroken voice, and she spoke in a stage whisper that had the curious effect of drawing you towards her, physically. "Next Monday, there will be no six-thirty class, but there will be an extra class on the following Monday at seven-forty-five. On the Tuesday of the first week, to accommodate the people who can't attend the Monday makeup on the second week, the usual five-forty-five class will be held at six-thirty instead. That means, obviously, that the seven o'clock class will be canceled on that first Tuesday. Unless I decide to cancel them both, plus a third. I was going to print out a new schedule, but I don't want to be forced to pass that expense on to you." She took a tissue out of a box beside her pillow and blew her nose. "Given the number of makeup classes I'm considering holding, I cannot offer anyone who has prepaid for the semester a refund. Now, a couple more quick things. On Wednesday, Shira will substitute for Chandra. That means, obviously, that Shira's regular class that morning will be canceled. The makeup Shira class will be the

Chandra class, so there will not be a refund for that cancellation. Please call first because I'm thinking about canceling all the classes at the end of the week due to a peace vigil I might be holding."

I couldn't tell if anyone was absorbing this information, but most of the other students were listening attentively and at least making a noble effort at appearing engaged. As far as I could tell, everything had been canceled and no money was being refunded. Dotty settled herself into the pillow, getting ready for what turned out to be round two of the announcements.

"I'm afraid I have some bad news. Mika Panjellini's hamstring workshop on the second Saturday of next month is going to be canceled again. She's back in the hospital." This announcement was greeted with a collective groan of sympathy that I joined in on so that Dotty wouldn't think I lacked empathy. "If you've already prepaid for the workshop, I can, if you insist, either refund you some portion of the four hundred dollars or apply a bigger portion of it to a full-day workshop on shoulders I might be thinking about offering next June. And by the way, Tony and I are trying to find a place in Truro for the month of August, so if anyone has a three- or four-bedroom house on the ocean they'd like to loan us for the month, see me after class. Now. Shall we begin? We have one newcomer today, and I hope you'll all welcome him. What's your name?"

"William Collins," I said.

"What is it again?"

"William Collins."

"I'll try to remember. It's easier if you've prepaid for the entire semester and I have it on record. Don't compare yourself with anyone else, just follow along as best you can and be in the posture you're in, not the posture you think you ought to be in because I'm telling you to get into it. Is that clear?"

"Absolutely." Her words were addressed to me, but she was making eye contact with everyone else, the more reliable paying customers, I suppose.

"Unfortunately, I won't be able to explain everything and slow down the entire class and change my whole plan for this evening simply to accommodate one person who's never practiced yoga before and is paying for the class strictly on a drop-in basis."

"I understand completely."

"I'd like the people who've prepaid for the entire semester to move up to the front of the room so I can give you more attention."

Once the bodies had been reshuffled, Dotty again struck a gong.

"Close your eyes and choose an intention," she advised. "Why are you here tonight? What is it you'd like to accomplish? Identify it. Commit to it. Breathe into it."

Whatever thoughts I'd had about enriching my spiritual life, or even, more fleetingly, about coming to terms with the question of love, had been pushed aside by Dotty's rambling monologue. The front wall of the room was covered in a mirror and when I opened my eyes, I saw Kumiko standing in the first row, glaring at me.

"Lift your shoulders," Dotty instructed, "and open them like a big, multicolored umbrella. Your head is a proud, strong flying saucer. Bend from the waist like a wide-brimmed hat. Think about a stained glass window and breathe into it. Do not forget your intention for the evening. Why did you come here? What is it you want to get out of this class?"

I looked back at Kumiko and mouthed, as clearly as I could, "I want the rent."

ʃo ʃo

"That was so, so unyogic of you," Kumiko said as we drove home. "You used me. You claimed you want spiritual fulfillment and you dragged money and commerce into the class. I don't know if I'll be able to go back."

"I'm sorry," I said. "But I've worked in advertising and real estate, and in neither field have I heard so much discussion of finances as I did in that class. I have a question for you."

"More demands. What more can I do for you, William? What?" She looked out the passenger side window, driven, apparently, to despair.

"It's a simple question. Your real name—what is it?"

Automatically, without realizing what she was doing, she said, "Esther."

I gloated silently the rest of the way home, and then, as we were driving up the hill to my house, I said, "It's a very pretty name. Esther."

uncluttering

"I don't understand why it's taking you so long to clear out the marine's condo," Deirdre said at our next staff meeting. "I thought she'd agreed to the plan for uncluttering it."

"She has," I said. "It's a complicated situation. I had to rent a storage space and a U-Haul. She had to get prepared. Then she threw out her back. Then she had some hip problems. Then there was an ankle issue." Even for Marty, the litany of health complaints seemed excessive. I'd begun to wonder if, despite her initial enthusiasm for selling, she was stalling for time. Her whole relocation plan struck me as ill conceived, perhaps more a product of Edward's coercion—fueled by his desire to make changes—than anything she'd thought through seriously. "The newscasters haven't lost interest, have they?"

"Not yet," Deirdre said. "They're fiercely tenacious. Like a couple of hideous leeches."

"I'm afraid *I've* lost interest." Mildred tossed the listing sheets onto the conference table. "This is the hottest real estate market in history, so if you can't unload this place, William, something is wrong. I resent the amount of time we spend at these meetings on this place. I have a psychotherapy practice I have to attend to. I have a family."

I was certain that everyone else in the office was tired of discussing Marty's condo, but fortunately, there was more general resentment of Mildred than of me, and the mysterious newfound respect of at least a couple of my coworkers.

"You seem to be implying," Deirdre said, "that you're the only person with a family here. And just how do you define family? As I understand it, William is deeply involved in family life."

"More than one family life, in fact." Exactly what Jack thought he meant by that was unclear to me, but I was touched by the fact that he was willing to rush to my defense.

"The apartment will be cleared out this weekend," I said. "You can arrange the newscaster showing for Sunday morning."

"Fine," Deirdre said. "I'll stagger the appointments so no one's killed during the walk-throughs. And you don't need to be there, William, if you have something else to do."

"I'll be spending quality time with my families," I said.

I ended up hiring a couple of teenaged brothers who lived down the hill from me to help move out Marty's excess belongings. Like most of the teenagers you saw these days, they were unaccountably tall and big boned, as if they were the products of genetic tampering. Their father was a plumber, a grim man who was significantly younger than me and always appeared to be covered by a thin coat of dust. He spoke exclusively in the form of complaints, apparently irritated by life's every detail beginning the minute he woke up. I liked listening to him complain, mostly because his disapproval of everything and everyone else made me feel he liked me. "They'll do it," he said when I asked him if his kids would like to make a few bucks. "They're lazy and unreliable, but if I tell them to do it, they will."

They showed up that Saturday morning, tall and droopy-eyed, as if they'd just been dragged out of bed. Although one was reportedly two years older than the other, they looked like twins and had identically taciturn personalities. The three of us crowded into the front seat of the van I'd rented, and as I drove them to Marty's, I tried to make conversation. It wasn't until I started nattering on about real estate that I realized I knew nothing about the subjects that might interest them—sports teams? cars?—and that the substance of my usual friendly small talk—the housing market primarily—was completely outside of their world. Fortunately, my existence didn't register on them. They communicated with each other in mumbled, sleepy insults, most of which came out as garbled variations on "Shut up" and "Fuck you."

Edward let us into Marty's apartment. He and I hadn't been in touch since Didier's unfortunate interruption of my phone call with him, and I was so happy and relieved to see him, I went to throw my arms around him. But halfway into the embrace, Charlaine rushed in from another room and growled at me with such conviction, I retreated.

"What are you doing here?" I asked. "And very nice sweater, by the way."

"I'm helping," he said. He snapped his fingers, and Charlaine sat at his feet. "Marty needed some prompting. Who are these?"

The brothers looked at each other, baffled by something as complicated as a request for an introduction.

"Danny and Jimmy. Or the other way around."

Edward looked at the sleepy brothers, assessed the situation, and calculated what needed to be done. "Which one of you is the brains of this outfit?" he croaked.

They shrugged in unison, but then the taller of the two pointed to his brother and said, "He is, I guess."

"In that case, he's in charge of everything. Danny? You give the orders about how to move stuff out of here. You figure out angles and doorways, all that."

Marty was observing in the background, suited up in her biking shorts and clutching one of her canes. "Any scratches, gouges, or chipped paint and you deal with *me,*" she said. "If you do it right, William will give you a bonus."

The brothers woke up immediately and seemed, at the same time, to relax. They'd been handed a job, they knew the system, their limits, and exactly what their roles were. Now they could get to work.

"We're a good team," Marty said. "You see how we handled that, William? We took charge and laid out the rules. Now everyone's happy. Don't Dither."

Deirdre had been right about clearing out the condo; the more the brothers carried down to the street, the better it looked, larger and, oddly enough, more inhabited. As I watched them work with Edward overseeing, I tried to figure out a way to apologize to him for the phone call and for lying about Didier and dinner. But every time I began, I realized there was more background information I'd have to give, more rationale for my behavior, more confessing about what I'd been doing for the past year. And Edward's hostile stares in my direction weren't inspiring me to open up.

While the brothers were lugging a red love seat down the stairs, I went into Marty's study to see how much was left to be hauled out. There were several boxes stacked in a corner, and I opened the top one. The carton was filled with parking tickets, some of them, based on a quick scan, recent. The second box contained a stack of papers from collection agencies, and the third was full of late payment notices and what appeared to be threatening letters from the IRS. I've always suspected that everyone has a drawer somewhere in his house filled with unpaid parking tickets, but three boxes? It was completely out of character for Marty, or Marty as she and Edward portrayed her. At least her financial ruin was neatly organized.

I was closing up the boxes when Marty came into the room, and we exchanged a glance. "Those stay," she said, in a firm voice.

"Right. I wasn't sure."

"Assume Nothing, William. It's one of my rules."

"I know that."

"I'm dealing with my finances the way I deal with my finances."

"Absolutely. You don't need to explain to me."

"Of course I don't need to, but I did. And remember, I explained it to *you*. No one else." She put down her cane and walked across the small room with no sign of pain or discomfort. "What time are the newscasters coming to look at the place tomorrow?"

"Early afternoon. I won't be here, but someone from the office who's been dealing with them will be. She's very professional. I think you'll hit it off."

That struck me as highly unlikely, but there was no harm in pretending. Marty nodded and held up a thick manila envelope. "Make sure they get this before we meet. It's my promotional material."

When Marty was at her most audacious and demanding, her eyes looked especially pleading, a complete contradiction. And now, as she was ordering me around, she looked almost as if she was about to weep. "I'm planning to do a hard sell of my company the minute they walk in the door. It'll help if they have this information."

"One piece of advice," I said.

She held up her hand. "No thanks. You don't think I got this far by listening to anyone else's advice, do you? I offer advice, that's what my career is all about."

I could hear Edward's hoarse voice coming from the next room, alternating between giving the brothers orders on what to move and how to move it and asking them questions about their school and their parents. I'd always found Edward's interest in other people one of his most endearing traits, even if he tried to mask it with constant disapproval.

"You do know," I said, "how much Edward is counting on this move?"

"What's that supposed to mean?"

"It's a question. I just want to make sure you and he aren't operating on completely different assumptions."

"Assume Nothing, remember? You're not Assuming Nothing, William, I can tell."

"He's already started looking at real estate in San Diego. For all I know, he might have made an offer on something. I would hate to see him disappointed."

"Really? Then look at your own behavior. You think I'm out to hurt him? He's doing combat duty every day. It's something I know about, OK?" She nodded toward a bulletin board where she'd tacked up photos of her deceased fiancé. "What *you* don't know is that he's been having panic attacks on the damn planes. He's on pills for it, but they're not helping much."

"Pills? What kind of pills?"

She shook her head in disappointment at being asked such an obvious question.

I couldn't stand the thought of Edward, rigid with panic, speeding through the subzero ether at thirty thousand feet. Despite the crowding on planes, air travel has always struck me as peculiarly lonely.

"He hasn't mentioned any of this to me," I said.

"Maybe that's because he figures he won't get any satisfaction from you. Maybe he doesn't feel safe being vulnerable in front of you. Call me as soon as you have the exact time of the showing tomorrow."

When the truck was loaded, one of the brothers stood patiently on the sidewalk waiting for me while the other listened to Edward, the nondriver, explaining the virtues of a standard transmission.

"Why don't you come with us?" I said to him, putting my arm around his shoulder. "We'll unload this stuff, unload Danny and Jimmy. I have to go to an inspection for Charlotte and Samuel, and then we can all go to a movie or take a walk. Something." Anything was what I meant.

"Sentimental weakness," he said. "Besides, I've got other plans."

inspection

On my advice, Charlotte and Sam had hired Ken O'Leary, a burly little man with a bad back, to do the inspection on their apartment. Of the many inspectors I'd worked with over the years, I liked Ken best. He was thorough and efficient and had an amusing way of being exasperated by almost everything he saw in a house or apartment. He would go into a state of despair and disbelief at

the condition of the roof, the dampness in a basement, the inadequacy of the smoke detectors, at the sheer stupidity of the owners
who had allowed a particular contractor into their house, almost as
if every flaw was a personal affront. He'd look at the circuit break-
ers and sigh and mop at his face with his hand as if he'd just been
told discouraging results of a major medical test. It made the potential buyers feel as if they weren't in this alone, as if someone
with professional authority was taking on the burden of their purchase. Best of all, in the end, he'd shrug, ask the buyer if she still
liked the place, and then recommend going forward. "I've seen a
lot worse," he'd say, a comment that everyone found comforting,
no matter how many sheets of paper he'd covered with serious
problems that needed immediate attention.

I was standing outside the building with Ken, waiting for
Charlotte and Sam to show up, weary from the move earlier that
morning, and frustrated by my own inability to talk to Edward.
Even if I didn't know exactly what it was I wanted to tell him.
Temperatures had soared once again to midsummer levels, but the
tree we were standing under was shedding its leaves in autumn
style, a weird juxtaposition of seasonal cues. When I commented
on this, he shrugged.

"End of the fucking world. Serves us right. Greedy bunch of
shits we all are."

Ken had been living in Boston for forty or more years, but he
still had the faint traces of a brogue and a lyrical way of describing
assorted structural problems and code violations. He was polite,
nearly erudite, when talking to potential house buyers, but with
me he tended to use graphic scatological images to describe everything.

He was wearing a weightlifter's leather belt around his waist,
an item that gave him excellent posture, squeezed his soft body
into an hourglass shape, and somehow helped him do his job. His

blue eyes lit up his whole face and made me think he'd probably been a successful womanizer at one time.

"How's your wife?" I asked.

"Worse, poor thing. But we're going forward. It makes you appreciate every moment you're given."

I'd been working with Ken for ten years now, and in that time, his wife, a mysterious woman who never appeared at any of the parties or real estate events Ken went to, had been in a courageous battle with an assortment of indeterminate ailments. Her condition was always described as "worse," and from what he said, he seemed to think her remaining days could be counted on one hand. Sometimes I wondered if this invalid status wasn't a family myth invented to add tension to their lives and to force them to wring joy and poignancy out of every minute.

I opened up my folder on Charlotte and Samuel. *Late again,* I jotted down. *Marital meltdown? S's affair discovered? Outdated word? Affair? Infidelity. Fcking around. Kate good in bed? Long legs. What to do about Edward. How to help. Looked espec cute and sad with longer hair. Natural blond? Wld like to have kissed him. Sentimental weakness? Is that so bad?*

Charlotte's silver car pulled up in front of the house, and she climbed out, alone and exasperated. "I'm going to kill him," she said, hitching her bag up to her shoulder. "I waited and waited for him to show up, and nothing. I hate when he works on Saturdays. I hope this doesn't throw off your whole day."

Ken was particularly smooth in the presence of women. "Not at all," he said. "I can tell you right now, very nice condo conversion. We don't know what we'll find on the inside, but it looks splendid from here."

We started in the basement of the house, and Ken was immediately peeved by a lack of proper lighting in the entryway.

"Code violation number one and we're not even in the door."

He looked crestfallen, as if the managers of the building had let him down personally with this oversight. I often wondered what it would be like to be attuned to every problem festering in the walls and under the counters and floors in a house, and to know, as he seemed to, the significance of every mysterious household odor. Like most people, I preferred to live in a state of hazy half awareness about such things.

He carried a leather briefcase with him, and from this he extracted vials to take samples of mildew he spotted crawling up a wall. He took out a towel and laid it on the floor so he could reach behind a bank of washing machines without getting his clothes soiled.

"Oh, oh, oh, I don't like what I'm feeling back here. Not good, not good at all."

I looked at Charlotte and shrugged.

Ken fearlessly tasted water from a small puddle he found in a corner of the floor to see if there was oil seeping out of the burner. I'd seen him do this before and it never failed to endear him to potential buyers who felt he was putting his own health at risk for the sake of their purchase. "I think we're safe here," he said. "But you see over there?" He shook his head and gave a doleful sigh. For a man of sixty, he had boyish hair that was always falling over his forehead. "That beam. Trouble of the very worst variety. Supports sixty percent of the weight of the house and it has about it the look of a weary traveler ready to collapse from exhaustion."

He took a small silver flashlight from his briefcase and crawled behind the hot water heater.

"I hope you're not too discouraged about all of this," I told Charlotte. "He finds every flaw, no matter how small, and then you have to choose which ones matter to you."

"Like dealing with a husband."

"I imagine so."

"How's your sex life?" she asked.

"It's nonexistent."

"That's the goal, apparently. Do you miss it?"

"No," I said. "Not at the moment, anyway. Although there's something about the ritual I miss. I can't put my finger on what it is. Do you miss drinking?"

"I feel lonely without it." We were standing in the dim light of the basement, and her hair was falling around her face in disarray, and it sounded like an especially heartfelt declaration. "Like right now, I am very certain I'd care a lot less about Samuel and where he might or might not be if I knew you and I were going to go out and have a drink after this. But we aren't, so once we go up-stairs, I have to look at this apartment in bright sunlight, and when we're done, you have to go home and clean."

We made our way out of the dark basement and up the stair-case into the increasingly warmer air of the floors above. The own-ers of the apartment had started packing and the odd corners of the rooms and bays of windows, the very things that gave the place so much charm, were exposed now, and it was easy to see how much of the space was decorative and unusable.

Charlotte wandered from room to room tugging at her lower lip.

"Buyer's remorse," I said. "Not that you've actually bought it yet. Everyone goes through it. You probably went through it with the house in Nahant."

"We didn't buy the house in Nahant," she said. "We inherited it from Samuel's uncle. My husband's always been lucky with money and real estate. He gives the illusion of being a successful businessman, but in many ways, he's just a lucky businessman."

She arranged herself on a window seat and looked out at the warm day. I was leaning against the mantelpiece. I opened up the folder and began scribbling again. *Lucky businessman. Same thing as successful? Hedges against loneliness: Sex, booze, furniture polish, Mr. Edward. Samuel's affair with Kate. More good luck?*

"Sometimes I resent him for being so lucky," Charlotte went on, "even though I benefit. I hope you're not writing down what I say."

"Just scribbling. Details I should bring up with you later."

"The counselor was always taking notes. I found it completely unnerving. It made me think my words mattered."

I put the papers back in the folder and closed it up. "I have a terrible memory for details."

"It's a plague, the memory problem. Either that or a blessing. And speaking of things I'd rather forget, I don't suppose you've read the books I gave you, cover to cover, word by word."

The mention of those books made me think about her manuscript, and I searched her face, trying to see if she was really asking me about that. I told her, truthfully, that I'd looked at them. "There was one that interested me. I think it had the word 'zowie' in the title."

She dismissed my comment with a wave of her hand. "No one reads them. They sell hundreds of thousands of copies, but no one reads them. Knowing that makes them much easier to write."

I heard Ken O'Leary let out a cry of discouragement from somewhere in the back of the apartment, and I excused myself and went into the kitchen. Despite his age and his back problems, he always managed to dismantle a room single-handedly and then put it back together. The stove and the refrigerator were in the middle of the floor, and he was standing against one wall in a puddle of rank black water. The refrigerator, he explained, had been leaking here, onto the hardwood floor, for, he was guessing, nearly ten years. There was serious rot, and probably leakage into the floor below. "And that's only the beginnings of the problems," he said. "It's a major shit storm here."

When I went back into the living room, Charlotte was still sitting on the window seat, gazing at the trees.

"A few minor glitches," I said. "Nothing to worry about."

She shrugged and turned, and I saw that she was crying. Within seconds, her head was in her hands, and she was sobbing. Although tears are a routine part of nearly every movie I've ever seen, they're a rarity in my everyday life, and I was horrified and probably a little thrilled by the sight of Charlotte bent over with her shoulders heaving. After a moment, the thrilling part wore off, and I stood there, watching her, feeling frozen and completely inept. "Is there something I can do?"

"No, absolutely not." She pulled a pack of tissues out of her shoulder bag and cleaned up her eyes and her face. "I used to cry a lot when I was younger, and then I went through a dry period of maybe twenty years when I never shed a tear. Now, everything gets to me. I'm sure it's hormonal or an indicator of my middle-aged psychological state." She blew her nose and stuffed the tissues back into her bag.

It was then that I saw the folder I'd been keeping on them sitting on the cushion beside her. She caught my gaze and laid her hands on it, her pretty fingernails more incongruous and pointless than ever.

"It's not news to me," she said. "It's really not news. I'd call it terribly harsh confirmation of nagging suspicions. More than suspicions. Let's face it, it's easier to pretend something isn't happening if you assume you're the only one who knows it is."

I moved the folder from the cushion and sat next to her. A few of the crasser phrases I'd jotted down raced through my mind as I took her hand and made an attempt at a mumbled apology.

"Well, it's not as if it's your fault, is it? Don't worry about that part. In some ways, I'm grateful. The lack of complete sentences and the awful abbreviations made it a little easier to take."

When Ken had completed his inspection, he came into the living room and presented his case. It was an old house. It had been badly maintained for many decades and then badly broken up into oddly shaped rooms with structural flaws. The electrical systems were insufficient and the windows would soon have to be replaced. There was the water damage and the rot.

"Would you advise buying it?" I asked him.

"Frankly," he said, "I wouldn't."

Usually, he was much more cautious and diplomatic in his pronouncements. I felt obliged to tell Charlotte that she should go over the papers carefully with Samuel and give it a day or two. There was still time to back out without losing too much money. There seemed to be no shortage of reasons for rethinking the purchase.

"What do I care about the electrical systems?" she asked. "I'm not buying electrical systems. I'm trying to buy a second act here. This will do as well as any other. It's the perfect place."

one big sudden something

The next day, I was sitting at my desk, answering calls and waiting for word on the reaction of Deirdre's clients to Marty's apartment. If one of them actually made an offer, it would be a relief. If Edward's apartment was going to sell, then it was better for everyone, Edward especially, if Marty's sold quickly.

Most of the people who call in on Sundays to make inquiries were easy targets: young two-income couples whose lives and relationships were still upbeat enough to make them completely uninteresting. Generally speaking, they were first-time buyers who had good jobs, no aversion to debt, and undeveloped tastes. They liked

gadgetry. They wanted steam showers, Jacuzzis, and any other feature that wasted water. If you caught them at the right moment,
you could make a tidy commission with minimal effort. Despite
that, I didn't much care for working with them. They arrived
loaded with facts and figures they'd gleaned from Internet searches
and took offense at questions about their personal lives.

But after what had happened with Charlotte the day before, I
figured I should do my best to avoid all personal questions for the
time being.

Avoid inquiries, I wrote on a notepad. *Young couples with money,
no issues, no affairs. Avoid taking notes.*

Shortly after noon, I got a call from my mother. She sounded
uncharacteristically glum and opened up the conversation with an
accusation. "You're depressed," she said.

"You're attributing your mood to me. That's called projection,
dear."

"And that's called condescension, *dear.* I happen to know very
well what I'm doing, William. I'm calling you with sad news, and
I want to hear you deny you're depressed before I deliver it. Is
that so terrible? Is it going to require years of psychotherapy to
expunge?"

"Funny," I said, "I don't remember hearing you use the word
'expunge' before. Is it one of Jerry's?"

"We do vocabulary together every few days. It's supposed to
prevent Alzheimer's."

"I'll have to invest in a dictionary. What's the sad news?"

"Death, of course."

"Could you narrow it down a little?"

"Please don't get sarcastic on me. Even when you live in a
mortuary like I do, it isn't pleasant to report on someone's death.
What did you have for supper last night?"

"I hope that question is an irrelevant non sequitur," I said. "A friend made me a beef stew with a French name. It took hours. If you like, I can get the recipe from him."

"You might as well get me Rollerblades. That whole cooking thing seems so antediluvian to me. I'm surprised anyone bothers with kitchens anymore. But I'm pleased to hear you've got someone cooking for you. That's progress."

"You could call it that." *Expunge, antediluvian,* I wrote on my notepad. *Progress?* "Can we get to the obituary now?"

"If you insist. I had a call this morning at six A.M. that would have woken up any person with normal sleep patterns. It was Rose Forrest's brother. He'd miscalculated the time change and didn't seem to understand it once I explained it. Anyway, that's the news."

"Rose?" I said. "But I saw her so recently. What happened?"

"The brother was vague. She had everything wrong with her, you yourself said she looked bad. In the end, I gather it was something massive. One big sudden something."

I didn't know what to say to my mother. In theory, Rose was a relatively minor character in my life whose relevance had ended more than a decade earlier with my father's death. It occurred to me then that she'd never sent me the boxes of unused gifts she'd given to my father. One more bit of unfinished business in her life. The sad thought of those boxes tossed into a Dumpster somewhere struck me like a blow.

"The brother let slip that she was eighty-five, a big shock. Older than me." She paused, and as was so often the case these days, I heard the soft typing of a computer keyboard. Even my elderly mother had become a multitasker. When the typing stopped, she said, "I hope you're not too upset about Rose."

"It isn't as if I knew her all that well," I said.

There was an empty silence on the other end of the line. She seemed to be waiting, with patience, for me to say something else.

"I knew her a little bit," I said. "Beyond her working for Dad. I had lunch with her a few times after he died. Infrequently but regularly."

"I know that."

"Oh?"

"I'm the one who suggested she call you when she was in Boston. Your father's death was a loss for her, too, and she had no way to mourn it, no way to acknowledge to anyone that it was a loss. I thought you could handle it. After all, I could, so it didn't seem like such a burden for you. You're so much less judgmental than your brother."

Part of the pleasure of my meetings with Rose had been their secrecy, and the way they'd made me feel I had a special relationship with my father, albeit an imaginary one. Perhaps I should have been relieved to learn my mother had been aware of it, but instead it made me feel irrelevant and strangely betrayed by her. "So she knew that you knew . . ." I couldn't force myself to make it more specific than that.

"I have no idea. We were all civil, that's the important part. It helps everyone maintain their dignity. But it's all in the past. I was never truly miserable, and now I'm happy."

"With Jerry?"

"With Jerry."

"I suppose next you'll be sending him to see me."

"Hardly. He lives too far away. Anyway, he and I have decided to never meet. It's much more romantic this way."

"Never?"

"It's imperfect, it's incomplete, but I have the illusion of having a companion, of being in love, and of being loved. And in many ways, it feels more real than the last few decades I was married to your father. Why spoil it by meeting? Your generation wants everything, that's your problem. It's all right to want everything and even, for a short while, to look for it. But at a certain point, you have to take stock of what you've got. You're not young, you know. Even if we weren't all about to be blown up, you still wouldn't have forever."

mutual interest

I stayed at the office until Deirdre put in an appearance after showing Marty's condo. It was nearly five o'clock by the time she arrived. I let her settle in, make an angry phone call to her beloved husband, and check her e-mail. Finally, I sat on the corner of her desk and casually asked about the showing.

She gave me a piercing look, as if she was about to scold me, and then, apparently having changed her mind, relaxed her mouth and said, "I'll grant you this, the condo looked better. The dog was there as part of the show—more on that later—as well as some little friend who is apparently connected to you as well. He, I might add, did his best to keep things on track and prevented the dog from eating anyone. I brought the husband over first and he liked it. Later in the afternoon, I went back with the wife. I fully expect one or the other, possibly both, will be making an offer."

The confusing part was that Deirdre's tone was so sour.

"It all went well," I said. "There's going to be an offer. Why do I sense there's a problem?"

Deirdre lifted an immense padded envelope out of her shoulder bag and tossed it onto her desk. Marty's promotional material.

"This is the problem. Not once, but twice, I had to sit in the living room and listen to an hour-long pitch your friend gave about herself and her business and the horrible *dog* and how she would be a perfect subject for a profile on one of their broadcasts.

They were both fascinated, and I suppose there'll be an in-court battle over who gets credit for discovering her. One more marvelous contribution to our culture."

I'd assumed that allowing Marty to discuss her business had been a simple matter of courtesy. It hadn't occurred to me that someone might go for the idea. "I suppose that's more good news," I said. "If they liked her and the condo, there are two feathers in your cap."

"I feel exploited," Deirdre said. "And frankly, I'm much more comfortable being the exploiter. Hopefully, we'll have these two in a bidding war within the next twenty-four hours and some cash will change hands."

esther

Esther was proving to be a more reliable tenant than Kumiko ever had been. Since my spiritual awakening in the yoga class and her inadvertent revelation of her real name, she'd paid me close to a thousand dollars in cash. It was a small dent in the total amount she owed by now, but it was a dent.

As she was turning over a money envelope to me one morning, she said, "I think it helped that you stopped doing my ironing. It makes you seem more like an authority figure and less like staff."

"I'm glad you feel that way. I have an old iron I'm not using anymore, and I'd be happy to give it to you, if you'd like. Permanent loan. It's excellent quality."

"Thanks, but I've hired someone else."

I opened up the envelope in front of her and counted out five crisp $100 bills. It was a big relief to get these payments, but every time I made a deposit, I was reminded of the fact that she could have been paying me all along and for some reason had chosen not to. "I think I'm going to have to charge you a little extra for the use of the garage," I said. "What do you think would be a fair price?"

"You're the one in real estate, William. You tell me."

"Let me think it over. It won't be much."

She sighed and started to head back to her apartment, but then changed her mind. "I'm not a bad person, you know."

"I didn't say you were."

"When you let me move in without checking references or asking about finances, I figured you didn't really need the money. It's not like my trust fund is all that big, and I resent turning over a chunk of it every month to someone who's so casual about the whole business."

"I'll try to be more stern and professional."

"Thank you. And just so you know, you really don't have a clue about how to iron pleated skirts. I can show you, if you like."

"I appreciate that. But it's probably a skill I can live without."

an offer

A week later, the male half of the newscaster couple made an offer on Marty's apartment. It was $25,000 below what she wanted, but she told me she had no intention of turning it down. The newscaster had already made an appointment to spend two days with her the following week to get footage of her for a ten-minute profile to be broadcast on their show, *New England Innovators*. If the offer had been fifty thousand under asking, she still would have taken it, just to stay in his good graces. She mentioned something about Going for the Better Good, another slogan from her seminar, and then explained that she had to get off the phone; she had an appointment for a manicure, a piece of news I found so shocking, I hung up without saying good-bye.

Now I had three closings pending, not spectacular business given the real estate boom, but good enough to satisfy Gina that I was making a serious effort and enough to make me feel the irresistible pull of momentum. It was good news for Edward as well, and since I finally had something positive to tell him, something I thought he'd enjoy hearing, I called his cell phone.

"I'm in Seattle," he said. "It's early, William. I had a late night."

"With your pilot, I assume."

"Assume Nothing."

It was the first time I'd heard him use one of Marty's slogans, and because he'd uttered it in a brittle tone, laced with disapproval eerily similar to Marty's, I recoiled. I passed along the good news about the condo.

"You shouldn't have brought newscasters over there," he said. "You know what a publicity hound she is. I'm glad she accepted the offer, but we'll see where it goes."

His voice was more groggy and raspier than usual. I shouldn't have made any assumptions about the pilot; he could have been up pacing the floor of his hotel room in a sweaty panic attack. "When I was over at Marty's the other day, she told me you've been having some problems."

"Oh really? If I wanted to discuss them with you, William, I would have told you myself."

"Now that I know, let's talk about it."

"It doesn't help me to talk about it. I'm taking some medication, but I hate the way it makes me feel. My schedule for the next few weeks is horrible. The weather across the country is horrible.

The airline is letting people go and the rest of us have to take up the slack and the workload is horrible. I have a horrible head cold. I'm going to hang up now. I'll call you when I get back to town, all right?"

He didn't wait for me to answer.

the neighbors

What I was enjoying most about *The Mandarins* was everything that the author of the introduction had derided. The hypnotically leisurely pace, the extravagant set pieces, the abundance. Reading it felt like a luxurious reminder of all the free time I had, now that I'd given up the computer. Even on nights when I didn't see Didier, I'd come home and prepare a meal for myself, forgo the lure of the vacuum cleaner and the ironing board, and sink into the rich, chatty world of the book, a world where DVDs and laptop computers and cellular telephones did not exist. The sprawling, untidy nature of the novel seemed to be connected directly to its extraordinary intelligence. You couldn't imagine any of these characters scouring their sinks with carbonated beverages or caring too much about folding their towels.

I was stretched out on my chaise longue one night, reading more and more slowly, when Charlotte called to talk about the closing for their condo.

"What are you doing this evening?" she asked.

"Reading," I said. "Something I've been trying to get to for years."

"No doubt it's about management style for the new millennium. Don't answer that. I'm just calling to see if we can postpone the date of the closing. Not for any of the reasons you might guess. It's for a reason you probably wouldn't guess." She paused, as if waiting for me to suggest something. After a moment she said, "You're no fun, William. It's our anniversary. Samuel suggested we go away for a few days."

"Very nice," I said. "A surprising development. A positive development."

"I thought so, too. *He* wants to go to Bermuda, but I suggested something a little closer to home. I think it will be a happy anniversary."

It was clear she wanted me to believe this, even if she didn't herself. After assuring her that the date could be changed without much trouble, I began to think about her manuscript. I still hadn't decided the best way to get it back to her. Simply giving it to her and explaining myself would have been the most honest way to handle it, but I couldn't imagine the mechanics and discussion involved. I wasn't a good liar, and I knew I'd feel compelled to qualify my response to the stories, and after all the other trouble I'd caused her, that plan of action struck me as heartless.

"What do you do with a big rambling house like that when you go away?" I asked. "I suppose you have to get a house-sitter."

"You're forgetting," she said. "There's no crime out here, discounting domestic violence and the occasional murder in a family of good standing. It's one of the reasons the real estate prices are so high. No one locks their doors. I mean, thank God, because there are about eight doors on this house, and I couldn't stand having to wander around making sure each one was closed, never mind locked. When the neighbors go away, we look in on their houses. What terrifies me is that I'm going to walk in on neighbors A and B doing something inappropriate in the house of neighbor C, or worse still, in my own house."

Unlocked doors and people wandering in and out at all hours. It seemed like a solution to the manuscript problem, and although it wasn't beach weather, it might be nice to drive to Nahant one more time.

mrs. didier

Marty had sent out several bulk e-mails announcing the date and time the profile of her would be broadcast on *New England Innovators*. Her e-mails were half self-promotion and half unconvincing hype about the show itself. The latter reached a potential audience of two million people, she claimed, which I took to mean that if everyone in the Greater Boston area with a television set tuned in to watch her, the audience would be in the neighborhood of two million.

I was excited about seeing Marty on TV. There's something inexplicably thrilling about the sight of someone you know on a television screen, even if you don't have much respect for the program, even if you barely know the person in question. I invited Didier to watch it with me, but he complained about the quality of my set and suggested that I come to his apartment instead. "I have a big flat screen with stereo speakers I bought to keep my mother amused. She hates American TV, but she finds it easier to take than America itself."

"She's still here?" I asked skeptically.

"She is here, Mr. Collins. I told you she was here but you never believe anything I say. You two can have a big conversation in French."

I was amazed by the invitation to Didier's apartment. In all the time I'd known him, he'd come up with a series of increasingly elaborate excuses to avoid inviting me over, or even to giving me his address. Now he was simply asking me to visit because he had a better television set, as if this were the kind of thing he did all the time. There was something so radical about the invitation and about the casual way he'd made it, that I sensed it didn't signal a new beginning to our relationship, but was more likely an ending of some kind. I dressed for the occasion in an Italian suit that had cost me close to a thousand dollars, even at the consignment shop.

Didier's building turned out to be a couple of short blocks from Edward's. It was an old factory that had been converted into famously expensive apartments. Whenever I'd tried to imagine where Didier lived, I'd pictured a small studio with heavy drapes and dusty antique carpets, ashtrays heaped with cigarette butts, and the smell of sex clinging to the upholstery. I was shocked when Didier opened the door to his apartment and I saw behind him a wall of windows blazing with the lights from nearby buildings and reflected up from the street, five stories below. He gave me a series of right-cheek, left-cheek pecks and welcomed me in. "What is this outfit, Mr. Collins? You've come directly from work?"

"A funeral," I said quickly. "I didn't have time to change."

"My mother will be impressed. She loves death."

Although I generally prefer small, even cramped rooms, I was dazzled by the bright expansiveness of his place, the high ceilings, and polished walnut floor. Far from being cluttered and dusty, it was a masterpiece of midcentury understatement and was so crisp and expensive, I thought I must be imagining the whole scene. I complimented him on his taste and his tidiness, although it seemed highly unlikely he'd done either the decorating or the cleaning.

"Yes, Mr. Collins, I know. You thought I lived in a terrible little hovel with no windows and cigarettes and perfume that smells like animals. You thought I was ashamed of how terrible it was. But instead, I was maybe a little ashamed that it was so nice."

He led me into the living room, and there, sitting on a classic piece of Le Corbusier leather and metal, was a golden-haired woman he introduced, unapologetically, as "Mrs. Didier."

"*C'est M. Collins,*" he said. *"Le type que je t'ai décrit."*

I understood enough to get that at least I'd been mentioned to the matriarch.

"*Enchanté, madame,*" I said and shook her hand. I then added the one sentence in French I can speak with a semblance of fluency: *"Je m'excuse de mon français. C'est très, très limité."*

"Ah, well," she said, "if your English, Italian, Spanish, German, or Flemish is better, we can try any of those."

Mrs. Didier was neither thin nor fat, but appeared to have a solid, sensible body, encased tonight in a very smart woolen suit that was probably an ancient, well-preserved Chanel. At least I didn't feel overdressed. She was smoking a cigarette with elegant nonchalance. Her hands were mottled with age spots, the skin loose and veiny, but her face was a splendid example of careful renovation. Her forehead and eyes were completely unlined, and her neck was taut. All of it was unmistakably artificial, but her appearance didn't reach the level of horror movie excess that often went with this territory. As one tends to do in these situations, I began admiring, not the bone structure and features of the face itself, but the skill of the surgeon who had reconstructed it, and Mrs. Didier's wisdom in seeking him out.

"I wasn't expecting such a beautiful woman," I said.

This comment inspired her to slowly grind out her cigarette, slip on a pair of black, heavy-framed glasses, and make a more thorough examination of me. Finding me as uninteresting as she'd suspected, she took off the glasses and shrugged. "I like your socks," she said.

"I'm coming from a funeral."

"You can't be all bad then, can you?"

Sitting on a leather sofa and taking in the surprising surroundings, I had to conclude that Didier had been more truthful with me about his work life than I'd assumed, and that the confusing stories about the trips abroad and his employment in the family business had very likely been accurate. He and Mrs. Didier chatted in what sounded to my untrained ears like formal French while I tried to piece together why seeing him like this, as a three-dimensional human being with actual family on the furniture and actual artwork on the walls, made him more interesting but less attractive to me.

At nine o'clock, Didier switched on the television set, and after a series of mishaps with the remote control, the big, impressively flat screen was filled with an image of Deirdre's divorcing newscasters, joking and smiling at each other as if they were the happiest couple in the world. "These are boring people," Didier said.

"I suspect you're right. I think you'll find Marty more interesting."

There was a profile of a shopkeeper in Rhode Island who sold nothing but magnets, and then a feature on a swarthy little glassblower in northern Maine. There was a long, tiresome series of advertisements for local businesses, and finally, the newscaster husband said, "Now let's meet a New England entrepreneur who's giving anger and hostility a good name."

"I didn't know it had a bad name," the wife joked. "Around our house anyway."

Marty appeared on-screen, microphone in hand, pacing back and forth across a stage, shouting at a roomful of people who sat cowering on folding chairs. The camera pulled back to show Charlaine poised at a corner of the stage, baring her teeth at the intimidated audience.

"This is your friend?" Mrs. Didier asked.

"Yes," I said. "That's definitely Marty."

"He is brutal."

"She's a woman," I said.

Mrs. Didier laughed at the suggestion and put on her glasses again. "This country," she said dismissively. *"Je comprends maintenant, chéri, pourquoi tu ne peux pas trouver une femme."*

She understood why her son hadn't been able to find a woman? Or had she meant a wife? Either translation raised a number of fascinating questions that it was impossible to ask at that moment. I looked over at Didier, but he was engulfed in cigarette smoke, grinning one of his enigmatic grins.

There were shots of Marty stomping and screaming, riling up a group of people by pumping her fists into the air, eliciting bestial cries of outrage and fury. Then, in a stunning slam cut, she was shown curled up on her living room sofa, professionally made up, dressed in a pink sweater, looking soft and stereotypically feminine. "It's not about being angry," she said softly. "It's about being active."

The next image was of one of Marty's clients, huddled in a corner of a room weeping into a napkin while Marty screamed at her; and the newscaster (Tom, they were all named Tom) said, in a cheerful voiceover, "But if this isn't anger and hostility, it sure looks like it. And maybe that's exactly what everyone wants and needs in this time of terror alerts and posttraumatic stress—a little righteous aggression."

"It's not about fear," Marty said, sitting on her sofa, a few of the stuffed dolls from her bedroom visible on the windowsill behind her. "It's about faith in yourself."

The piece rambled on in this incoherent fashion, mixing Marty's kind, gentle words with contradictory images, and shots of her jogging along leaf-strewn paths with faithful Charlaine at her heels. Next came the testimonials from people who'd been in her training seminars, including one woman who claimed, through a shower of

tears, that she'd lived most of her life as a recluse after an unspecified violent attack in her youth, and that upon finishing Marty's
training she'd begun to "live her dream" and had opened up a
chain of successful restaurants. There was a lot of sobbing, and
many references to September 11 as either the motivating factor in
taking the seminar or justification for having done so.

Didier and his mother seemed to find the entire ten minutes
hysterically funny, as they commented on the clothes of the people
on-screen, the simple-minded attitudes, and mostly, Marty's stunning audacity. But by the time the profile ended, I think even they
were impressed with Marty's self-confidence. The whole piece finished with a brief shot of one of Marty's previously traumatized
clients walking peacefully through a park, holding the hand of her
large husband, as if, in the end, this simple act of intimacy was
what required the most courage and determination. As if this ultimately was the goal.

"That is a sweet story," the newscaster wife said to her husband.
"I guess the world needs more rage."

"Please," the husband joked. "Just not in the kitchen."

As soon as Didier clicked off the television, Mrs. Didier pushed
herself out of her chair and excused herself. *"Après ça, il faut que je
mange.* Interesting to have met you."

She walked carefully down a long hallway and disappeared
around a corner.

"She's an imposing figure, Mr. Didier. You might say intimidating."

"You might if you were her son. So, now you know everything
about me, Mr. Collins. You can see I've had nothing to hide all
along."

"I'm stunned. But even if you had nothing to hide, you hid it
well."

"I do my best. I'm going back to Brussels with her the end of next week, Mr. Collins. I won't be seeing you for a while. You will have to find someone else to not fuck."

"I'll try. It's not so easy, you know, Mr. Didier. There is one thing I have to ask you about. The wife. I didn't know you were looking for one."

"Oh, yes. But not looking very hard. It's mostly to please my mother." He settled himself back on the sofa in a brief, naughty sprawl, as if, once again, he were in control of our relationship. "Don't be so surprised."

"So she doesn't know—"

"She knows everything. What do you think? Appearances matter in my family, and it would be nice to produce an heir. I am the only child."

An heir. I'd never heard anything quite so odd as the prospect of Didier being a father.

He led me to the front door of the apartment. From somewhere down the hallway, I could hear the sound of a garbage disposal, grinding up food in the sink. I loved the idea of Didier's elegant mother in her Chanel suit stuffing leftovers down the drain.

Before opening the door, Didier reached up and patted my face. "You didn't tell me who died, Mr. Collins."

"Ah. No one at all. I had a feeling we might not be seeing each other for a while. I wanted to look nice for you, Mr. Didier, to leave you with a good impression, I suppose."

"Yes," he said. "I knew that. I just wanted to make you admit it." He ushered me out the door, and I heard it lock behind me.

midnight call

My phone rang at midnight. I was sitting on the chaise longue in my bedroom, reading the final pages of *The Mandarins* with regret. Since I'd turned forty, no one ever called me after 11 P.M., so I was expecting more bad news of the death and destruction variety.

It was Marty. As a testament to the power of mass media, I felt a surge of gratitude that this TV personality was actually phoning me.

"You were incredibly charismatic," I said, "and the footage of the seminars was riveting. On top of it all, you looked beautiful."

I could practically hear her shaking her head in disappointment. "Let me tell you something, William. I don't really give a shit if I look beautiful or like a rabid dog. One of the key lessons in my seminar is You Don't Look at Your Own Looks. So why care? What I do care about is that I've been tracking my Web site, and in the past two hours alone, I've had sixty hits. They're broadcasting the segment again this weekend as part of a best-of-the-week wrap-up. This is major."

"It . . . sounds it. And after seeing the show, I'm not surprised. You've earned it."

But even this comment, which I'd meant sincerely, raised her suspicion. "I appreciate the praise, but I don't need the condescension, especially not tonight. I'm calling to tell you that I'm pulling out of the sale." She waited for me to say something, but not wanting to Step in Her Shit, I Kept My Mouth Shut. "I could call Tom myself, obviously, but I figured the professional thing to do is to let you handle it."

"What about San Diego?"

"I'm not walking away from a business opportunity like this. You can't buy this kind of publicity."

"And Edward? He's been counting on this for months."

"Let me tell you something, William," she said. "The only way to help someone else is to ignore them completely and take care of your own needs. Think about it. So the best thing I can do for Edward is to take care of me. But someone needs to take care of Edward, and you're the most likely candidate. That's the real reason I'm calling you this late. He's in trouble."

"What kind of trouble?" I looked out the big picture window of my bedroom at the lights of the Boston skyline. Planes were circling the city, even at this late hour. "What are you talking about?"

"He's stuck in Montreal. He called me a couple hours ago to tell me." ·

"Stuck? How can he be stuck?"

"He was flying in from Chicago almost a week ago, and he had a major panic attack. Now he won't get back on a plane. I guess you didn't notice he'd dropped out of sight. The airline is threatening him with a lawsuit or some bullshit. I told him to get on a bus, but he's too freaked out to do that."

"Does he know you're not moving?"

"We discussed it. OK, William, he thinks I'm abandoning him. I suppose I am in some ways, but I can't help it. I'm Not About You."

"No."

"He also feels abandoned by you, which is a lot more to the point. He can't get on a plane anymore, he can't work, his apartment's almost sold so he's got nowhere to live. He's talking about buying a place up in Canada and staying there. Something about wanting to leave the country. If you were a real friend, you'd go get him."

"Of course I'll go," I said. "What's his phone number?"

"I have no idea."

He'd refused to tell Marty where he was staying. He'd left the hotel where the airline had put him up, and he'd thrown away his cell phone so their lawyers couldn't reach him.

"My God," I said. "It sounds like a full-scale nervous breakdown. What about the pilot, does anyone know how to get in touch with him?"

"Oh grow up, William. There's no goddamned pilot. That was to make you jealous. Just go up there and start looking."

"That doesn't sound very productive. The closing on his apartment's in a few days. Maybe his lawyer knows how to get in touch with him."

"When in doubt, call a lawyer. I have to get off. My Web site is officially going through the roof."

Closing

Because Edward was so small of stature, because he wore a little blue uniform to work, because he sought out the company of unavailable married men, because his job involved aimless travel in the air above the surface of the world, I tended to think of him as childlike and inconsistent, simultaneously irresponsible and self-sufficient. But the truth was, he was one of the most consistent and reliable people I knew, and infinitely more adult than me or any of my friends. He had a lot of silly affectations—the refusal to get a driver's license, the long, pointless delay in getting a computer—but the more I thought about those, the more they seemed like examples of his steadfast certainty of who he was and what he wanted from life. I couldn't bear the thought of him undone by panic, wandering aimlessly around the cold streets of Montreal.

I'd given him the name of the lawyer he was using for his end of the sale, and I called several times, leaving ominous, vaguely worded messages.

"We're closing on his apartment in two days," I said when the lawyer finally called me back. "I've been having a little trouble getting in touch with Edward, and I wanted to make sure everything's set."

"I've got it all written down," he said. He was an older man, and he had a deep, gruff voice I'd known Edward would find appealing. Unfortunately, he also had the lawyerly skill of never saying more than he intended to say.

"So Edward's planning to be there?"

"I'm handling the closing. He's given me power of attorney in this, and he's chosen not to be there."

He refused to say more than that, and since I thought it might be best to hold my tongue as well, the conversation died for a surprisingly long time.

"I know he's in Montreal," I finally said. "I don't suppose you'd be willing to tell me exactly where or how I can get in touch with him."

"I'd be happy to give him a message."

"That would be something. Tell him I'm trying to reach him. Tell him to call me."

I still had hope that Sylvia would come to her senses and cancel her plans at the last second, but even if she did, it wouldn't solve anything. And she wasn't likely to; she was so enthusiastic about buying the condo, it was exhausting.

"You know, I'm ashamed of that sex book I wrote, William," she told me one afternoon. "I'm not ashamed of my behavior or my success, of course, but the whole topic seems so dated to me now. Sex. Does anyone care anymore? I doubt it. It's all so pretragedy, twentieth century, isn't it? You were very prescient to stay above the bodily fray. It's all about real estate now. Real estate is the sex of the new millennium."

The closing on Edward's condo was held at his lawyer's office in an ancient brick building behind the Cambridge courthouse. It was a small firm, and the lawyers who worked there handled the closing with bored efficiency, although in this case, they were late. Sylvia and I sat around the conference table, drinking coffee and waiting for everyone else to show up. She looked as exuberant and ridiculous as ever, in her mod clothes and her big turquoise eyeglasses.

"You're giving me a very peculiar look, William," she said. "Admiring, or dismissive? Clue me in."

"Neither," I said. "I was just thinking that I never imagined I'd be at an actual closing with you. I'd been expecting our old relationship to go on for years. I'll miss it."

"I probably will, too. But I'm so self-absorbed I won't realize it. I could come in and pretend to be apartment shopping from time to time."

"I wouldn't object to that," I said. "But it wouldn't be the same."

"It might be better, for all we know. I'm sorry about little Edward. I don't suppose it's serious, do you?"

"I suppose it is. I just have no idea how to find him. Montreal isn't exactly a small town."

Sylvia brightened at the mention of the city, obviously thinking back to one of the ecstatic, outdated adventures she'd written about. But then she sighed and said, "I could never live anywhere but here now. My contempt is what inspires me. It's just a matter of getting his address," she said. "Then you can go and claim your bride."

There was always a surprise at a closing, an unexpected problem with the deed, a revelation about a roof leak, or an upcoming assessment that no one had mentioned; but in my experience, the problems never changed the outcome. No one had ever backed out of a deal at that point, no matter what came up. Even when it seemed as if it might be better to stall, the momentum, combined with weariness, its counterpart, always carried the day. I imagined there must be an equivalent in marriage, at least for some people, an eleventh-hour revelation or realization, something that changes everything except the outcome.

There was a problem with the condominium fees in Edward's building and a bookkeeping error on the part of Edward's lawyer's firm. This resulted in a series of sharp exchanges between attorneys while Sylvia and I discussed the weather and the dire predictions of an early-season snowstorm that night.

In the end, of course, it was resolved. All of the papers were signed and there was a series of handshakes. "Now what?" Sylvia asked.

"That's it," Edward's lawyer said. "We're done."

"You just have to move in and live there," I told her.

"Oh, dear," she sighed. "The hard part. I suppose it's now or never."

Outside, the sky had turned steely, and the light was fading quickly. Sylvia wasn't dressed for the weather, but then, in all the time I'd known her, she'd never dressed for a season or made any concessions to climate. Despite her extreme slenderness, she appeared to be completely inured to temperature. I was wearing my expensive, funereal suit, and a topcoat that was short on me but was made of such high-quality cashmere, I'd taken the consignment owner's advice to buy it anyway. And still, the cold air had penetrated the layers of expensive wool and entered my bones. Snow was looming, gathering in the flat gray sky. You could feel it pressing down on the low curtain of clouds.

"I want to take you out to dinner," Sylvia said. "It's the least I can do. I'm quite moved by the whole process although I'm so emotionally detached, you'd never guess it. There's a new Portuguese fish place around the corner that's notoriously horrible. I've been dying to try it."

"You're generous," I told her, "but I have to drive out to Nahant. I have to return something to a friend."

"Oh, William," she said. She stuck her glasses on her face and gazed at me through the thick lenses. "I'm feeling so alone right now. I bought a small apartment that I'll live in solo for the rest of my life. I mean, thank God, but even so. Can't you change your plans for me, *carino?*"

"It's a small window of opportunity. I'm sorry."

She thought this over for a minute. "I think I'll slip back into that office and try to talk your friend's lawyer into going out with me. He's very handsome, isn't he? And I'm sure he's seducible, don't you think? A well-preserved seventy, which should make the seduction easier."

"I don't know. I suspect he's married."

"Irrelevant, of course. Either way, he'll be flattered by the attention."

We said our good-byes and I wished her luck with the lawyer.

"What's his name again?" she asked.

"Kurt."

"Kurt. I'm sure I must have had one of those but I can't recall where or when."

As I was walking up the street, I heard her call my name and turned to see her dashing toward me. "I almost forgot," she said. She reached into her overflowing bag and pulled out an envelope bulging with papers related to the signing. From this, she extracted the corner of an envelope with a Montreal address written on it in her handwriting.

"I assume it's your friend Edward's address. The lawyer had it written down on the folder, under Edward's name, and he stuck the check right next to it. I thought it might be of some use to you."

ſnowſtorm

It started to snow while I was stopped in traffic on the Tobin Bridge. It was much too early for winter to begin, but in that moment when I was suspended over the river, high above the green water with a view of the harbor and airport in the distance, the whole dark, raw season blew in off the ocean. My car rocked in the wind. I'd planned my exit from the city poorly; it was the worst hour for traffic, a Friday, and there was now the added complication of the weather. Charlotte's manuscript sat in a white paper bag on the floor of the passenger side of the car, and I glanced at it occasionally, feeling as if at any moment I was going to be pulled over by a cop and arrested for carrying around something that didn't belong to me—specifically, Charlotte O'Malley's yearnings.

As I looked ahead to the line of stalled traffic, I felt a little catch in my stomach, a flicker of panic and paranoia. What if the bridge collapsed right now? What if the truck ahead was loaded with explosives and the suicidal madman at the wheel, just at that moment, decided to detonate it? But then I remembered that I had no phobias about bridges in general, none about this bridge in particular, and no overwhelming fears of terrorist explosions. I was having sympathetic worries that harmonized with Edward's. I tried to shrug them off, but in the end, I decided to give in to them. It was soothing to feel my way into Edward's peculiar and paranoid view of the world, which maybe wasn't so paranoid at all.

Montreal. Another half-baked escape idea of Edward's, this one even more senseless than San Diego. As far as I knew, he had no friends in Montreal and didn't know anyone in the entire province.

I'd once dated a man who claimed that Montreal was the height of North American culture, and he and I went there frequently over the course of our ten-month off-and-almost-on relationship. In preparing for each trip, there would be a lot of discussion about superb restaurants, about rushing to buy tickets to some show in pre-Paris tryouts as soon as we hit town, about a great little chocolate shop in a remote neighborhood. As soon as we'd checked into our hotel, he would start to talk about strip clubs and saunas and the number of each in the city and how many new ones had opened up and which we would go to that weekend and in what order. The restaurants? "I'm not hungry." The plays? "You'd be bored." The chocolate? "I'm on a diet." In my mind, the city was a confused blend of sleazy glamour, furtive sexual encounters, and dignified European charm. It made a certain amount of sense for someone like me, but none at all for Edward. The idea of him even considering buying there made me so angry, I was sorry to have his address. Eventually, I was going to have to call him and try to persuade him to leave Canada and face reality either in Boston or San Diego.

By the time I crossed the causeway onto Nahant, the air was filled with broad, wet feathers of snow, coming down in earnest. It wasn't sticking to the macadam yet, but it was clinging to the dried grass along the sides of the road like a sticky chemical that had been sprayed on. A spell of false winter with lovely false snow that would hopefully melt away in a day or so.

There was a cove near Charlotte and Sam's house, a tiny public beach with a small parking lot. I left my car there for fear of alarming any of the watchful neighbors, and walked up the road in the snow, clutching the bag with Charlotte's manuscript inside my woolen coat. The pathway that led around the side of the house to the waterfront was lit with low, dim lanterns, but the house itself was reassuringly dark. I stood for a moment on the porch where Edward and I had met Kate and turned to look back at the city across the water. The buildings and the lights were obscured by the storm, and the wind was blowing all that wet fluff back into my eyes. I was struck by the folly of my mission as soon as I turned the knob on the door and pushed it open. I should have just thrown the manuscript away.

The living room was cool, and smelled of furniture polish and lilies. A spotlight on one of the neighbor's houses was shining through the bare trees and flooding the floors and walls with a pretty purple glow. From what I could tell, it was as tidy and spotlessly clean as a room in my own compulsively arranged house. I followed the route I'd taken when I'd come for the party, into the kitchen, and up the back staircase. But I had such a strong craving for something alcoholic, I went back into the kitchen and opened up the fridge. I pushed a few things around and saw three bottles of beer in the back. No one would notice if one was missing, and if they did, each could blame the other, another of the many advantages of being part of a couple. I twisted off the cap and downed half the bottle in one gulp as I went up the staircase through the servants' quarters. "I should drink more often," I said aloud; I suddenly didn't care half as much about what I was doing, and any residual sadness about the closing on Edward's apartment melted. I had his address. The fact that I was here in this house alone while Charlotte and Samuel were off celebrating their anniversary struck me as testament to the fact that somehow or other, my friendship with them and my straddling both sides of their relationship had paid off. I'd done some actual good.

Despite the snow and the late hour, Charlotte's top-floor study was blue, with light coming in the skylights, and there were shadows from the branches of the naked trees flickering across the walls. I set down the beer and took the manuscript out of the bag, opened the desk drawer, moved aside some papers, laid it inside neatly, and quietly slid the drawer shut. That mission accomplished, I sat on the corner of the desk and finished off the beer, feeling foolishly virtuous.

I was casually looking through Charlotte's desk calendar, trying to see if there was anything about me written on it, when the phone rang. More startling still, the door to the roof deck opened, and Charlotte came in.

Her hair was covered in snow, and she was holding a glass that was empty except for a few ice cubes. She looked at me, slightly indignant, but not especially surprised.

"I like your coat," she said and shut the door behind her. "I wish I'd had it outside there. It's freezing." She set down her glass, leaned over, and brushed the snow off her hair. When she straightened up again, she was a little unsteady on her feet, and it was obvious she was drunk. The phone stopped ringing, leaving in its wake a big silence that had to be filled. "Are you going to tell me," she said, "or do I have to ask you?"

"I thought you and Samuel were going away," I said. It was a lame response, but the fact that she'd been drinking made everything seem easier.

She considered this comment and took a seat on the sofa. "I don't know what question that's an answer to, but I don't think it's the one I was going to ask."

"Ah. And I suppose that question, the one you were going to ask, would be: What the fuck are you doing here, William?"

"I don't use the word 'fuck' in that way very often. It's easier for men to pull it off somehow. But that's the gist of it, yes."

The nice thing about being discovered breaking into her house was that it made taking the manuscript seem like an insignificant offense. I explained it to her, stressing my interest in reading her work as a way to get to know her better. She listened, pouting, and tugging on her lips, and I couldn't help but think she was taking pleasure in my discomfort. When I got around to telling her how much I'd enjoyed reading the stories, she held up her hand and flapped her fingers at me.

"Uh, uh, uh. Please. If you read them, fine, you read them. But praising me is beyond the call of duty. You could have thrown the manuscript out. I probably wouldn't have noticed." She stroked her neck and closed her eyes, and for a minute, I thought she was going to fall asleep. "Tell me," she said, keeping her eyes shut, "what you liked *least* about the stories."

I stalled for a minute, and then I said, "The endings, I suppose. They're all too happy."

"Oh, that. Well, that's your problem, not mine." She said it with a surprising amount of vehemence. "What else?"

"Truthfully, nothing else. I enjoyed them, even if I felt bad about the way I came by them."

"That sounds like appropriately lukewarm praise." She finally opened her eyes and looked around the little study as if she was expecting to see it changed in some way. She appeared slightly more sober, almost as if she'd taken a brief nap. "Do you think I'm talented?"

"Yes," I said. "I do."

"I always wanted to think I was talented, but I'm not convinced. So I settled for being loved, which has many of the same advantages. Except you're dependent upon someone else, aren't you? I know I'm not a very appealing drunk, William. It's one of the reasons I stopped drinking. But you can guess why I might fall off the wagon tonight." She held her hand out to me. "Help me up, please. We'll go downstairs. I'd love a sandwich."

the center of my life

She sat at one of the counter stools in the kitchen and directed me toward the necessary ingredients and utensils: a roasted chicken and mustard in the refrigerator, bread in a box on the counter, knives in the appropriate drawers. The house was chilly, but she was wrapped in a big sweater and either because of that or because of what she'd been drinking, she didn't seem to notice. There was something so peculiarly intimate about standing at her kitchen counter, using her knives to cut up the chicken she'd roasted, that I felt at last I could ask her what had happened to her weekend anniversary plans.

"You'd have to ask Samuel that question, and he's not here at the moment. As you clearly noticed. The official word is a business crisis of some kind. What was I supposed to do when he called, challenge him on it? 'Is that *really* why you're canceling our anniversary trip?' If you don't want an answer, you don't ask the question. Maybe a thin spread of mayonnaise before you close up the bread."

"Have you ever thought about leaving?" I said, as I sliced the sandwiches in halves and put them on plates. "I often wondered if you were buying the apartment for yourself."

She laughed at this suggestion, not drunkenly, but with genuine amusement.

"A minute ago you were criticizing me for imagining inappropriately happy endings for my poor, mixed-up characters. Now you're doing the same thing with me; imagining me moving into my large lovely apartment on a pretty street and happily starting all over again. No, that's not where I'm headed. I don't believe in that kind of ending for my life."

We took our sandwiches into the living room, and she turned

on a single light in a far corner of the room. We ate side by side on the sofa, watching the snow pile up on the balustrade around the porch.

"I hope you don't regret buying the apartment," I said. "I feel responsible, at least partly. I can guarantee you it's a good investment, if nothing else."

"Responsible? Don't be ridiculous. Besides, it's perfect. Or nearly. It won't solve all our problems, but it will make some things better. It wouldn't have happened without you. I made a few attempts with other real estate agents over the past year, but we never quite clicked. You, on the other hand, were the ideal medium. We're going to have to sell this monstrosity soon, to pay the bills, among other things, and when we do, I'll make sure Samuel gives the listing to you. I can't imagine it selling for less than a million."

"You easily can double that figure," I said, thinking about my rich cousins.

A medium. Of course. I bit into my sandwich. How stupid of me to have thought I was a friend—a different category altogether.

"What about you?" she asked.

"Me? What about me?"

"What are your plans? You need plans. I don't think you can just go on like this forever. There's as much about you in those notes you took on us as there is about our marriage. Even if the bulk of it is wedged unconsciously between the lines."

"I'm the medium. Do mediums need plans?"

She sighed and put down her plate. "Well, I'm sorry, William. I know it wasn't a very nice thing to say, but after all, it's not my fault if you choose to be on the outside of your life. You probably disapprove of me for choosing to stay." She touched my face tenderly, but the look in her eyes wasn't especially sympathetic. "At least I'm at the center of my life, no matter how complicated it is or even how second rate it is."

I stayed for another half hour, and as I watched the snow swirling in off the ocean, I mulled over her words, trying to think about the center of my life, and how I could formulate plans around it. I brought the plates into the kitchen and left them in the sink, then went back to the living room, put on my coat, and wound my scarf around my neck. Charlotte had her feet tucked under her on the sofa, and looked once again as if she was about to doze off.

"William," she said, sleepily. "I have a strange request. I'd like you to leave that scarf here."

"My scarf? Whatever for?"

"Leave it draped over the back of a chair somewhere in the house. Samuel will see it, and wonder whose it is. He won't ask me, of course, but it will bother him. It will equalize things in a tiny way that will matter only to me. I'll get it back to you, of course."

I liked the idea, but not nearly as much as I would have liked it a few hours earlier.

"I'm afraid I can't leave it," I said. "I'm driving up to Montreal tonight, and it's bound to be even colder up there."

"Montreal? But our closing's on Monday. You'll be back for it, won't you?"

"I don't know. Someone will cover for me if I'm not."

I slid down the slick hill to my car. The whole neighborhood seemed deserted, as if everyone were hunkered down for the storm. My car swerved as I backed out of the little lot, and I nearly went off the road. Someone slowed down in passing, and then, as if changing his mind, continued on. I was fairly certain it was Samuel, but I don't think he recognized me.

anyone

Because I'd had no intention of driving to Canada when I'd left my house earlier that day, I had no maps with me, and no change of clothes or shaving kit or shampoo. But it was a direct drive from Boston to Montreal, and even I would have had a hard time getting lost.

Somewhere in Vermont, the weak signals of classical music stations failed, and I was reduced to shifting back and forth between a variety of loud talk shows that bore stunning similarity to one another. The hosts railed angrily against the world and the callers called in drunkenly to support their rants, and everyone tossed around a lot of unsubstantiated suppositions and thinly veiled racism as excuses for blowing things up—people, buildings, whole countries. The confusion and fear of the past year had hardened into a thirst for explosive revenge, if not against the perpetrators of disaster, then—please—against someone. Anyone.

an empty bench

I crossed the Champlain Bridge over the St. Lawrence River as the sun was coming up. The buildings of the cold, foreign city were steaming in the frail morning light, and the mountain rising up behind the glass skyscrapers was a black shadow. It was too early to head to Edward's address, so I went first for breakfast. In the restaurant bathroom, I made a feeble attempt at cleaning up and washing away the telltale signs of my all-night drive. Sleeplessness is never an attractive ornament, but I hadn't realized quite how damaging it was at my age until I looked in the bathroom mirror.

Maybe, to be optimistic, my appearance lent gravity and urgency to my face, to my reasons for being there. Edward couldn't doubt my sincerity, looking the way I did.

The address Sylvia had written down was on a north-south street in the Plateau, a working-class French neighborhood that, like most working-class neighborhoods these days, had been taken over by the upwardly mobile. But not entirely. Decay and disrepair stood side by side with polished renovation, giving the whole neighborhood the schizophrenic feel that's so prized by investors. It was bitterly cold, but there was no snow on the ground here; the storm I'd driven through hadn't come this far north.

Edward's building was leaning more toward the decay and disrepair side of the gentrification equation. The sign outside indicated that it was a house of temporary rentals "for students and others." I waited on the sidewalk until the front door opened. A man wearing two coats, clearly an "other," came out.

If the outside had a certain amount of antique charm, to use the most relevant real estate euphemism, the inside combined the less appealing features of a dormitory and a boardinghouse, all overlaid with the faint smell of cigarettes and age. How had my meticulous friend ended up here? I wondered.

I cruised up and down the hallways until, on the third floor, I came across one door that was partly open, with a thin cloud of marijuana smoke drifting out. I knocked, the door swung open, and I saw two young people of indeterminate gender sitting on the bed, passing a joint back and forth, intently studying a fashion magazine. They looked up at me with the silly, easily pleased look of the stoned.

"I'm looking for a friend," I said. "He's in this building, but I'm not sure which apartment he's in."

"Sorry, but I don't know a lot of people here," one said, clearly a boy, possibly Dutch, judging from the accent.

I described Edward, and he said, "Oh, older guy? Long hair?"
Older? "That could be him," I said.

The second person spoke up, twin to the first but a girl this time. "He's the one who fixed the toilet down the hall?"

"Yes," I said. "I'm sure that's him. Do you know which room he's in?"

"It's number twenty-two," the boy said.

"Twenty-four," the other corrected. "He's bad with numbers," she explained.

The boy held the joint up and smiled, offering it to me. "It's a little early," I said, but of course, what I really meant was, it was much too late, unfortunately, for me to sit around a dorm room at nine in the morning, smoking pot.

There was no answer when I knocked at number twenty-four. I tried the knob, but it was locked. I pressed my ear to the door, but the room was silent.

"If you see him," I said to the stoned couple, "can you tell him William is looking for him? You'll remember the name, won't you? Or at least what I look like?"

They gave me confused glances, and I realized of course that I'd long ago passed into the Invisible stage of life; my appearance hadn't registered on either of them and they wouldn't have been able to describe me, even if staring at me directly.

"Is he usually here during the day?"

"I think he's taking French classes," the girl said.

With that, they both lost interest and began speaking in their own language, pointing things out to each other in the magazine.

On the street, the cold air had the opposite effect on me from what it usually did, and instead of feeling revived, I felt so suddenly and completely exhausted, I nearly dozed off standing up. I'd left my car on a street beside a park, and when I went back to claim it, it was gone. All the cars that had been there were gone.

Towed, a more careful reading of the sign revealed, for reasons related to a road construction project.

Halfway up the block, I saw a house with the unmistakably overdone paint job and window treatments of a bed-and-breakfast. I'd have preferred an anonymous hotel, and the free parking would have saved me a lot of trouble. But it was preferable to nodding out on a park bench. The owner was an irritable man, portly and gray-haired, and when I tried to explain in French that I wanted a room, he cut me off and said: "I know you want to practice, but I don't have time. Anyway, I'm American."

He handed me a series of forms to fill out, and as I did so, I asked him how long he'd been living in Canada. "A year," he said. "Almost exactly. It was time to get out. Is that what you're doing here? Planning an escape?"

"No," I said. "I'm not."

"If you change your mind and decide you're interested in buying an apartment, which I'd strongly suggest, I can help you. I have my real estate license."

He led me up two flights of stairs to a tiny room under the eaves. The ceiling was so low, it was impossible for me to stand straight without brushing my head. "How much is it again?" I asked.

He repeated the price. "But if you end up buying something through me, I'll reimburse you fifty percent of the room rate for the first week."

I collapsed on the bed, and when I woke up, the room was shadowy and freezing. It was twilight. I reached out and touched a radiator beside the bed, but it was cold, and I couldn't figure out the complicated system of knobs that turned up the heat. There was one small window across from the bed, and from it, I could see the park with its barren trees and its long, serpentine pond, clogged with leaves and the thin shimmer of an icy crust, just beginning to form. The soft, yellow streetlamps had come on around the pond, and people were out with dogs, bundled up against the cold, hurrying from one part of their lives to the next. Tight jeans and turtlenecks and women in high-heeled boots. A little boy on the sidewalk below was screaming something in French to his young mother. I was about to turn away when I spotted a man, sitting on a bench just across the street, reading a newspaper in the dim yellow light. He had on a leather jacket and a green woolen hat that covered his hair and didn't suit him at all. But it was unmistakably Edward.

"I know you're trying to get away from everything," I practiced as I splashed water on my face at a little sink wedged into a corner. "I know you've been unhappy and everything seems crazy, but we both know this plan isn't going to work out. Come back with me, and we'll figure it out together. I have plenty of room in my house. It won't be perfect, but we'll be at the center of each other's life. You've been at the center of mine for years now. I'm sorry I didn't realize it sooner."

I ran down the staircase. The cold and the noise of the street hit me with a pleasant shock when I opened the door. I walked out into the winter twilight with a mission, but by the time I'd dodged the traffic and crossed into the park, the bench was empty. I buttoned up my coat and wrapped the scarf around my neck more tightly. There weren't that many places he could go. I wasn't worried. I knew where to find him.

Acknowledgments

Many thanks to The Ragdale Foundation, The Boston Athenaeum, The Newton Free Library, Wellspring House, and La Bibliothèque Nationale du Québec. Also to Chuck Adams, Denise Roy, and Denise Shannon. Also to Cynthia Liebow. Also to Kimberly Diaz, Emily B. Petrou, and Nancy Gorman. Also to Helene Jacob, Philippe Le Sage, Florence Martin, and Antonio Interlandi. Also to John Morley. Also to Sandrine Calabria. Also to Sebastian Stuart. Also to Jonathan Strong, Morgan Mead, Scott Elledge, and Ann Colette. Also to Amy. Also, most especially, to Anita.